THE FORTUNES OF TEXAS

*Follow the lives and loves of a complex family
with a rich history and deep ties
in the Lone Star State*

HITTING THE JACKPOT

The Maloneys of Chatelaine, Texas,
have just discovered they are blood relations
to the Fortunes—which makes them instant
millionaires. But their inheritance comes with
a big secret that could change everything
for their small-town family...

Gigi Fortune is used to men wanting her for her
money, but her new attorney Harrison Vasquez
is not impressed. He is sure the "poor little rich
woman" means nothing but trouble. The more
time he spends with her, though, the more he
realizes he's been underestimating her—and his
thoughts veer from "never" to "possibly forever"!

Dear Reader,

I'm always thrilled when I'm asked to write a Fortunes of Texas book—and not just because I'm a huge fan of the series. It's exciting to read the outline of the upcoming stories, and it's fun to collaborate with the other authors, making sure various settings and recurring characters stay consistent.

But when Harlequin invited me to take part in the 2023 Fortunes of Texas series—my twelfth Fortunes book—I was hesitant. The past two years were especially difficult to navigate. Not only did I weather the pandemic along with everyone else, but I also faced various family trials and losses that took a hard hit on my creative process. Could I give another story my all? Would I be able to finish it on time?

But I love the Fortunes, so I agreed. And I'm glad I did. As the story began to come together, and as I got to know what made Gigi Fortune and Harrison Vasquez tick, my muse stirred to life. And I found joy in writing again.

Have you gone through something similar? If so, I hope that the 2023 Fortunes of Texas series and my contribution, *Self-Made Fortune*, will help you once again believe in dreams, love and happy-ever-afters.

May you find the same joy in reading this book as I did while writing it!

Judy

P.S. I love hearing from my readers. You can contact me through my website, JudyDuarte.com, or at Facebook.com/JudyDuarteNovelist.

Self-Made Fortune

—

JUDY DUARTE

HARLEQUIN
SPECIAL
EDITION

Special thanks and acknowledgment are given to Judy Duarte for her contribution to The Fortunes of Texas: Hitting the Jackpot miniseries.

HARLEQUIN®

SPECIAL EDITION™

Recycling programs for this product may not exist in your area.

ISBN-13: 978-1-335-72461-8

Self-Made Fortune

Copyright © 2023 by Harlequin Enterprises ULC

For questions and comments about the quality of this book, please contact us at CustomerService@Harlequin.com.

Harlequin Enterprises ULC
22 Adelaide St. West, 41st Floor
Toronto, Ontario M5H 4E3, Canada
www.Harlequin.com

Printed in U.S.A.

USA TODAY bestselling author **Judy Duarte** has written more than sixty books and novellas for Harlequin Special Edition and Kensington, earned two RITA® finals in the inspirational category, won two Maggies and received a National Reader's Choice Award. She lives near the coast in Southern California with her personal hero.

When she's not cooped up in her writing cave, Judy enjoys traveling with her husband and spoiling her grandchildren—an array of talented kids who call her Nana.

Visit the Author Profile page
at Harlequin.com for more titles.

To Toni Wiebe, elementary school teacher,
farmer's wife, loving mom and grandma, 4-H supporter,
awesome baker, Facebook friend—
and a Special Edition reader.

This book's for you, Toni!

Chapter One

The Chatelaine Report: With all the Maloney men now off the market, have we seen the end of the Fortune saga? Not quite yet, Chatelaine. A woman has recently come forward declaring her own connection to the Fortune family. We reached out to Reeve Fortune, the CEO of Fortune Metals and FortuneMedia for comment, but he declined to respond. His sister, Gigi Fortune, bluntly says "Mariana Sanchez is a liar."

Gigi Fortune stood in front of the massive mahogany desk that once belonged to her great-grandfather, Walter Fortune. She'd never met his son, her grandfather. Phillip Fortune, Sr. died when her dad was a teenager. But she'd had a special relationship with Walter, the dear old man she'd called Grampy. Even now, a quarter of a century beyond those childhood days, it seemed that he'd been the only adult who'd really had time for her.

She dribbled lemon oil onto the desktop, then took a soft cloth and polished the wood with smooth strokes. Her maid took care of all the other rooms in the house, but her home office had always been more than the place in which she worked. It was where she found solitude.

She inhaled the lemony scent of the oil and took a moment to reflect upon the times Grampy would stop by her house and take her to work with him. He'd let her sit at this very desk, and she'd put on his reading glasses, drink pretend coffee from his mug and draw pictures for him to display on his office wall. He'd had one of them, a childish sketch of a little blonde girl steering a spaceship to the moon, professionally framed. It adorned her home office wall now.

"Gigi," Grampy had said time and again, "you'll be running Fortune Metals one day."

Maybe, if Grampy hadn't died twenty-three years ago, she might be in charge of the family mining enterprise. But he'd had a stroke when she was nearly sixteen and passed away from complications a year later. Unfortunately, her father, Phillip Jr., didn't have the same philosophy when it came to women in business.

She replaced the lid on the bottle of lemon oil, the citrusy scent another reminder of the hard candies Grampy used to keep in his desk drawer and in his car.

When her dad decided to repurpose Grampy's old office and get rid of the furniture, Gigi insisted upon keeping the desk and bookcase, as well as a few other personal items that held little value to anyone other than her.

She glanced at the wall, where she'd hung a shadow box that displayed his reading glasses, the coffee mug that bore a Dallas Cowboys logo and the fedora he used to wear...especially during football season. Grampy had been a huge Cowboys fan and used to take great pleasure whenever someone mistook him for Tom Landry, the former head coach.

Her cell phone rang, drawing her from her sweet memories. She glanced at the display and smiled when she spotted Diana Dawson's name. Diana was the talented young CEO of Stellar Productions. Gigi had been so impressed by the whiz kid she'd met at Chatelaine High School that she'd encouraged the young woman to attend college and given her the seed money to start the business. Then she'd hired Stellar Productions to record her podcasts.

Gigi snatched her smartphone and took the call. "Hi, there. How's my favorite CEO and Chatelaine High School alumna?"

"I'm not sure," Diana said, her voice a little shaky.

Gigi stiffened, her senses on high alert. "What's the matter?"

Diana paused, then blew out a sigh. "I have an offer from a company that wants to buy out Stellar Productions."

"Wow. That's exciting. Congrats." That could prove to be lucrative for the woman who'd grown up in Chatelaine and came from humble beginnings. "Are you going to sell?"

"It's a hard offer to turn down. But it's kind of like…" Diana's words stalled.

Gigi knew exactly what she was going to say. "Because it would be like selling your baby."

"Yeah, that's about it."

"So who made the offer?" Gigi took a seat in the tufted leather chair behind her desk.

"You don't know?"

Should she? "I don't have a clue."

"FortuneMedia."

"What?" Gigi bolted upright and damn near dropped the cell phone. Her younger brother was behind the sale? She let out a huff and slowly shook her head. "Actually, I had no idea." She and Reeve were only three years apart, and they'd once been incredibly close. But they weren't anymore, even though they'd once lived in the same gated community in Corpus Christi. But his move to a huge house across the water from Corpus proper had nothing to do with the fact that they rarely socialized.

"I'll probably sell," Diana said. "Reeve said he'd keep me on for at least a year—maybe longer. Only trouble is, I think there's going to be a noncompete clause. At least, for a set period of time."

Gigi bit back a curse. No way would she allow anyone other than Diana to record her podcasts, especially someone affiliated with Reeve. "When do you need to give him an answer?"

"Soon, I guess. You think I should take it? Or turn it down?"

"Don't do anything hasty, Diana. Send me the deal. I'll do a little research and get back to you later today."

"Thanks. I really appreciate you. And the encouragement you've always given me. College was never on my mom's radar. I don't think I would've pursued a degree if you hadn't suggested it. And I never expected to get a full ride."

"I'm a life coach who specializes in empowering women. That's my job. It's what I do. Remember?"

"Yep. And that's why 'Gigi's Journey' is such a popular podcast."

"Maybe so. But, Diana, you have a real gift when it comes to marketing."

"Aw, thanks. Gosh. I'm sorry, I gotta jam. I have a documentary I need to prepare for, so I'll talk to you later."

When the call ended, Gigi set the phone on the desk, leaned back in the chair, the springs creaking, and tapped her fingers on the desktop. "Dammit," she muttered. "Wasn't running Fortune Metals enough for you, Reeve? Now you have to poke your nose into my business?"

She heaved a sigh, then reached for the cell and dialed her brother on his private line.

"Hey," Reeve said, "I was just going to give you a call."

Uh-huh. Sure. "I'm not surprised. But I already know why. I just talked to Diana at Stellar Productions."

"She told you about my offer to buy her company?"

"Yes. And I'm not happy about it." Reeve had started FortuneMedia while he was still in college, but recently he'd been buying out other similar operations. Once he owned them, he began making internal changes to the companies and stirring things up. Lately, though, he'd become even more image-conscious, in her opinion, anyway. In fact, he'd even threatened to sue a blogger over something he didn't like.

"What's not to be happy about?" he asked. "Your protégée will end up with more money than she's ever seen in her life."

"I get that. But that's not the point."

"I disagree."

Gigi loved her brother, but they had different philosophies regarding life, money and happiness. In fact, these days their last name seemed to be the only thing they had in common.

"Actually," Reeve said, "aside from Stellar Productions, I'm glad you called."

"Oh, yeah?" They didn't usually have much to talk about these days.

"Actually, a woman by the name of Mariana Sanchez contacted me and claims to be related to us."

That wasn't news. For the past several months, the Sanchez woman had been trying to contact her, but Gigi had ignored her efforts. Mariana was probably another fraud who'd found Gigi through the internet. There'd been others before her claiming to be related to the Fortunes.

"Money brings out all the fortune hunters," Gigi said, a hint of sarcasm creeping into her tone.

"Maybe so, but Sanchez claims to have proof that

she's Walter Fortune's granddaughter. And she's talked to an attorney."

"There's no way Grampy would have cheated on his wife or abandoned a child."

"You're probably right. But I decided to take a pro-active approach and hired an attorney."

"Hired?" Gigi's senses reeled. "Are you talking about someone who isn't with the firm you have on retainer?"

"I decided to go another route in this case."

Gigi snatched a pen and reached for her notepad. "Who'd you hire?"

"His name is Harrison Vasquez. He just joined the firm of Bentley, Donovan and Tyler. One of my associates said he really knows his stuff and encouraged me to give him a chance. I'm meeting him at his office this afternoon."

Give him a chance? What was her brother up to? "Why didn't you tell me about this sooner? I've got a lot going on today."

"No problem. I don't expect you to go. I just wanted to give you a heads-up that Mariana Sanchez could contact you."

There he went again, giving her the pat-on-the-head treatment like their father always did. "What time is the meeting?"

"Two o'clock. But don't worry, sis. I've got it covered."

Sure he did. Gigi bit back a snappy retort.

"Anyway," Reeve said, "I gotta go. I need to leave in an hour, and I still have some work to catch up on."

"All right. We'll talk later."

But it'd be sooner, rather than later. If her little brother thought he was going to that meeting alone, he had another thing coming.

A quick internet search provided Gigi with the location of the law offices of Bentley, Donovan and Tyler, which were on the eighth floor of Brighton Towers. She took time to freshen up, change into her power suit and apply the appropriate matching makeup. Then she was off to surprise Reeve.

Fifteen minutes later, she steered her white BMW into the parking garage and found a stall near the lobby entrance. Then she grabbed her purse, locked her car and headed into the building. Once inside, she joined several others gathered at the elevator doors, all dull and business-zombie-like, except for one man who stood out.

Six feet tall, more or less. Black hair. Brown eyes. An olive complexion. Square-cut jaw. Broad shoulders that filled out a designer suit—stylish and tailor-made for him, no doubt. He also wore an alluring aftershave— something that reminded her of sea breezes and white-sand beaches.

She wasn't looking for a guy or a relationship right now, but she wasn't dead, either. A good-looking man who cut an imposing figure still turned her head. She looked around and stifled a smile. Another woman had taken note of him, too.

The elevator doors opened, and they all stepped inside. The eighth-floor button was already lit, so Gigi walked to the back of the car, then turned and faced the front. The handsome man stood just to her right, and in spite of herself, she couldn't help but steal another glance his way and inhale his scent. Dang if that didn't give her a tick of arousal, which was ridiculous. Besides, she'd ended a dating relationship recently and wasn't eager to strike up another.

He turned to her and offered a polite smile that didn't last. Then he lifted his left wrist and looked at his watch, the kind serious athletes favored. She couldn't help noting that he wasn't wearing a wedding ring, although that didn't mean anything. It certainly hadn't meant anything to her ex-husband, the lying cheat.

The elevator dinged, then the doors opened to the fifth floor, where the other passengers got out, leaving Gigi and the mystery man alone. She checked him out again, but refrained from starting a conversation. After all, what was the point? Besides, she wasn't in the mood for fun and games.

The elevator dinged. Eighth floor, which was her stop. When the doors opened, she stepped out and glanced at the directory on the wall.

Mystery Man exited, too. And even though he had an opportunity to address her, he didn't. Odd, though. It was usually Gigi who kept her focus on business and did the ignoring. Maybe she was losing her appeal. But so what? Forty was the new thirty, right? She really didn't care.

Okay. Admittedly, deep down, she did care. The man stepped away to answer his phone, and she walked past him and continued to the law office, which was just to the right of the elevator. She picked up her pace and, after opening the glass door, she entered the lobby and paused at the reception desk, where a middle-aged red-head was talking on the phone. She offered Gigi a smile and lifted her index finger, signaling that she'd be just a moment. That is, until Mystery Man approached the desk. The receptionist brightened and abruptly ended the call.

"Did you have a nice lunch?" Mystery Man asked.

"Yes, I did. I ate outside in the alcove. It sure is a nice day. Too nice to be indoors."

"I hear you, Jessica."

"Oh! By the way, your new client is already here." She nodded toward the corner of the lobby.

Gigi scanned the reception area, where her brother was sitting, nearly hidden by a potted palm tree. No way. What the heck? She glanced back to Mystery Man. *This* guy was the attorney?

Her brother had his head down and was scrolling through his phone. *Jeez, Reeve. You've got to take your work everywhere?*

"Excuse me, ma'am." Harrison Vasquez brushed past her, crossed the room and approached her brother with an extended arm. "Good afternoon, Mr. Fortune. I'm sorry if I kept you waiting."

Reeve got to his feet and slipped his cell phone into the breast pocket of his jacket. "No problem. I haven't been waiting very long." Reeve smiled at the attorney before he looked over the man's shoulder. When he spotted Gigi, his smile faded. "I, uh… I see my sister's here."

Gigi's presence had clearly caught Reeve off guard,

but it shouldn't have. This meeting was about *family* business.

"Your sister?" Harrison turned, smiled and offered Gigi his hand. "Nice to meet you, ma'am."

"Same." *Ma'am?* He'd called her *ma'am?* Like she was some old maid? She supposed she was heading in that direction. Not that she had any plans to change that. But seriously!

"Please," Harrison said, "come with me. I'll take you to my office."

Gigi made a point of stepping in front of Reeve and following right behind the attorney, leaving her brother to trail behind as they headed down the hall and to an office on the left.

While Harrison opened the door, Reeve caught up, tapped Gigi on the shoulder and muttered, "You didn't have to come, you know."

"Yep, I know."

Harrison pointed to the chairs facing a dark oak desk, which seemed as outdated as the rest of the furniture, including an empty bookcase. A withered plant that needed water rested on top of the file cabinet, next to a small hammer and a box of nails, which appeared to be waiting for someone to hang the pictures and diplomas that were on the floor, leaning against the wall.

"I'm sorry about this mess." Harrison gestured for them to take a seat while he rounded the desk and pulled out his leather chair. "I'm still unpacking and trying to get settled."

Reeve pulled out a chair for Gigi, then took the seat next to her. "No problem."

Maybe not to him, but Gigi saw a red flag. "First day on the job?"

"First week."

That wasn't a good sign. "Just passed the bar?" she asked. It was a valid, if direct, question. The family had plenty of top-notch attorneys on the payroll. Why put a newbie on retainer?

Harrison leaned back in his chair. "Actually, I passed the bar nearly fifteen years ago."

"Harrison used to be a JAG attorney," Reeve said. "And he comes highly recommended."

JAG, huh? Gigi hadn't seen that coming. He must have cut a fine figure in uniform. "So why did you leave the military?" He didn't look old enough to be retired.

"It wasn't an easy decision. I loved what I did. And the travel. I was stationed in various places around the globe, most recently in Hawaii. But my parents are getting older, so I decided it was time to be a civilian and find a law firm that's closer to home."

"That's why you left? Don't you have siblings who can help out?" she asked. Not that it was any of her business, but he'd made a pretty big life change.

Yet, he seemed unfazed by her questioning. "No, I'm an only child, Ms. Fortune. And I'm glad I can be there for them. My folks and I have always been close."

"I see." And she supposed she did, although she couldn't relate. Not that she didn't love her parents, but after her father retired early, he and her mother moved to France, and she only got the occasional FaceTime call. It had hurt at first, but she was beyond that now.

"What's your specialty?" she asked.

"Besides being a good attorney?" His mouth quirked into a grin, and his brown eyes sparkled.

Damn good-looking and a smart aleck, too. Just like Anson. Her ex-husband had been an attorney. Heck, Gigi had put the guy through college and law school. And a lot of good that had done her.

"All kidding aside," Harrison said, "I really appreciate your trust in me. I know my reputation for investigation and discretion got me this case, and I promise I won't let you down." He looked at Gigi with sincerity. "Please know that I'm very good at what I do."

"Our friend Tyson speaks very highly of you," Reeve said.

"He's a great guy. I'll have to thank him for the referral." Harrison flipped open the legal pad. "So tell me—what's going on?"

"I'll lay it all out for you," Reeve said. "A woman named Mariana Sanchez claims to be a descendant of our great-grandfather, Walter Fortune. I think she's trying to stake a claim on his estate, and I want you to make sure that doesn't happen."

Harrison took notes, then looked up. "Has she mentioned anything about money?"

"No, not yet," Reeve said. "I just heard from her this week."

"Just this week?" Gigi leaned back in her seat and crossed her arms. "I've been getting letters and calls from her for months."

"What?" Reeve scoffed. "Are you serious? Why didn't you say something before now?"

"How many months?" Harrison gazed at her with a

furrowed brow. "Has she made any other contact with you? In person?"

"No, she's only reached out with letters and voice messages to my business." She shrugged. "This started maybe six months ago. I chalked the woman up as just another con artist, or crackpot, or both. They usually burn out after a few weeks if I ignore them."

Reeve clicked his tongue. "Hell, Gigi. No wonder she's talking to a lawyer. She thinks she's entitled to restitution because you ignored her."

"Oh, come on, Reeve. She isn't the first person falsely claiming to be a Fortune, and she won't be the last."

Reeve shook his head. "I'm sorry, Harrison. My sister isn't taking this seriously, but I am."

"I'm not suggesting the woman is completely harmless," Gigi said. "But I feel safe. Enough." Okay, she was starting to sound a little reckless. But she lived in a gated community that provided twenty-four-hour security.

"Did you bring the correspondence she sent you?" Harrison asked.

"No, I'm afraid not." She'd been in too big of a hurry to get here. But now she was questioning herself, which went against her grain. "I saved her voice mails on my home-office line. The letters came by mail, and I have them in a stack, next to the shredder."

"Don't shred them," Harrison said. "I need them."

Reeve sighed. "You didn't think to bring them with you?"

Gigi didn't respond. She wasn't inept. She just wasn't

as concerned about this woman as Reeve seemed to be. Until now.

"Has Ms. Sanchez mentioned money?" Harrison asked. "It's probably her endgame."

"Not so far," Gigi said. "Just that she wants to get to know her family. But if she's a Fortune, then I'm Santa Claus."

Harrison lifted an eyebrow and granted her a mild grin.

"I have to agree with Harrison," Reeve said. "That Sanchez woman has to be after money."

"We'll proceed with that assumption, that she doesn't intend harm." Harrison looked at Gigi. "Do you have any idea where she lives?"

"The return address is a post office box in Rambling Rose, Texas."

"Do you think she knows where you live?"

"I don't think so. She's approached me through my business address, which is a post-office box." But her actual office was at her house. Gigi hadn't been worried. Yet, the way Harrison looked at her with a mixture of alarm and concern made her realize she wasn't taking this seriously enough.

Those expressive brown eyes. The way they lingered on her for an extra beat. The slight quirk of a smile. That handsome face. She bet he did look sharp in that dress uniform. She shook off the vision. Where had that come from? *Focus.*

Harrison lifted his gaze to hers. There was a buzz between them that she couldn't ignore, but then he cleared his throat and made another note. His manner shifted back to strictly business. Good. That was for the best.

"Ms. Fortune," Harrison said, clicking his pen. "Your brother has a valid point. He's concerned about your safety, and so am I."

She looked at Reeve and then back at Harrison. "It's not a subtle point you two are making."

Harrison merely studied her. Waiting for her to crack? To admit defeat?

She might've taken note of him in the elevator, but she didn't find him particularly charming now. Not when he seemed to be teaming up with Reeve against her—as if it was her fault that Mariana was coming at them.

Was it? Insecurity gripped her for the briefest of moments. Had she inadvertently created a huge family problem by not taking the woman seriously?

"All right, then." Harrison set down his pen. "I'll need those voice mails and letters."

Gigi nodded. "I'll scan them and send them to you via a secure link."

Harrison shook his head. "I need the originals. You make copies for yourself, and I'll have a paralegal stop by and pick them up tomorrow. Is that acceptable?"

"Why do you need the original letters?" she asked.

"This is an investigation. The originals may have clues that won't translate with a copy."

Reeve cleared his throat. "Just give them to him, Gigi."

"I was just asking a question. Of course, you can have the originals and anything else you need for this investigation." Gigi gave Harrison her address, as well as her phone number.

"There's a guard at the gate," she added, "so I'll need the name of whoever is coming."

"I'll call you in the morning." Harrison stood, apparently not trying to run up the clock…and the bill. She saw that as a good sign.

Reeve got to his feet, and Gigi followed their lead.

Harrison saw them to his office door. "Ms. Fortune, is ten o'clock a good time for one of the paralegals to stop by?"

"Sure. I'll be home until noon. But do me a favor."

"What's that?"

"Call me Gigi." Enough with the old-maid reference.

"All right. Please call me Harrison." He flashed her a charming smile, reminding her of her initial attraction. And she stuffed that right down where it belonged.

As she and Reeve made their way back to the law-office lobby, she felt compelled to look over her shoulder, to see whether Harrison was watching or whether he'd already returned to his office. But she would take the power position, as if he hadn't had any effect on her feminine stirrings.

Reeve stopped at the reception desk for some reason. She could have continued through the doors and to the elevator. Instead, she paused.

Unable to help herself, she glanced over her shoulder and spotted Harrison still standing in the hall, just outside his office, his gaze aimed at her.

His expression both annoyed and thrilled her at the same time. Her heart rate spiked for a moment, then hit a speed bump. She knew the signs of attraction, the mutual spark of allure, that dangerous urge to give in and follow that magnetism right into bed.

She shoved open the glass door and left the office. *Keep walking*, she told herself. *Far away.* It wasn't as if she hadn't had sex since her divorce. But she no longer allowed her heart—or her feminine urges—to overrule her head.

And she certainly wouldn't do so now.

Chapter Two

Under most circumstances, Harrison would have sent a paralegal to Gigi's house to pick up the letters and make note of the voice mail messages, but this case was different. If he handled it right, the Fortunes could retain him for other projects, which would be a huge boost to his budding civilian career. So Harrison called Gigi and told her that since he was in her area, he'd be the one stopping by her home office.

He'd also done his homework. Walter Fortune and his late brother, Wendell, had been co-owners of a silver mine near Chatelaine, Texas, which had made the family exceedingly wealthy, even by Fortune standards. Walter's only child, Phillip Sr., died while Phillip Jr. was in high school. When Phillip Jr. retired, he and his wife moved to France, leaving both adult children in Corpus Christi…and Reeve in charge of Fortune Metals.

At thirty-seven years old, the megamillionaire was not only the CEO of the family mining operation and its subsidiaries, but Reeve had also begun to diversify early on. While in college, he'd started FortuneMedia, which was steadily growing and expanding.

After meeting him yesterday, Harrison found him easy to peg. He had a commanding presence and wasn't used to taking no for an answer.

But Gigi? She wasn't easy to figure out. She had a podcast called "Gigi's Journey" and appeared to be a life coach, which was interesting. Still, he wasn't quite sure what a woman who'd been mega wealthy since birth would know about coaching other women on how to find success. Maybe, after stopping by her house this morning, he'd have a better understanding of her.

He had to admit, he was curious about her. Before they'd been introduced yesterday, he'd caught her looking at him in the elevator, but he'd been so focused on the two-o'clock meeting and making a good impression on her brother that he'd passed on engaging in a conversation with the beautiful blonde rocking a stylish black business suit.

It had taken every ounce of his self-control to ignore the way her long, wavy hair had been swept up into a topknot, revealing a pair of diamond studs. Or how those big brown eyes and full lips… Well, she would have been a major distraction yesterday. Actually, she still was.

He might be wrong, but he'd sensed a mutual attraction had passed between them in the office. But he knew better than to get involved with a client…or a client's sister. It wasn't smart or ethical. Besides, they ran in completely different circles and didn't have a damn thing in common, other than this case.

His cell phone rang, drawing him from his musings. He glanced at the display in his Audi and saw an incoming call from his mother.

He answered with a smile. "Good morning."

"Yes, it is. Should be warm and sunny. I hoped to catch you before you got to the office. I don't like bothering you at work. *Am* I bothering you?"

"Nope." His mom would never be a bother. "In fact, I'll be on the road for a few more minutes, so I'm free to talk."

"Your dad and I wondered if you'd be coming to town next weekend."

Now that Harrison could make the drive home in just a couple of hours, he planned to visit them once a month. "I don't see why not. What's up?"

"The Chatelaine Bar and Grill is having a Cinco de Mayo celebration on the patio next Friday night, and your dad and I thought you might want to join us."

His parents had been married nearly forty-five years, yet they still made a point of having "date night" once a week. And the Chatelaine Bar and Grill was one of their favorite places to go, although it was about the only nice option in town. "Sure. Sounds like fun."

"I don't know what the plan is on the fifth," his mother said, "but there's usually a DJ and sometimes dancing."

"Papa's dancing again? Those cortisone shots in the knee must be working."

"No, not really. This time the injection didn't seem to help as well as the last one, so I've been gently pushing him to schedule the knee-replacement surgery he's been putting off."

"That's for the best, but ouch."

"He can't put if off any longer. Which reminds me. He'll have to find someone to cover those ESL classes he teaches on Saturday afternoons."

"Shouldn't be too hard."

"You'd think, but he's pretty fussy. And listen, I hope he doesn't embarrass you next Friday night."

A grin stretched across Harrison's face. "What's he up to?"

"He's going to wear a sombrero and serape. He wanted me to dress up, too, but I'd rather not go in costume."

His dad could've been a comedian, had he not decided to teach high-school Spanish and auto shop, a career he'd retired from recently. The kids had loved him. But Mama was a nurse and was more low-key. She preferred the straight-man role when it came to Papa's shenanigans.

Up ahead, Harrison spotted Lone Star Estates, one of the most exclusive gated communities in Corpus Christi. Even the bushes and flowers needed to apply for membership.

"I'd better let you go, Mama. I'm just arriving at my client's place."

They said their goodbyes and ended the call, just as Harrison pulled up to the guardhouse. "Captain Vas—" Oops. Whenever he saw a guard at a gate, he went on autopilot. He cleared his throat. "I'm Harrison Vasquez. I'm here to see Gigi Fortune. She's expecting me."

The guard consulted his clipboard. "Yes, sir. Have a good day."

Harrison nodded and drove through the gate when it opened. He followed his GPS past several Southwestern-style haciendas, expecting one of them to be hers. Instead, the route ended in front of a smaller model, the runt of the neighborhood, although it was still impressive. The yard was landscaped beautifully, with a green lawn and a colorful array of flowers along the walkway. He parked at the curb, grabbed his briefcase from the passenger seat, exited the Audi and made his way to the front door, the air smelling of a mixture of freshly cut grass and roses. He rang the bell, which sounded more like the deep resonance of a cathedral gong. Nice digs. Impressive. But too fancy for him.

Moments later, Gigi answered the door, her makeup light and natural, yet perfect.

"Good morning." He glanced down at his briefcase, which gave him an opportunity to give her a quick and discreet once-over. She wore an oversize hot pink top that revealed a bare shoulder and a pair of black yoga pants, her feet bare, and her toenails boasting lavender nail polish.

When he lifted the briefcase and his gaze returned to her pretty face, she offered him a half smile. "Counselor, come on in."

He entered the foyer and looked into what he assumed was the living room. He took in his surroundings, only to be a bit surprised. He'd expected something cold and conservative, but she'd used splashes of bright color to warm the white plaster walls and dark hardwood floors. Her furnishings, leather sofas and chairs, were definitely upscale, but she'd topped off the decor with a few vintage pieces. In the far corner, he spotted a baby grand piano.

"Do you play?" he asked, as she closed the front door.

"Excuse me?"

He nodded toward the corner. "The piano."

"Oh. Yes, although I'm not that good. My mother insisted I take lessons when I was a child. I hated them, but I'm glad I play now. I think she assumed I'd inherited her musical abilities, but I'm afraid I'm just average. I did inherit what she called her cankles."

"Cankles?"

She grinned and pointed to her foot. "Calves that don't taper down to the ankle. Just one solid line."

He didn't see that at all. Only a shapely leg, a welldefined ankle draped with a delicate gold chain and a foot with a high instep. "They look good to me."

She touched his arm with a friendlike intimacy that surprised him. "Thanks. But at best, they're average."

On the contrary. There was nothing "average" about Gigi Fortune. "You're being too modest."

She laughed. "Never. Not my style. Anyway, you're here for the correspondence. It's in my office." She turned and led him down the hall, past a formal dining room and a cozy-looking library.

Her place reminded him of his commanding officer's house. Colonel Binghamton came from old money, but he'd dedicated his life to the service. Was Gigi like that? Was she dedicating herself to service by coaching women? Or was it an ego trip? He'd like to think that it wasn't.

He couldn't help but notice the way her long blond hair tumbled over her shoulders and down her back, bouncing with each step she took. Or the way her hips swayed in a natural, alluring, way. He knew from his research she was divorced, but he wondered if she had a significant other.

Enough of that, Harrison. Keep your mind on your work...and not her sexy backside.

Gigi led him into an office with a mahogany desk, where several letters and a card were lying on the top. She pulled out a chair from an antique table that held a cut glass lamp—probably an antique as well—and dragged it to the desk. "Have a seat."

While he did as instructed, she pulled out her tufted leather chair and sat behind the desk.

"I assume this is what she sent you." He pointed to the envelopes. "Did you make yourself copies? Can I take these?"

"Please do."

After he'd reviewed each of Mariana's letters, as well as an Easter card she'd sent recently, he placed them back on the desktop. "You're right. She didn't mention anything about money. Is it possible that she wants exactly what she said? To get to know you and her biological family?"

Gigi slowly shook her head, those blond wavy curls swaying around her neck. "No. In my experience, everyone wants money, especially if they think someone has more than they do."

"You have a point." Harrison certainly was motivated by money. If he hadn't had the will to succeed and better himself, he never would have joined the military in order to get through law school without ending up with a slew of student loans.

Gigi let out a soft sigh. "At times, I wish I would have been born poor. Some things might have been easier."

"Oh, really?" The comment took him by surprise, and he leaned forward. "In what way?"

She shrugged. "Expectations and family baggage, I suppose."

Harrison bit back a scoff. "You think poor families don't have expectations or baggage? Barely meeting your basic needs sucks on so many levels."

She eyed him carefully. "Were you? Born poor, I mean."

"My family didn't struggle financially, but they were far from rich. Putting me through college and law school would have been a big hardship. And unfair to them. They've worked hard all their lives and deserve to enjoy their retirement."

"So you joined the army?"

"Yes. And it provided me with a wealth of education."

"You mentioned wanting to be closer to your parents. Are they in Corpus Christi?"

Most people had no idea where his small community was located, but the silver mine owned by Fortune Metals wasn't too far from there. "They live in Chatelaine."

"Really?" She leaned forward and placed her forearms on her desk. "I know it well. My great-grandfather used to take me to town with him when I was a child. He and I were very close. Mom called me his shadow."

Harrison rubbed his chin. Interesting. He hadn't sensed much warmth between her and Reeve. But apparently, she had some close family ties, too. Or had them, once upon a time. From his research, he'd learned that Walter Fortune passed away twenty-three years ago. "I'm sure you'd still recognize Chatelaine. Not much has changed. There's the same old gas station with one pump. And the sign out front still says 'Welcome to Chatelaine. The Town That Never Changes. Harv's New Barbecue straight ahead.'"

"I know. I drive through it every time I visit Chatelaine High School."

"My alma mater." He couldn't imagine why she'd go there. Not that it was actually located in Chatelaine. It was just outside of town and served two small communities. "You visit regularly?"

"It's one of the Fortune family's charities. And the school could use all the financial help it can get."

He bristled. Slightly. He wasn't sure how to take that. He wasn't ashamed of his humble roots or the small town in which he'd once lived. But he had fond memories of the school and the teachers who'd seemed to take an active and supportive interest in their students, so he shook it off. "You mentioned that you had a couple of voice mail messages from Ms. Sanchez."

"Actually, just one." She reached for her desk phone and pushed a button. A beep sounded, followed by a woman's voice. *"Hello-o-o, Miss Fortune. Or maybe I should call you Gigi. This is Mariana Sanchez, your long lost relative. Anyway, I'd love to meet you for coffee someday soon. There's so much to talk about, so much I'd like to know. Weekdays are best for me, 'cause I work evenings in the kitchen at Roja. It's a restaurant at the Hotel Fortune here in Rambling Rose. And then I spend the Saturdays cooking out of my food truck at Mariana's Market."* The woman let out a rather loud cackle. *"Anyway, like I said, we have lots to talk about. I'd love to hear from you."*

She left her number before disconnecting. Another beep sounded, and Gigi hit the stop button. "What do you think?"

Harrison let out a sigh. "It's hard to say. Do you mind playing it again? I'll record it with my cell phone."

"Not at all." She reached over to replay the message, while he set up his phone, then took out a pen and his legal pad.

"So what's your plan?" she asked.

As he jotted down a few notes, he said, "How about this? I'll take a drive out to Rambling Rose and do a little research."

"You'll talk to her?"

He nodded. "If she's approached by your attorney, it might scare her off. And while I'm in town, I'll poke around a bit. Do some investigating."

"Alright. When do you think you'll be able to do that?"

"I've got some free time on Friday. I'll go in the afternoon and spend the night. I'll visit the restaurant where she works. Then, the next morning, I'll check out Mariana's Market."

Harrison slipped the letters into his briefcase, and they both got to their feet at the same time. Gigi walked him toward the front door. When they reached the foyer, her steps slowed. "Do you mind if I ask you a personal question?"

He couldn't promise a completely frank answer. "Only if I can ask you one."

"Deal." She folded her arms across her chest, the pink fabric of her oversize shirt pulling snug over her breasts. "Is Harrison your real name?"

"Yep."

"I mean, it…" She paused, bit down on her bottom lip.

"It seems more British than Latino?"

She glanced down at the floor. When she looked up, her cheeks bore a rosy flush. "I'm sorry. I didn't mean for it to sound that way. And it's really none of my business."

"No problem." He smiled. "My dad is a huge *Star Wars* fan, and he insisted on naming me after his favorite star."

"Aw," she said. "Harrison Ford. I should have known."

"My mom tried to talk him out of it. She'd wanted to name me Miguel, after her father. She claims that she only agreed to Harrison because it was better than naming me R2-D2."

At that, Gigi laughed, and her pretty face brightened, losing that tight expression she seemed to wear most of the time. A grin tugged at his lips. Damn. When she lowered her guard, she was downright approachable.

"So what was your personal question for me?" she asked.

"I'll take a rain check."

"You mean I'll owe you one?"

He liked the sound of that and gave her a wink.

Their gazes locked, and he felt a jolt of electricity. No. Not that, he told himself. Having a "thing" with a client was off-limits, especially this one. No way did he want to mess up the opportunity to provide more legal services to the Fortunes.

He looked away and opened the door. "Thanks. I'll call you after my investigation." Then he walked out into the morning sunshine, dragging behind a bit of regret.

Gigi stood in the doorway and watched Harrison saunter to his car, his steps determined, his shoulders broad and straight. The sunlight glinted off the dark curls of his hair.

The man was full of surprises—he was a former JAG attorney. An alumnus of Chatelaine High School. And attractive as all get-out, too.

Once Harrison had slid behind the wheel of his late-model black Audi sedan, she returned to the foyer and closed the door.

She knew better than to be swayed by a man's good looks, or by her physical reaction to him. But honestly, there was a stirring within her, something about him that drew her attention. She recognized the signs. She recognized the red flags, too. She'd hadn't been celibate after her divorce, but she hadn't dated very much. Most men seemed to be more interested in going out with her because of her last name.

She sucked in a deep breath and slowly let it out. At forty, she had been deemed "too old" by men who were eager to start a family. Apparently her shelf life was limited. So she'd resigned herself to the fact that she probably wouldn't have children. Sometimes, when she considered the possibility, a dark cloud rose up and shadowed her usual sunny demeanor.

But if truth be told, she'd rather remain childless than have a loveless marriage with a "Fortune hunter."

The jury was out on Harrison, of course, but she couldn't be too careful. Still…

She headed to her office, snatched her cell phone from the desk and sent a text to her brother telling him Harrison had come and gone.

Moments later, Reeve responded.

Did he get what he needed?

She informed him that indeed he had and she added a note about his plan to visit Rambling Rose to check things out.

Good. That's a relief. To me, anyway.

She typed a check mark next to his comment. It was a bit of a relief to her, too. She added another text.

We should have some answers by Monday.

Three dots popped on the screen, indicating he was typing out a response. Then the dots disappeared. He was probably distracted by something or other.

She bit down on her bottom lip, then typed out her message, choosing her words carefully. I've been thinking... I should have taken the Sanchez woman more seriously. I do now.

No response?

Nothing snarky?

Was Reeve still distracted?

Her fingers flew across the keyboard as she typed again. I know you're busy. I've had more contact with her, so I'll take the lead on this and keep you posted.

A thumbs-up emoji popped up on the screen, followed by his response.

Makes sense. Thanks.

Gigi smiled as she replied. Just trying to help the family.

Yourself, too?

Maybe so. Her thoughts drifted to Harrison. He was a handsome man, and she could be wily at times. But rather than respond to Reeve's insinuation, she'd left any further rebuttal unsaid.

On Friday morning, Harrison packed for an overnight trip, then, after a one-o'clock meeting with a new client at the office, he made the long drive to Rambling Rose, an up-and-coming Texas suburb located halfway between Austin and Houston.

Prior to setting out today, he'd done an internet

search and read up on the community Mariana Sanchez called home. Twelve or thirteen years ago, Rambling Rose had been a forgotten blue-collar town with a few ranches on its outskirts. Then, after it was featured in a documentary about Texas's best kept secrets, a flood of out-of-towners moved to the area and scooped up real estate at cheap prices and then gentrified everything in sight, much to the chagrin of the locals.

With the development of Rambling Rose Estates, a gated community of expensive homes, millionaires began moving in, and the community seemed to change overnight.

Initially, he suspected Mariana Sanchez had seen a better way of life and then come up with a plan to acquire some wealth of her own. But upon further research, Harrison learned that several branches of the Fortune family lived there. And that brought up another question. Why didn't Mariana claim to be related to the Fortunes who lived in Rambling Rose? Plenty of them had opened up businesses—a hotel, a restaurant and any number of other endeavors. So why seek out Gigi and Reeve?

Harrison clearly had his investigative work cut out for him. In the meantime, he reserved a room at Hotel Fortune before leaving his office. Several hours later, at a quarter to four, he arrived at the impressive, Spanish-style building with a white stucco exterior and a red tiled roof.

After pulling into the porte cochere, he'd barely shut off the engine when a valet approached with a welcoming smile. "Good afternoon, sir. Will you be checking in? Or just here to dine with us?"

"I'm checking in." Harrison exited the car with his backpack and handed the keys to the valet.

"Can I get your bags?"

"No need. This is all I have. I'll only be here one night."

"The front desk is located to your left," the valet said. "And Roja, our onsite restaurant, is to your right."

Harrison couldn't ask for a better place to stay. Once he had the keys to his room, he'd settle in and freshen up. Then he'd head for Roja, the restaurant where Mariana Sanchez claimed to be a cook.

Thirty minutes later, he stood at the dark-colored hostess stand, the word *ROJA* on the front in raised red lettering. A twentysomething blonde approached with a spring in her step and a bubbly smile. "Hi, y'all. Welcome to Roja. I'm afraid the restaurant won't be open for dinner for another thirty minutes or so. But the lounge is. And we have a bar menu."

"No problem," Harrison said. "Point me in the right direction."

The effervescent blonde laughed. "I don't mind takin' ya there. Come with me."

Harrison followed her past a cozy, but empty, dining area and into the lounge, which was filled with men and women in business attire—a professional crowd. Not surprising on a Friday afternoon at the end of a workweek.

He took a seat at a table for two near a window that looked onto the street. He'd no more than reached for a small menu when his cell phone rang. He pulled it from the pocket of his sports jacket and glanced at the screen. When he spotted Gigi Fortune's name, a smile tugged at his lips. "Hey," he said. "What's up?"

"Did you get a chance to talk to that Sanchez woman?"

"No, not yet." Apparently, Gigi was the impatient type. But dang. He'd just got into town. "I'm just doing a little recon this evening."

"Just to get you up to speed," she said, "I'm going to take the lead on this case. Reeve's pretty busy right now, and I'm the one who's had the most contact with her."

When Reeve had touched base with Harrison earlier today, he'd pretty much told him the same thing. "Understood. I'll definitely keep you posted. But I don't think I'll have much to report until tomorrow afternoon."

"What's on the game plan?"

He looked around to make sure no one was listening, then cupped his hand over his phone and said in a quiet voice, "I'm going to visit Mariana's Market and see what I can find out there. I'll mosey around like a tourist, ask a few questions then check out her food truck."

"And tonight?"

"I'm already in the Roja lounge. After dinner I'll pay my compliments to the chef and the kitchen staff."

"I doubt Mariana's the actual chef. Maybe a line cook. Isn't Roja an upscale restaurant?"

"You're right. Either way, I'll call you on my way back to the city. Unless you'd like to meet me someplace and discuss it in person."

She didn't respond right away. "Where'd you have in mind?"

He hadn't given it much thought.

"I mean…" She cleared her throat. "I don't think it's a good idea for us to discuss it in public. Why don't you stop by my house on your way home?"

He didn't blame her for wanting to keep their conversation private. "Works for me. I'll call you when I'm on the road."

Should he show up with a bottle of fine wine?

Damn, Harrison. What's the matter with you? Gigi Fortune is a client. And that's all she'll ever be. No wine. No roses. No wild-ass romantic assumptions. The only thing he'd bring to the table was a solid representation of her family's interests in this case and a fair and justified bill at the end.

Chapter Three

Harrison enjoyed a tasty prime-rib dinner at Roja, but as luck would have it, Mariana Sanchez had taken the night off. But that didn't mean he couldn't quiz his waitress about her.

The twentysomething woman with purple streaks woven into her dyed black hair put the bill on the table. "Yeah, she's off tonight. She's got some big event going on tomorrow at Mariana's Market."

He'd already checked her business license, and it was up-to-date. "Where, exactly, is her market located?"

"On the south side of town. Just follow Main Street down until it turns into a dirt road." She eyed him carefully. "Are you a friend?"

"I'm a just a friend of a friend," Harrison said, reaching for his wallet. "While I'm in town, I wanted to say hello. Do you know her very well?"

"Well enough." She tilted the empty tray in her hand. "My boyfriend and I have only been here a few months, but you can't live very long in Rambling Rose before meeting her. She's a longtime local and town legend. She and her mom started it all years ago with just a food truck. After her mom passed away, she kept everything going. It's really popular. People come from all over to buy and sell."

"Mariana's Market, right?"

She nodded. "My boyfriend has a band, and sometimes they play there. They're really good—if you like country music—and they draw a pretty nice crowd."

"That's a great way to get known."

She nodded. "Yep. Too bad it's only open on Saturdays. But it's super busy. Everyone around here calls it a flea market, but it's more than that. Vendors sell anything you can think of—baked goods, handmade crafts, artwork and the best produce. You never know what you'll find there. The place is huge. And her food truck is right at the center of it all."

"So she owns the land?"

"I'm not sure about that, but she's definitely in charge and rents out booths. She lets my boyfriend's band play there, and doesn't charge them. They don't have to pay her, either, but she gives them lunch and lets them put out a tip jar."

"Sounds like she's a real entrepreneur." And always ready to make a buck.

"Yep. That's her. But she's generous. You'll be hard-pressed to find anyone in Rambling Rose who doesn't like her."

"Is that a fact?" Harrison wasn't convinced. But he didn't persist. Instead, he paid the bill and left a nice tip.

After calling it a night, he woke up early and snagged a cup of java and a muffin at a coffee shop nearby. He made a mental note that the small but bustling town seemed to have civic pride. Merchants swept the sidewalk in front of their closed shops. A gardener clipped the elm trees that shaded the buildings.

After he checked out of his room, he asked the valet— a different one than the day before—to bring his car.

The young man handed him his keys. "Here you go, sir."

"Thanks." Harrison peeled off a five-dollar bill from his money clip and gave it to him. "Can you give me directions to Mariana's Market?"

"You bet." The valet directed him to the outskirts of town. Ten minutes later he spotted an open-air marketplace that took up several acres. And it was packed with vendors, buyers and lookie-loos. Mariana Sanchez had to be making bank on the rentals.

He parked in a crowded graveled lot, next to a large white shuttle van. Las Palmas Senior Living was painted on the side.

No doubt about it. Mariana's Market drew a large crowd. He'd just slid out of the driver's seat when a redhead wearing a white polo shirt with a Las Palmas logo returned to the van.

"Good morning," he said, offering the woman a smile.

"It sure is." She unlocked the side door and retrieved

a small brown purse from one of the seats. "Or it would be if someone wasn't so forgetful."

"Someone forgot something?" he asked.

"Yep. Helen Marshall. She was about to buy a brownie from the bakery truck and realized she'd left her purse in the van. I offered to loan her the money, but she wouldn't have it. She's on a shopping spree today."

Harrison chuckled. "What all do they sell here?"

"You name it." The woman locked the van door. "But most of our residents consider this a weekly social outing."

He walked along with her to the edge of the market.

"You must be new here, or a tourist," she said.

"Yep. I heard you couldn't visit Rambling Rose without checking out this place. And eating lunch at Mariana's."

"Her meat-loaf sandwich is to die for. I mean, that's what I heard. I'm a vegetarian."

"I'll keep that in mind."

They entered the market, where the sounds of laughter filled the air, along with the smells of baked items and grilled meat.

So far, nothing made sense. Mariana was a good cook. And from the looks of things, a sharp businesswoman. Sharp enough to fleece his clients?

Various customers had formed lines in front of the makeshift shops. Next to a man selling wood carvings, four older men had set up a card table under an awning and were playing cards. A small crowd had gathered around them.

"See what I mean about social outings?" the van driver said.

Harrison nodded. Wasn't that the truth?

"Well, the bakery truck is right over there." She pointed to the right. "And that sweet, gray-haired woman at the front of the line, patting herself and looking for her handbag, is Helen. So I'd better solve her problem and leave you to wander."

Harrison nodded. "Thanks. Have a good day."

Before continuing on, he paused by the card table, where the men were playing gin rummy. One fellow with a head of thick white hair took a draw from his cigarette, then tucked it behind his ear while he withdrew a card from the stack and pondered his next play. And he continued to ponder as a swirl of smoke curled into the air above his head.

"Come on," the man to his right said. "Make up your mind, Cotton Head. We ain't got all day."

"Keep your pants on, Norm. I'm thinking. Planning my strategy." Cotton Head studied his hand, trying to decide which card to throw away.

Harrison figured the dropped-bill game would work on these guys. He took another five from his money clip, then eased toward Norm. He swooped down and pretended to pick up the bill off the ground. "Looks like someone dropped this."

"Not me," Norm said.

Harrison set the bill on the table, but no one picked it up.

"You guys play here often?" he asked.

"Every Saturday morning," Norm said. "I'd invite you to join us, young fella, but it's a four-man game."

"Yes, I know. My dad is a gin player."

"I know a guy who's trying to set up another foursome. I could give you his number."

"I'm not a local," Harrison said. "I was told to check out the marketplace. Looks like it offers a little bit of everything."

"Yep. Check out the farmers' market on the east side. My wife runs a booth selling candied figs and strawberry jam."

"Nice to know. I'll pick some up after I get a bite to eat. Got any recommendations?"

"Only one. Mariana's food truck. Folks rave about her meat-loaf sandwich, but she makes a mean breakfast burrito."

"I take it you know her."

"You betcha. She's a great gal. Natural-born cook and fundraiser."

"Oh, yeah?" Did any of those funds make their way into her pocket?

Norm chuffed. "For Pete's sake, Cotton Head, I ain't got all day. Throw down a card already."

As the pondering gin player finally removed a card from his hand, the balding man across from him said, "Your hair's on fire, Cotton Head."

"He's right," Norm said. "You should've put out your cigarette."

A glance at Cotton Head's right ear told Harrison the men weren't just "blowing smoke."

Norm picked up a disposable cup and tossed the contents, ice and all, at the smoldering cigarette, the liquid splattering the side of the man's face.

"Oh, for cripe's sake." Cotton Head shook a finger at Norm. "Why in the hell did you do that?"

Harrison just chuckled, then continued to wander past a variety of vendors. Every now and then, he'd strike up a conversation with someone willing to chat. They all seemed to say the same thing. Mariana Sanchez was a friendly sort. A good cook. Jovial. A lot smarter than she looked.

Hmm. Smart enough to make her claim fly?

He purchased a couple of used books on aviation and Texas history he thought his dad would enjoy, noting that the saleswoman had a jar of tickets on her table, like many of the other vendors had set on theirs.

"What's going on?" he asked her. "Are you having a raffle?"

"Kind of," she said. "It was Mariana's idea. Most of us are donating a prize. I'm giving a copy of *Cujo*, autographed by Stephen King himself."

"Who's going to benefit?" he asked. Mariana?

"Greg Miranda," the woman said. "The kid suffered third-degree burns, and his folks don't have medical insurance, and he's got a big hospital bill."

"So a good cause, huh?"

"There's always someone in need around here, and we do what we can to help out. If you want to buy a ticket, there are a few high-school kids walking around and selling them."

Harrison nodded, then took the books he'd purchased for his dad and continued on his way. When he reached the center of the marketplace, he spotted a red, black and white vehicle with chrome trim. Green swirly letters on the side spelled out *Mariana's* in a fancy cursive font. Several people had already begun to fill the seats at the folding picnic tables set up out front.

He had to admit, the mouthwatering aroma coming from the truck sure smelled good.

A matronly woman with ruddy cheeks, warm brown eyes and bleached blond hair pulled into a bun popped her head out the open window and called in a graveled voice, "Clayton! Your breakfast burrito is ready."

As Harrison reached the food truck, a short, stocky man with a military-style haircut neared the window and reached for the foil-covered paper plate she held out. He must have whispered something funny, because the woman let out a raucous laugh.

Another man eased toward Harrison and gave him a nudge. "You in line, buddy?"

"Yes," Harrison said. "I'm sorry. Didn't mean to hold up the line."

"You look like a newbie. And there's a lot to take in."

Harrison hadn't meant to stand out. "Just visiting. I was told not to miss coming to Mariana's."

"That being the case, you're at the right food stand. Mariana makes a hell of a breakfast. You like menudo? Bet you don't even know what it is."

"Actually, I do. It's a traditional Mexican soup known as *pancita* or *mole de panza*." But not too many people could make it better than his mother.

"Order it. You won't be disappointed."

Harrison looked at the woman taking orders at the window of the food truck. "Is that Mariana?"

"The one and only."

Harrison nodded, then made his way to the open window, where the yellow-haired woman in her sixties stood.

"How can I help you, sweetie?"

"First of all, I'd like a bowl of your menudo." He reached for his wallet. "Then, if you have a moment, I'd like to talk to you. In private."

"I'm pretty busy. You wanna rent a booth? Come back at closing and we'll talk. But now's not a good time. Lunch rush is starting, and I got a special event going on. We're selling raffle tickets and taking donations for a teenager who was injured while saving a handicapped neighbor from a fire." She pointed to a table to Harrison's right. "You can give me a check or cash. Everyone here has donated prizes."

"Sounds like a good cause." He pulled out his wallet.

"You bet, sonny. How many tickets do you want?"

Harrison handed her a fifty, and she counted out ten tickets.

"Write your name and phone number on the back of each one, then put your tickets in that jar over yonder for that basket of fruits and veggies, or drop them at any participating vendor's booth for their prize. Good luck."

"Thanks." He tucked the tickets inside the cover of the book on aviation pioneers. "So when can you find time to talk to me?"

"After five," she said. "When people start shutting

down." She looked him up and down. "Haven't seen you around here before. What's on your mind?"

"I represent Gigi and Reeve Fortune."

At that, she brightened. "Well, in that case I guess I can spare a few minutes right now."

He bet she could.

She glanced over her shoulder. "Maggie, you're gonna have to take over for me. I need to take a break."

She winked at Harrison, then nodded toward an empty table with two folding chairs. "Have a seat. I'll be with you in a two shakes of a lamb's tail."

Late Saturday afternoon, following her special presentation of Adulting 101, a class on college or career planning and living on their own, that she taught to the junior and senior girls at Chatelaine High School, Gigi realized she'd never make it home in time to meet Harrison. She was eager to find out what he'd learned in Rambling Rose. So she gave him a call. He didn't answer immediately, and disappointment sparked. And not just because of the Sanchez woman. She liked talking to him for more reasons than one.

About the time she thought she'd have to leave a message, he answered. "Hey. I was just going to call you."

Her heart zinged at the sound of his voice, and, as much as she hated to admit it, Mariana had very little to do with that zippity-do-dah beat.

"What did you find out?" she asked.

"Well… It's hard to say for sure. Mariana has a big personality and appears to have a soft heart, but I can't rule out the possibility of her being a con artist. She's got an interesting story to tell. I didn't get out of town as soon as I'd wanted to, so I can meet with you and give you a complete rundown on Monday."

Not until Monday? "Got big plans this weekend, huh?"

"Not really. But while I was in Rambling Rose, I purchased a couple of books for my dad. And since Chatelaine wasn't that far off the interstate, I think I'll surprise him and my mom."

Gigi's heart rumbled and tumbled, then slipped back into a normal beat. "You're going to be in Chatelaine?"

"I will be in about an hour and twenty minutes."

She gripped the steering wheel as if she could steer her excitement into a matter-of-fact tone, licked her lips and cleared her throat. "Believe it or not, I'm here, too. And I thought I'd stay over. Well, I'm not exactly *in* town. But at the LC Club. But just for the night."

"In one of the condos?" he asked.

"No." Reeve had a condo at the lake but rarely used it. He'd said she was welcome to stay there, but she never took him up on the offer. Admittedly, ever since her father had begun grooming Reeve to take over the family's businesses, she'd tried to distance herself from her brother, and from feelings of jealousy and disappointment. "I stay at the hotel when I'm in the area." She bit down on her bottom lip. "We could meet here… if you have time."

"Actually, sure. I'm not in a hurry to surprise my folks. The LC Club must have a bar. Maybe we can find a quiet table where we can talk."

"Sounds good." A prickle of excitement shot up her

spine, and she did her best to tamp it down. This was business, not pleasure. "I'll meet you in the lounge."

"Sounds good. I should be there in about an hour. I'll see you then."

Gigi ended the call, but when she returned her full attention to the road, she realized that she'd made a wrong turn and ended up on a street she hadn't been on in ages, the one on which the old hardware store was located.

"Well, would you look at that," she muttered. The building had been remodeled. And a Grand Opening banner hung across the front of the deep covered porch with the words *Remi's Reads* written on it.

A bookstore? In Chatelaine?

Two old whiskey barrels filled with an array of colorful flowers flanked the double-wide front doors.

Unable to quell her curiosity, she parked along the street, then entered the new shop. She hadn't been there long when she spotted a fiction book one of her clients had raved about. She picked up a copy and read the story highlights on the inside-cover flap. She loved to read, but didn't indulge that pleasure often enough. Her blog and life coaching kept her busy, and the titles she did read were mostly nonfiction.

But what was it they said about all work and no play? Gigi decided to purchase the book and tucked it under her arm. When she neared the checkout desk, she overheard a name that stopped her. *Fortune Maloney.* She listened and picked up some of the conversation, but she couldn't hear all of it. Liam? Lincoln? Somebody had inherited something. Long-lost heir. The Fortunes. Engaged to Remi. Lucky girl.

Unfortunately, the women speaking stepped outside, leaving Gigi intrigued, although not in an especially good way. She scanned the bookshop and spotted an attractive young woman with long red hair who appeared to work there. Or, at least, she seemed to know her way around.

"Excuse me," Gigi said. "This is a great bookstore, isn't it?"

The woman turned to her with a smile. "It sure is."

"Do you know the owner?"

The redhead pointed to the pretty woman behind the counter, a brunette with long hair, a creamy complexion and big brown eyes with long lashes. "That's her. Remi Reynolds."

Bingo. "Oh, yes. She's engaged, right? To…gosh, I can't remember his name."

The woman nodded. "Lincoln Fortune Maloney."

"Any relationship to *the* Fortune family?"

As if suddenly uneasy about the line of questions, she stiffened. "I'm afraid that's all I know. Will you excuse me?" Then she turned and walked away.

Okay, so Gigi didn't have the investigative skills that Harrison was supposed to have. She'd need to tell him what she'd heard and let him take it from there.

But wasn't it interesting that Mariana wasn't the only one claiming to be a Fortune? At least this so-called Fortune hadn't approached her or Reeve. He was some other one of their shirttail relatives' problem.

After purchasing the book and gathering very little information, Gigi drove to the hotel at the LC Club, where she often stayed rather than making the two-hour drive back to Corpus Christi. The hotel was a sprawling building with several balconies and terraces that each offered a lovely view of Lake Chatelaine. The architecture not only had a rustic flare, but also a European elegance. The neutral color of the exterior went well with the red slate roof tiles. And the hotel, which had been built by the same contractor, blended perfectly.

She checked in at the front desk, took the key to her room and carried her small overnight bag to the elevator. By the time she'd settled into the cozy suite that overlooked the lake, she still had time to freshen up before meeting Harrison.

She went to the window and looked out at the lake. A pair of swans glided across the placid blue water, but underneath the calm surface, she knew their webbed feet were pumping wildly. That was sort of how she felt right now. Calm on the outside, but inside she churned to meet with Harrison.

She glanced at her Apple watch. Where had all the time gone? She hadn't meant to lollygag at the bookstore.

She hurried to the bathroom to freshen up. *It's business, remember?* Still, she took her hair out of the twist she'd been wearing, ran a brush through the long, wavy strands and let it hang loose. Then she freshened her breath and her lipstick.

"It's *not* a date," she told her image in the mirror.

The heck it isn't, her image insisted.

Ten minutes later, Gigi was seated at a table for two, trying not to watch the door and failing miserably. Thankfully, she didn't have to wait long.

Harrison sauntered in wearing jeans and a flannel shirt, no doubt trying to look the part of a Rambling Rose local. After a quick scan of the bar, he spotted her. A grin splashed across his gorgeous face as he made his way to her table. He'd no more than taken a seat when the cocktail waitress approached and placed a silver bowl filled with pretzels in front of them.

"Can I get y'all something to drink?"

"I'd like a glass of the Mendoza Winery chardonnay," Gigi said. "The reserve."

Harrison, who looked as comfortable in casual clothing as he did in a designer suit, ordered a scotch-and-water.

As soon as the server walked away, Gigi leaned forward. "So how did it go? Did you talk to her?"

"Yes, I did. And she had an interesting story."

"So you say. Do tell."

"Last year, a pink baby blanket with a letter *F* on it was sent anonymously to Steven Fortune. Mariana herself received a similar blanket, and so did Beau Fortune. Those clues, along with a photo of Fortunes' Foundling Hospital showing babies wrapped in that blanket, several engraved gifts and a poem, led the Fortunes of Rambling Rose to suspect that Mariana's mother, Maribel, had been left at the old foundling hospital by Maribel's mother, Luz Cortez. It's believed that Maribel was the biological daughter of Walter Fortune."

Gigi scoffed. "I find that hard to believe. What proof does she have?"

"Just the word of a man named Martin Smith, who claims to be the best friend of Walter's brother, Wendell. Do you know him?"

"No. I've heard the name, but never met him. I'd never met Wendell, either. Or if I did, I was too young to remember." Gigi paused, then shared the details she'd heard at Remi's Reads. "There are plenty of Fortune cousins in Texas, so who knows how they tie in, or where they got their inheritance."

The waitress returned with their drinks, and the conversation paused until she was out of range.

"I did hear that Walter and Wendell didn't get along," Gigi admitted. A thought struck her. How strange it'd be to discover a whole new family as an adult. Before she could allow herself to feel sympathy for Mariana, she hardened. "Find out what it will take to make the woman go away."

Harrison's demeanor stiffened, then he lifted his glass and took a swig. He didn't seem to be surprised by her request, but he didn't seem happy, either.

Had she said something to offend him?

"What's the matter?" she asked.

"Can I be honest?"

"You're my lawyer. I'd hope so." She braced herself.

He shrugged. "Something struck me as a bit hypocritical. For a woman who's in the business of listening to women's stories, I'd think you'd be a little more sympathetic toward Mariana."

Stunned—and speechless—Gigi stared into her wineglass. She found his comment irritating, mostly because he'd implied that *she* was the fraud and not Mariana. And it was so not true.

Or was it?

His tone softened. "I'll do the job I was hired to do,

but I believe she might be telling the truth. And to make matters even more plausible, she took a DNA test. According to Mariana, the results prove her relationship to the Fortunes."

At that, Gigi bristled. "You believe her?"

"She admitted that she went through one of those online ancestry companies, but said she's willing to take another DNA test, one that a court would recognize. I'll pursue that path further. And if that's true, I doubt that she'll just go away."

"True or not, we're not going to blindly accept her into our family. I did that once, when I married a man who only wanted access to my last name, and that was the biggest mistake I ever made. Just find out what it'll take to make her go away. That's what we hired you to do."

He shrugged. "Alright."

Gigi frowned and glared into her wine. How could people think they could weasel their way into the Fortune family—especially into their hearts?

"Are you okay?" Harrison asked.

"Of course." She turned off the frown, reached for a pretzel and popped it into her mouth. "Are you hungry? The restaurant opens for dinner at five."

He seemed to ponder the idea for a moment. "I'll have to take a rain check. I told my mother I was in the area, and she's making chili verde—one of my favorites."

"I thought you said you were going to surprise them?" Was he just using that as an excuse to ditch her?

He smiled. "I caved. I called them on my way here."

"I take it you're close to your parents."

"Yes, I am."

Gigi's parents lived in France and didn't stay in touch too often. Christmas. Birthdays. A rare FaceTime call. That was about it. "Must be nice."

"Most of the time. Do you come to Chatelaine very often?" he asked.

"Once or twice a month. I'll be here next week to record a podcast. And I also check in at the high school to see if I can fill a need—financially or otherwise." Like the special young women's event she held today.

"Next Friday?" Harrison asked. "Will you be staying over?"

"Maybe. Why?"

"Because Friday is Cinco de Mayo, and the Chatelaine Bar and Grill is hosting a fiesta on the patio."

Was he asking her out?

No, that seemed doubtful. Yet the thought of margaritas, a mariachi band and Mexican food was tempting.

The attorney sitting across from her, a broad smile revealing perfect white teeth, was tempting, too.

"If you're in town, join us."

"Sounds like fun," she said. And possibly a date. "I'll meet you there."

On Sunday morning, Harrison sat at his parents' breakfast table, drinking a cup of coffee and watching his mom prepare his favorite breakfast—huevos rancheros. The warm aroma of tomato and chili filled the air.

His dad, Andres, got up from his seat, made his way

to the stove and kissed Mama's cheek. "This is the first official day of your Mama's retirement, *hijo*. We'll have to go to dinner tonight and celebrate."

His mother had been talking about retiring for the past couple of years, something he and his dad had encouraged. She loved being a nurse, but she was prone to depression, and since she often took her patients' medical journeys to heart, the profession took an emotional toll on her. She'd always managed to carry on, but now, at her age, the twelve-hour shifts were physically exhausting.

"What do you plan to do with your free time?" Harrison asked.

His mother pulled three plates out of the cupboard and set them on the counter, next to the stove, then turned to face him. Her expression wasn't a happy one. "I have no idea. To tell you the truth, I'll probably go crazy sitting at home. Too bad I can't think of anything else to do in my 'second act.'"

"Since my retirement, I keep busy teaching that ESL class at the adult school," Papa said. "Makes me feel like I'm contributing something."

"And what do you contribute to your fishing and golfing buddies?" Mama asked.

Papa laughed and winked at Harrison. "Lots of laughs. And the pleasure of my company."

After filling Harrison's plate with a generous portion, she placed it in front of him. "More coffee? Orange juice?"

"No thanks. This is fine." Better than fine, actually.

Harrison rarely ate a big breakfast. But he'd never turn down one of Mama's homemade meals.

"My friend Gloria volunteers at the animal shelter, but… I'm allergic to cats." Mama tucked a strand of graying hair behind her ear. "I could volunteer at the hospital, and I'm not opposed to doing something like that, it's just that…" She sighed. "I don't know. I'm glad to have some time to myself, but I want to feel passionate about what I do."

"You can feel passionate about me, Sylvia, *mi preciosa*." Papa reached out and gave her a love pat on her bottom.

She waved him off while chuckling. "Yes, there's that, Andres. But that's not what I meant."

"You know," Harrison said, "I have a client who's a life coach. She helps women who are in transition learn to navigate a change, like widowhood, divorce, retirement." Harrison had no idea how Gigi would feel about working with his mother. But she might have someone she could recommend.

"That's probably expensive," Mama said. "And now we're on a fixed income. So I probably should figure something else out."

"Don't worry about money. I'll take care of any cost involved." Harrison lifted his mug and took a sip of coffee.

"A life coach?" Papa scoffed. "That sounds a little indulgent."

Mama shrugged. "Easy for you to say, Andres. You have your English-language classes and your buddies. I don't know what I want to do with all this new time on my hands. And certainly not just clean house and watch *Wheel of Fortune*!"

Harrison had his own personal *Wheel of Fortune* game going on. He didn't know where the ticker would land—success or failure in his new civilian life—but when he was around Gigi, he found himself holding his breath and watching the spinner.

What if he told his mother whom he was talking about?

He looked across the table at his parents. They'd both come from a generation and culture where a job was only a means to provide for their families, although they'd both found fulfillment in their respective careers. Now, they were financially set, even if they weren't rich, but they ought to both have something they found personally rewarding.

His father took a sip of his coffee. "I'm just saying, my generation never needed a 'life coach.' We just got on with our lives."

"Don't be so last-century, Papa. There's nothing wrong with life coaching. It can be very helpful." Harrison turned to his mother. "Mama, just so you know, Gigi Fortune is my client. She might not have time to take on someone else, but would you at least be willing to talk to her?"

Mama crossed her arms and eyed him carefully. She lifted one charcoal-gray eyebrow. "Gigi Fortune is your client? *The* Gigi Fortune?"

"Yes. I'm doing a little work for her and her family." Harrison dug into his spicy egg dish, savoring the hearty taste. When he glanced up, both parents were eyeing him, as if sizing him up. "What? Why are you guys looking at me like that?"

"Already asking the woman for a personal favor?" Mama asked.

Harrison shrugged. Was it too soon? Maybe. "Yeah, so? What's your concern?"

"You just started work at that new firm." Papa's brown eyes twinkled. "And it sounds like you've gotten to know her pretty well in a very short period of time. That is, if you feel comfortable in asking for a personal favor. Something else going on?"

"Papa, no." Harrison shook his head. "Just, no."

Besides, on the contrary, he didn't know Gigi Fortune very well at all, other than the assumptions he'd made on day one, a couple of which he'd had to reconsider.

"I assure you, asking Ms. Fortune isn't a problem. Courtesy between professionals." If he even broached the subject. Hell. Did he even want to go there?

"If she helps women navigate new seasons in their lives," Mama said, "I hope she's well beyond college age. I'm not sure I'd want to take advice from someone in their twenties."

"She's experienced, Mama. And for the record, she's in her late thirties, possibly forty. Is that old enough for you?"

Mama gave a slow nod. "She's about *your* age. And young enough to be my daughter. Still, I suppose she's old enough. Do you think we'd connect?"

"You like everyone, Mama. So I'm not worried. And just to be sure, I won't mention anything until after

Cinco de Mayo. She'll be at the Chatelaine Bar and Grill that night, and you can meet her there."

His mother shot a glance at his father, who broke into a dimpled grin. "Like I said. You seem to be getting to know her pretty well."

"Oh, no, you don't. Believe it or not, I never mix business with pleasure." A real no-no in the military ranks, and the civilian world as well.

"But you asked her on a date to Cinco de Mayo?" Mama asked.

"Not on a date. I just mentioned it, and she seemed to like the idea of mingling with the Chatelaine locals and letting her hair down a little."

"What color hair does she have?" Mama asked as she poured more coffee into Harrison's cup.

"She has long blond hair," Papa said. "And she's beautiful."

That was true. Harrison shot a quizzical glance at his father. "How do you know that?"

"I've never met her personally, but I've seen her a time or two at the high school."

"Is she a nice girl?" Mama asked.

"Oh, yes. Very," Papa said. "She's been exceptionally generous and supportive of the kids and the staff. Is she really your age, Harrison? I don't think she looks a day over twenty-five."

"She might look young, but she's older than that. And tough in a polite, professional sort of way." But she *was* definitely pretty. And blond. Slender. A cut and class above him, though.

Mama slipped a spoonful of sugar into her coffee. "Then I approve."

"Stop grinning like that, Mama. And don't either of you get any ideas. My relationship with Gigi Fortune is strictly business."

Still, Harrison knew where this line of questioning was coming from…and where it was going. His mom and dad had never made a big issue about it, but they'd like to have grandkids some day, and he was their only hope.

Unfortunately for them, being in the army and building his career as a JAG lawyer had been his focus. Sure, he'd had plenty of dates. And his libido was in fine working order. But setting down roots and getting married had never been a part of his playbook.

Well, it had been once—a couple of years ago, when he'd dated Sherrilyn. She'd been a single mom with two kids, and he'd been a little reluctant to go out with her at first. But it hadn't taken long for her and her sweet children to stir up warm feelings making him believe he could have a family of his own.

But then her ex came back into the picture, and she decided they ought to try and make a go of it. Harrison had understood why and got out of their way, but it still hurt. So he'd gone back to being single and unattached.

Maybe he'd find someone else someday. But not now. And not with Gigi.

"We're looking forward to meeting her," Mama said. "And helping her kick up her heels."

Papa nodded. "And shake out that long blond hair."

Something told Harrison he'd just invited trouble.

But it was too late to backpedal now. "Promise me you two won't do anything to embarrass me."

"No, of course not," Mama said.

Papa lifted his hand as if on the witness stand. "I swear. We'll be on our best behavior."

They nodded in assurance. Yet, Harrison had a sinking feeling Friday night might not turn out so well in the end.

Chapter Four

No matter how many times Gigi drove through Chatelaine, a sense of nostalgia settled over her. When she was a girl, and before Grampy's stroke, they would slip away from the Fortune Metals office and drive into town for a barbecue beef sandwich, followed by an ice-cream cone.

Now, as the sun slipped low in the west Texas sky, she felt that same old feeling as she passed the old gas station with one pump, the sign out front still welcoming people to Chatelaine, The Town That Never Changes, and directing them to Harv's New BBQ. She could almost smell the smoky, sweet aroma of seasoned meat on the grill and taste the smooth creaminess of a vanilla cone. The next time she ventured into town, she'd find time to stop at Harv's for a late lunch or an early dinner.

She glanced at the clock on the dash. She'd told Harrison she'd meet him at the Chatelaine Bar and Grill at six o'clock, but now she'd arrived fifteen minutes late. She'd blame it on unexpected traffic, but if truth be told, she'd spent too much time trying to figure out what to wear, a fact that irritated her. She hadn't been that fashionably insecure since her high-school days. Nevertheless, after rejecting the two other outfits she'd brought with her and finally deciding on a pair of black jeans, a red blouse and cowgirl boots, she'd taken numerous looks at herself in the full-length mirror in her hotel suite before she'd headed to the Chatelaine Bar and Grill.

As she slowed the white BMW near the entrance to the parking lot, she realized the place was really hopping tonight. It looked as if everyone in town had decided to show up at the bar and grill, and she had to park a block away.

A middle-aged couple entered the restaurant in front of her, and she followed them to the hostess stand. While waiting, she scanned the dining area. Red leather banquette seating and wood walls gave the place a masculine, old-school steak-house vibe.

"Do you have reservations?" the hostess asked the couple.

"We're attending the Thompson anniversary party. We were told it's in the back room."

The hostess asked Gigi, "Are you with the Thompson party?"

"I'm here for the Cinco de Mayo event on the patio."

The hostess pointed her in the right direction, then led the couple to their event.

Gigi strode through the bar and followed the sound

of mariachi music to the patio, which was decked out with twinkling white lights, a margarita fountain and a Mexican buffet. Smiling faces and laughter provided a festive, party vibe.

She'd barely glanced around before she saw Harrison seated at a table with an older couple—his parents, she assumed. He stood and made his way to where she was, near a large potted palm.

"I'm glad you made it." His eyes swept over her, and he smiled. "You look nice."

Her cheeks warmed. "Thank you." He looked nice, too. And he also smelled good, thanks to his musky cologne. But she bit back a comment that might make him think she was just returning the compliment.

"May I get you a margarita? Maybe a glass of wine? There's a full bar out here, as well as the one inside."

She smiled. "Considering the music, the food and the Southwestern atmosphere, a margarita seems appropriate."

"You've got it." He nodded toward the table he'd just left. "Do you mind if we sit with my parents?"

"No, not at all." Actually, doing that would be a lot more comfortable. And it would be easier not to get taken in by his expressive brown eyes and dimpled grin. Dang, he looked good in those jeans.

"Great. This way."

He placed a hand on her back, sending a spiral of heat to the spot and a tingle through her nervous system. She had to remind herself that this was just a business event. Not a date, even if her imagination tried to convince her otherwise.

He pulled out a chair for her, next to the one where

he'd been sitting. "Gigi, these are my parents—Andres and Sylvia."

Andres, a handsome older man who resembled his son, stood and took her right hand in both of his. "It's nice to finally meet you, Ms. Fortune."

"It's Gigi. Please."

Sylvia remained seated, a welcoming smile plastered across her face. "We're happy you could join us, Gigi. Please, sit down. We've heard so much about you."

"Oh, have you?" That set off alarms. What had Harrison told his parents? Cold, controlling, stuck-up rich girl?

As Gigi sank to her chair, Andres sat next to his wife. "I used to teach at Chatelaine High School. I'd like to thank you for the financial help and support you've provided to the staff, the students and the school."

"Oh, that's how you know of me."

Andres winked at his wife, then said, "Of course. I'm no longer teaching there, but I keep in touch with the staff. And they have nothing but good things to say about you."

"It's my pleasure," Gigi said. "I try to visit every time I come into town to make a podcast." She looked at Harrison, then to the empty chair beside hers.

"If you'll excuse me," Harrison said, "I'll go get a round of margaritas for everyone."

"Don't forget the chips, salsa and guacamole," Sylvia called out. "He's going to need an extra set of hands. Go help him, Andres."

Was that a ploy to get Gigi alone and to give her the third degree? The woman seemed pleasant, but Gigi scooted back her chair and raised her palm as she got to her feet. "Please, don't bother. I'll help him."

As she began to walk away, Sylvia lowered her voice, yet Gigi overheard her, anyway. "Andres, did you see the way he looks at her? Did that seem all business and professional to you?"

Gigi would have continued on to the patio bar and the margarita fountain, but a waiter carrying a tray of shredded beef who was heading to the buffet table blocked her path, enabling her to hear Andres's response.

"Don't get your hopes up, Sylvia. If it's meant to be, it'll happen."

Gigi wasn't sure if she should be pleased by their romantic hopes, or if she should feign a headache and call it an early night.

Harrison made his way to the margarita bar and stood in line behind a redhead dressed in a pair of snug denim jeans and a blue polka-dot blouse.

"I'd like two margaritas," she told the bartender.

"Comin' right up," the young man said.

Approaching footsteps sounded, and Harrison glanced to his right, where a smiling Gigi was approaching. "I thought you might want an extra pair of hands to carry the drinks to the table, as well as the chips and salsa."

"Don't forget the guacamole." He tossed her a playful grin. "I don't mind making a couple of trips, but thanks for the help."

Before Gigi could respond, the redhead turned away from the patio bar. Her eyes met his, and recognition dawned. "Hey! Harrison! What a surprise."

Yes, it was. He hadn't seen Suzy Walker in ages. Not that they were old friends. She'd been a freshman when he'd been a senior. She'd always been nice, but her brother, who was a year older than Harrison and a grade behind him, had made Harrison's life miserable from seventh grade on. So for that reason, he'd tended to avoid both of the Walkers whenever he could. But that wasn't necessary any longer. "Long time no see. How are you, Suzy?"

"I'm doing well. I go by Suzanne now, but I still answer to Suzy when I'm in Chatelaine, which isn't very often. I'm a psychology professor at Rice University in Houston, so that keeps me pretty busy."

Apparently, Suzy was a lot smarter than her brother. And while Harrison hadn't given her brother any thought after high-school graduation, he made the cordial and expected follow-up question. "What's Jason up to these days?"

Her brow lifted, and her lips parted. "You don't know? Jason joined the marines right after his senior year and died in Afghanistan almost twenty years ago. A chopper crash."

"I'm sorry to hear that." Harrison may not have liked the guy, but he hadn't wished him any harm. "We lost a lot of good soldiers, some of them my friends."

Suzy—or rather, Suzanne—nodded in agreement. Then she glanced at Gigi as if she'd just realized Harrison wasn't alone.

He made polite introductions, using first names only since he didn't want to give Suzanne any reason to think he was dating one of the Fortunes. Nor did he address their relationship. There was no reason to admit that he'd brought a client to the Cinco de Mayo fiesta. And even if they were kicking back and socializing this evening, claiming they were friends seemed like a stretch.

"Harrison and my brother were friends," Suzanne explained to Gigi.

Now that's what Harrison would call a *huge* stretch, but he didn't correct her.

Suzanne pointed to a table near the buffet line, where another woman was sitting. "I'd better get these drinks back to my cousin before she sends out a search party. It was good seeing you."

"Same here," Harrison said. "I'm sorry about your brother."

"Yeah. Me, too."

"Have a good evening," he added. "And a nice trip back to Houston."

As Suzanne carried two margaritas to her table, Gigi continued to study her back. He wondered what she was thinking. Making some kind of assessment, no doubt. Hopefully she'd keep it to herself. He didn't want to stir up any old high-school memories tonight.

When Gigi turned to him and caught his gaze, the sorrow in her eyes struck him like a blow to the gut.

"You okay?" he asked.

She waved her hand. "I'm all right. Sorry about that. It just struck me. I've been working with a woman who lost her husband in the military. She's having a hard time moving on."

He nodded in agreement, surprised to catch a glimpse of her softer side. "Sometimes service to your country requires the ultimate sacrifice, and I'm not just talking about military service. Firefighters, police officers, doctors and nurses, too. Sadly, it's not just those in uniform who make that sacrifice."

She placed her hand on his arm, connecting them in a surprising way and sending a warm, dazzling shiver all the way up to his shoulder.

Before either of them could speak, the bartender cleared his throat, drawing their attention. "What can I get you?"

Harrison ordered the margaritas, and moments later, he and Gigi delivered the drinks to the table, where his mother was sitting alone.

"Your father went to pick up the chips and salsa," Mama said. "That woman you were talking to. Was she Jason Walker's sister?"

"Yes, it was. I had no idea he'd joined the marines. Or that he died. Why didn't you tell me?"

"I'm sorry, honey. I thought I had. His death was so sad. It made me worry all the more about you."

"But I wasn't in combat."

"I know," Mama said. "But for the record, it's hard for a mother to shake her concern for her children, even when they're grown and gone."

Papa returned with a tray carrying four small plates, a basket of chips and bowls of guacamole and salsa. He'd even picked up a small platter of mini chimichangas. "I thought you might be hungry." He placed the appetizers on the table then lifted his salt-rimmed glass. "To a festive night out with our son and his beautiful companion."

Harrison nearly choked. He glanced at Gigi, who

merely smiled like a good sport and clinked her glass against Papa's, then Mama's. And his.

After the toast, they each took the first sip of their frozen drinks. They remained quiet for a couple of beats. Then Papa turned to Gigi and broke the silence. "Did you hear about the Latino firefighter whose wife had twin boys?"

Oh, brother. Harrison had heard that one a jillion times. But at least Mama had talked his dad out of wearing the sombrero and serape he'd taken out of storage.

"No," Gigi said, "I haven't heard that one."

Papa beamed, and his eyes twinkled. "They named them Jose and Hose *B*."

Gigi's furrowed her brow. "I don't get it."

Papa tilted his head as if dumbfounded. "Hose *A*... Jose? Hose *B*? Twins?"

"Oh." Gigi laughed, her voice a soft lilt. "*Jose*. Got it now."

"I'm afraid my dad always had aspirations to be a stand-up comedian." Harrison gave Gigi a nudge. "So you'll have to excuse his jokes. Some of them fall flat."

She grinned. "Like that one. But that doesn't bother me. My great-grandfather had a great sense of humor. At least, he enjoyed making me laugh. Although I'm not so sure he showed that side of himself to anyone else."

Interesting. When Harrison first met Gigi, he'd assumed that she didn't have a sense of humor and rarely laughed. But he'd been wrong. Maybe he ought to tell her a few jokes, just to hear that happy sound again and to see a joyful expression on her pretty face.

As the evening wore on, they enjoyed a second round of margaritas while the mariachi music continued to play. The conversation flowed surprisingly easy, especially for people of different ages and who had different financial and cultural backgrounds.

At a quarter to eight, Papa threw in the towel. "I'm afraid your mother and I have to leave. I have office hours for my ESL classes early tomorrow morning."

Mama leaned into Gigi. "Andres teaches several English as a second language classes at the adult school on Saturday afternoon and evening."

"I love that," Gigi said to Papa. "Even though you're retired, you're using your skills to help others."

"I'm happy for him. He's found something worthwhile to do with this time, something that makes him happy." Mama turned to Gigi. "Do you speak Spanish?"

"Not really. But I'm fluent in French."

Mama smiled softly, and her eyes appeared to mist. "I wish I was. I've always dreamed of going to Paris, and if I ever do, it would be nice to speak the language."

"It's a beautiful city," Gigi said. "My mother is French, so our annual family vacations always included a shopping spree on the Champs-élysées."

"How exciting. That street is famous for shopping. I'd love to see it, even if I couldn't afford to buy anything at those designer stores. Just to take it all in…" Mama let out a dreamy sigh. "And afterward, I'd stop at a sidewalk café and order coffee and croissants, warm from the oven." She reached across the table and placed her hand over Papa's. "Andres, speaking of retirement, can we plan that trip to Europe?"

"Maybe so, *mi amor*." Papa scooted back from the table, the chair legs scratching against the tile floor. He slowly got to his feet, wincing as he straightened.

"Darn that blasted knee." He blew out a sigh. "I guess I'll have to schedule that surgery before I take any walking vacations."

Harrison agreed. His dad should have had that knee replaced before now, but he kept putting it off.

"Sylvia," Papa said, "are you ready to go?"

"Yes, I am." Mama got up from the table, reached for her purse and slipped the strap over her shoulder. "I'm sure these kids would like some time alone."

"It was nice meeting you," Gigi said, her tone sincere.

"It's been a pleasure." Mama bent to give Gigi a warm hug. "I hope to see you again."

The gesture appeared to startle Gigi for a moment, then she smiled. "I'd like that, Sylvia."

Harrison had gotten to know Gigi on a different level tonight, and he'd come to actually like her. As a person, that is, and not just a beautiful woman. In fact, he was looking forward to spending more time with her this evening.

After his parents left, he asked her if she'd like a cup of coffee and a serving of flan.

She glanced at her Apple watch. "That sounds great, but it's getting late, and I have to wake up early tomorrow. I should get back to the hotel."

"All right." Harrison motioned for the waiter, and the twentysomething man hurried over to their table.

"Can I get you something?" he asked.

"Just the bill," Harrison said.

"No worries. It's already been taken care of. Mr. Vasquez paid before he left."

"In that case," Harrison said to Gigi, getting to his feet, "may I walk you to your car?"

"Sure."

As they left the patio, entered the bar and continued through the door that led to the dining room, Harrison felt the strongest compulsion to end the evening the way his mom had—by giving Gigi an affectionate hug. Not that he'd make a bold move like that.

But, hell. As her arm brushed against his, he was sorely tempted to take her by the hand and pull her close. He all but rolled his eyes at the stupid thought.

When they reached her white BMW, they paused by the driver's door. Gigi looked up at him wearing an expression that wasn't easy to read, but it reflected a vulnerability he'd never expected to see.

"I really had a good time tonight," she said. "Thanks for including me."

"I'm glad you came. And that you had fun."

"It was…more than that." Her words stalled. She glanced at her fancy boots, then up again. "Your parents are awesome and so down-to-earth. No pretenses. Just friendly chatter. In fact, I can't remember when I had such a pleasant and enjoyable evening."

Her admission took him aback.

"Your parents clearly love you," she added. "And each other."

"They're pretty cool. We've always been close."

As they continued to stand in the parking lot, she didn't seem to be in a hurry to leave. And quite frankly, he didn't want her to. If they'd been on an actual date, he might've made a move toward kissing her. He might've reached out and touched a long wavy strand of her blond hair. He might have moved it away from her face and swept it behind her shoulder, leaving his hand close to her cheek and—

Stop! She's not a date. She's a client. And a woman who could open the door for you to represent the Fortune family in another case.

But right this moment, with her gaze locked on his, with the springtime scent of her body lotion filling the night air…

Don't you dare touch her. Don't make the first move.

Without warning, Gigi reached out and gave him a brief, friendly hug that was over before he could blink. Yet it left him speechless. Stunned.

"Thanks for a great evening, Harrison." Then she turned, opened the car door and slid behind the steering wheel.

As she backed out of the parking space, Harrison continued to watch her go until her taillights disappeared.

Gigi Fortune may still be a client, but tonight she'd become a friend. Nothing unethical about that, right?

But what in the hell was he going to do about the urge to embrace her again…and give her more than a kiss goodbye?

Chapter Five

Gigi never cried. At least, she hadn't shed a tear since the day her divorce from Anson was final. But here she was, driving back to the LC Club hotel, with pent-up emotion ready to burst.

A lump formed in her throat, and tears welled in her eyes, threatening to spill onto her cheeks. She squeezed the steering wheel as if that might somehow shut off the waterworks and corral her skittish feelings.

What was going on? She'd just experienced an enjoyable evening, but here she was, falling apart at the seams and dealing with an unfamiliar emotion that bore a strong resemblance to sadness. And even envy.

Harrison and his parents seemed to exemplify a kind, loving family, something Gigi had never quite had as a child, or even now, as an adult. Yet she hadn't realized she'd been lacking anything until tonight.

Her mom and dad hadn't been very affectionate. A stiff hug or peck on the cheek was about all she ever got from them. Not that they didn't love her and Reeve. It's just that they didn't often show it. Not the way Harrison's parents did with those little love pats, private smiles and a wink here and there.

Harrison seemed to enjoy their banter. If one of his parents teased him in a playful way, he gave it right back to them. Their camaraderie had been sweet to see.

No, Gigi's family wasn't close like that. A tear slipped down her face, then another. She wiped them away with her fingers, leaving her cheeks damp.

When Sylvia had given her a hug this evening, she'd been stunned by the heartfelt gesture. Then a sense of longing had swept over her, leaving her unbalanced and somehow missing something valuable, even though Gigi Fortune had enough money to purchase anything she could possibly want or need. But what good was money if there was no one to come home to, no one to care about, to laugh with, to hug?

Another tear slid down her face, but this time, as she swiped it away, she scolded herself. *So what? You're forty years old and no longer a kid. Get over it.*

"Time to move on," she said out loud. Wasn't that what she told her clients? "Consider this the time for a new adventure in life."

Then…

"Oh, snap." She hitched a breath. She'd just hugged Harrison as if it was the most natural thing in the world to do. As if they'd been friends for years.

The hug had been completely spontaneous. Only

trouble was, Gigi wasn't spontaneous. *Ever.* She was a planner. And leaving like that, with so much unsaid, so much for Harrison to read into…

Dread and uncertainty raced up her spine. What had Harrison thought about it? Had she left him feeling as awkward as she was feeling now? Had she crossed the line in their attorney-client relationship?

Or worse. Had she given him the idea that she'd like to move past friendship and on to something more intimate?

She blew out a sigh. That was a possibility. She didn't want to admit it, but she'd been entertaining romantic thoughts about him from the moment they rode up in the elevator to his office. But she'd never act on that impulse. And she certainly wasn't about to do it now.

If he mentioned it, she'd blame the hug on that second margarita, even if she had barely tasted the tequila and didn't feel the least bit buzzed.

Besides, that brief embrace had been the friendly kind and not a sexual come-on. A man like Harrison could tell the difference. Gigi certainly could, even if she'd felt as if she might melt into his arms. And even if his warm, alluring scent followed her to the car and lingered in the air she breathed.

Either way, she doubted he'd even broach the subject. And there was no way in the world that she'd bring it up.

Poof. Just like that. That blasted hug had never happened.

By the time she pulled into the porte cochere at the hotel, she had begun to believe it herself. That is, until she got out of the car and handed the keys to the valet.

A light evening breeze ruffled her hair, releasing a hint of Harrison's cologne, and the bittersweet memory followed her for the rest of the night.

And she was unable to keep thoughts of him at bay throughout the weekend. But on Monday morning, she poured herself into her work. As she'd hoped, the Zoom meeting with Candice Robinson, her newest client, had finally taken her mind off him.

Candice had no idea what to do with her time, now that her youngest child, a daughter, had gotten married and moved to Florida.

"For the past umpteen years," Candice said, "my main focus has been my kids, while most of my friends spent their free time at the country club, taking golf and tennis lessons and perfecting their athletic skills. Even if I was ready to join them now, they won't want to play with a beginner."

"Are you and those women still friends?" Gigi asked.

"Sure, but there's only so many drinks around the pool or in the country club bar that I can stand. I'm not a fan of golf, and I've never played tennis. And to be completely honest, at my age, I'm not interested in taking up a new sport."

"Did you ever socialize away from the country club?"

"We had a book club one summer," Candice said, "but it fizzled out."

"How did you meet?"

"Our kids went to the same private school, so we were involved in the parents group and participated in the usual fundraisers. We went to all the games and plays. But the kids are grown and on their own now."

Candice let out a weary sigh. "I guess I'll need to find new friends, but I don't even know where to begin. I'd also like to do something worthwhile with my time, something that will help others."

Gigi belonged to the country-club set, too. Some of the women she knew not only played golf and tennis, but they also volunteered their time and money with various charity groups. "Maybe you can find a nonprofit cause you care deeply about."

"I'll have to give it some thought," she said. "But I'm open to suggestions."

"Great. It might take a while for you to find one you're excited to support. I participated in quite a few fundraisers for a variety of worthwhile organizations, but it wasn't until I became personally involved with Chatelaine High School that I found my passion."

Suddenly, the thoughts she'd been avoiding struck hard and fast: Chatelaine. Harrison. Passion.

Gigi ran her hand over her lips, then shook off the sensual turn of her thoughts. *Dang, girl. Get your mind back on work.*

She reached for the bottle of water she kept on her desk and took a drink. Then she refocused on the computer screen, and Candice gazed back at her, stymied yet hopeful.

"You might not need new friends," Gigi said, "just new interests. You might be surprised at how many meaningful projects and even jobs that you'll find appealing. I'm going to send a questionnaire I'd like you to complete. Once you email it back to me, we'll talk again."

Candice agreed, and they ended the virtual meeting.

While Gigi was jotting down a few notes to put in Candice's file, her cell phone rang. She glanced at the screen. When she saw Harrison's name, her heart jumped to her throat, and she considered letting it roll over to voice mail. Then again, Harrison was her attorney, and she was his client. He had every reason to call her. And she had no reason to be flustered.

She took a deep breath, then answered with the practiced, nonchalant tone she often used with her brother. "Hey there, Harrison. What's up? Have you heard something from Mariana Sanchez?"

How was that for pretending they still had an attorney-client relationship and that her parting embrace had meant absolutely nothing?

"No, not a word," he said. "Maybe meeting your attorney scared her off. Then again, she might be waiting to contact us until after she takes that second DNA test and has the results in hand."

"She'd have to compare it to mine or my brother's." Wouldn't she?

"Don't forget, there are plenty of Fortunes living in Rambling Rose."

"Maybe her so-far alleged Fortune connection is through one of them." And not through Grampy's line of descendants. She still couldn't believe he'd cheat on his wife.

"Anyway," Harrison said, "I'm calling because I'd like to meet you for a drink or dinner. I want to talk to you, and it has nothing to do with the case."

Gigi's jaw nearly fell to the floor, and she fumbled

the phone in her hand. She gripped it tighter to avoid dropping it.

Did she dare admit that she was free this evening? Even if she'd had something on the calendar, curiosity would insist that she change her plans.

Before she could respond, Harrison added, "I'd like to discuss something with you. And ask a favor."

So it had nothing to do with her hug. He wanted a favor. Relieved yet disappointed, she said, "Sure. What's on your mind?"

"Let's meet, and we can talk then."

"Sounds mysterious." Her curiosity was doing a real number on her, but she downplayed it. "When do you want to meet?"

"Do you have any free time this week?"

"The next few days are fairly open for me." Did that make her sound too available? Dang it. "I'm afraid I'm slammed on Friday and most of next week."

"Then what about this evening, after work?"

Her last meeting was at three o'clock. She'd suggested meeting Aubrey Taylor at the park on Skyline, where the newly divorced woman's children could play while they talked about Aubrey's new season in life. And it shouldn't take more than an hour, but she'd want to go home and change. "I should be free by five-thirty."

"Okay. To be on the safe side, let's make it—six o'clock."

"Where?"

"How about in the bar at The Flying Pig, that new restaurant on State Street?"

"Great. I love trying new places."

But there were two things Gigi *didn't* love—not knowing what Harrison had on his mind and how their conversation would unfold.

The meeting at the park with Aubrey went a lot better than either Gigi or she had expected. While Aubrey's twin preschoolers frolicked and played in the small fenced playground area, the mother and her life coach sat on a nearby bench where they could talk and watch over the children at the same time.

"I'm fortunate that Larry is taking his child support and alimony obligations seriously." Aubrey, a tall, slender blonde in her early thirties, lifted her disposable coffee cup and took a sip. "At least, that's one worry I don't have. So I'll be able to afford daycare when I go back to school. But gosh, Gigi. It feels weird to return to college at my age. I'll be thirty-six by the time I get a degree and thirty-eight if I go on for a masters."

"You're going to hit those two birthdays anyway. Wouldn't you like to have those two degrees when you do?"

Aubrey laughed. "Good point."

Gigi's Apple watch pinged with a notification. Glancing at it, she realized that their scheduled time was up—and she was due to meet Harrison soon.

Just minutes after four o'clock, Gigi scheduled their next meeting, then left Aubrey and her precious kiddos at the park and hurried home to get ready. After taking a shower and blow-drying her hair, she went to her walk-in closet and searched for the proper outfit to wear. She pulled out a pair of black slacks and a white blouse.

Then, realizing she'd need to give it a bit of pizzazz, she dug through the top drawer in the dressing-room bureau and removed a red silk scarf she'd purchased in Paris last fall. She laid it all out on her bed, then took a step back.

"Nope." She slowly shook her head. Even with the added color and elegance, that outfit was still too stiff and stuffy.

She rummaged through her closet again and landed on a classic black dress. Depending upon makeup, hairdo and accessories, it could be either evening or daytime attire.

It could also be sexy and suggestive, and the last thing in the world she wanted was for Harrison to think she had something other than business on her mind— even though she couldn't quell the memory of his heady masculine scent, which stirred a vision of his expressive dark eyes and a longing to gaze into them again.

"Oh, for Pete's sake. Get a grip, will you?" She slipped the hanger back in place and continued to search for something else to wear. She finally settled on a blue summery dress—more of a shift than a sundress—a white denim jacket and a pair of strappy sandals. The ensemble was a bit more feminine than her usual classic style, but at least it didn't make her appear strictly business-minded or overtly sexy.

Next, she fixed her hair, leaving the soft curls long and loose. Then she applied just the right amount of makeup, which would proclaim she had daytime on the mind, rather than evening. By the time she was satisfied that she looked her best, she grabbed her purse and headed to her car.

She arrived at The Flying Pig at exactly five o'clock, then remained in the white BMW long enough to be respectfully on time, without appearing to be overly eager. When she couldn't wait any longer, she got out of the car and neared the entrance, where pony-size brass pigs wearing old-style flight goggles flanked an open purple barn door that tempted customers to come inside.

A buzz of excitement sparked, and not because she was trying out an exciting new eatery. She'd waited long enough to hear what Harrison had to say and to learn why he wanted to have a face-to-face conversation.

The funky restaurant had already begun to fill with a happy dinner crowd. The unusual decor, what she'd call "farmhouse noir," seemed to merge American Gothic with the Twilight Zone. A fluorescent-colored mural on the far wall depicted a flying pig soaring over a barnyard full of animals that were gazing upward, and a befuddled farmer wearing tie-dye overalls and holding a glowing pitchfork.

Interesting, she thought. And creative.

She made her way to the hostess stand, where an older woman wearing a neon pink, prairie-style dress greeted her with a warm smile. "Welcome to The Flying Pig. Will you be joining us for dinner?"

That was doubtful. "I don't think so. I'm meeting someone in the bar."

The woman pointed her to an arched doorway. "It's right through there. And you're in luck. It's still happy hour. You should try the purple-cow martini. It's our signature drink."

Gigi strolled through the dining room and into the bar, where booths made to look like stalls had seat cushions made of black-and-white faux cowhide. Bright green lanterns with flickering yellow candles adorned each table.

She looked for Harrison, but didn't see him. Maybe he was running late, which was understandable. An unexpected meeting with a client might have taken longer than expected. Before heading toward an empty table, she glanced down at the blue fabric of her dress and the strappy sandals. They glowed purple from the black light above the bar.

A warm hand touched her shoulder, and a rich, baritone voice said, "Gigi."

She hadn't needed to spin around to know who was standing behind her. Harrison's alluring, sea breeze scent stirred her senses and nearly made her knees buckle. So much for thinking she would make a grand entrance. She slowly turned around. "Hi, there."

He offered a friendly grin, which should have eased her mind. Instead, it threw her even more off balance. Still, she managed to return his smile.

"This place is certainly…different."

"That's what I'd heard. And why I suggested it." He pointed beyond her and to the right. "There's two empty seats. Shall we?"

"Sure."

They walked together toward the table next to a window that provided a view of the tree-lined street. He pulled out a chair for her, and she took a seat.

He sat across from her. "I'm glad you could make it today. I wanted to talk in person."

"Well, here I am," she said. "What's on your mind?"

Harrison hadn't planned to launch right into his reason for meeting Gigi today, especially when she was rocking a blue dress that belied her usual tough, no-nonsense persona and reflected a softness he hadn't expected to see. The outfit suggested that she was approachable. And touchable.

"Let's order a drink first," he said, motioning to a server wearing a neon green shirt and black slacks.

The young man, who'd dyed the tips of his spiked hair green, approached bearing a toothy grin. "Good afternoon. What'll you have?"

Harrison pointed an open hand to Gigi, signaling for her to order first.

She eyed the server. "I heard the purple-cow martini is good."

Harrison found that a bit surprising. He'd pegged her for choosing a high-end wine. Maybe a fancy French Bordeaux. Or possibly champagne.

"What's in that drink?" she asked the server.

"Blueberry liqueur, grenadine syrup, a hint of lemon and vodka."

"Hmm. I'll have that."

"Good choice." The server turned to Harrison. "And how about you, sir? It's happy hour so we have a two-for-one going."

"Do you carry anything from the Mendoza Winery? Maybe one of their reds?"

"Yes, we do. And they're all one of the Mendoza reserves."

"Then I'll have the merlot," Harrison said.

When the server returned to the bar to get their drinks, Gigi leaned back in her seat and crossed her arms. "If you've been trying to drive me crazy with curiosity, you've done a good job."

"Sorry about that. It's just that I wanted to pick your brain and get your opinion."

She smiled. "I always have one."

"I'm not surprised."

The server returned with a tray holding their drinks, as well as a silver bowl filled with a variety of pretzels and other flavored snacks to munch on. When he left the table, Harrison lifted his wineglass in a toast, and Gigi followed suit, raising her purple martini, which had a thin, curly lemon peel dangling from the glass.

"To what I hope is a new friendship," he said.

Her smiling expression drifted momentarily, then returned, and she clinked her glass against his. "Yes, friendship. I had a good time Friday night. I enjoyed spending it with you and your parents. So I guess it's safe to say we're becoming more than clients. Friends."

He wasn't sure what he'd expected her to say. It wasn't as if they were skating around a budding romance, although the thought had crossed his mind more than once, especially after she'd hugged him and he'd felt her breasts press softly against his chest and inhaled her springtime scent. But it was best this way.

"That leads me to what I wanted to talk to you about," he said.

She arched an eyebrow, and her demeanor stiffened. "Go on."

"My mother has needed to retire for a while, but she's uneasy about it and isn't sure what she's going to do with her time."

Gigi settled back in her seat, apparently more relaxed. And not as defensive. "She said as much on Friday night. Do you think she'd agree to meet me, either via Zoom or Skype? I can also visit her in person the next time I'm in Chatelaine."

That's what he'd hoped she'd say. And getting her to agree had been easier than he'd thought it might be. "That would be great. I realized that you work with a lot of women who are..." He paused. "I mean those who have a lot more money and connections than my mom has. My parents have plenty to see them through retirement, but they don't have an abundance of cash on hand."

"First of all," she said, a hint of annoyance biting her tone, "my clients run the gamut. And my podcasts are aimed at women of all ages and socioeconomic levels."

"I didn't mean to offend you."

She shrugged. "I guess it was an easy assumption for you to make. Most of my clients don't have any serious financial concerns, but they all have made mistakes or been hit by some unexpected turn of events. Or, like your mom, they're facing retirement but still have a lot to contribute to their communities and society. Many of them just need their confidence boosted. Believe it or not, I can relate to women who come from different walks of life."

"I didn't mean to imply that you couldn't."

"That said," she added, "I really like your mother. And I'd be happy to talk to her."

"I'll cover the cost," he said.

"When pigs fly." She smiled. "No pun intended."

Damn. Was one of her consultations that expensive?

"No, really. I can afford whatever you charge."

"Don't be silly, Harrison. I wouldn't charge her."

"I'm not looking for a freebie."

"I never charge friends for my services." Gigi took a sip of her drink. "Hmm. They were right. This is really good. But strong. One more of these and I'll be seeing purple cows and flying pigs."

Harrison laughed. He liked a woman with a good sense of humor. He lifted his wineglass, took a drink and savored the merlot, which was every bit as good as the Mendoza label would suggest.

"Thank you, Gigi. I appreciate you taking on my mom."

"My pleasure." She reached into her purse and withdrew a business card. "You have my contact info, but give her this and tell her I'm looking forward to hearing from her."

He watched her study the dwindling purple drink in her martini glass. "Do you mind if I ask you a personal question?"

She glanced up and smiled. "You can ask, but depending upon what it is, I might not answer."

"Fair enough. How'd you become a life coach?"

She looked back at her martini and lifted the glass, but rather than take a drink, she placed it back on the table. "It's a long story, Harrison, so maybe another time? Suffice it to say, I got married right out of high school and was divorced ten years later. At twenty-eight, I no longer knew who I was or what I wanted out of life. And when I figured it out, I decided to help other women who had to face new circumstances."

She didn't have to go into detail. Harrison got the picture, loud and clear. Her divorce had knocked her off her feet. "I'm sorry. That must have been very difficult for you."

"My divorce? Yes, and that's one reason why I'm skeptical of Fortune hunters." She didn't say it, but the experience had scarred her and left her wary of men. He suspected that was why she'd been opposed to meeting with Mariana Sanchez.

"I made the most of it," Gigi said, "I went back to college, something I should have done ten years earlier."

"It's never too late."

"That's what I tell my clients." She lifted her glass and this time took a drink, polishing it off. "One of the first courses I chose to take was called 'The Psychology of Personal Growth.' I got an A in the class…and had an epiphany. I decided to help women like me, who were facing a new season in their lives through divorce, widowhood, empty nest, retirement or whatever."

"I'm impressed."

She waved him off. "Don't be. I wasn't trying to toot my own horn. You asked how, and I told you."

"I'm glad you did."

"And for the record," she added, "I don't go around sharing my history with people, not even my clients. But I do allude to it when I need to."

Harrison motioned for the server and said, "Would you like to have dinner in the dining room or have appetizers in here?"

"I'm not especially hungry."

Something told him she'd lost her appetite after that brief but painful trek down memory lane.

"Yes, sir," the server said as he approached the table. "What can I get you?"

"We'd like to see the bar menu." Harrison turned to Gigi. "Would you like another martini or maybe something else to drink?"

"The purple cow was very good," she said, "but I'd like to switch to wine. And I'll have whatever he's having."

"Two merlots," the server said. "I'll be back with your wine and the menu."

An hour later, they'd managed to finish their second drinks and fill up on an artisan cheese platter, walnut raisin bread, dried dates and fresh apples and grapes. All the while, they kept the conversation light. He much preferred a smiling Gigi over one that appeared pensive.

They rounded off the evening with crème brûlée. When the server returned with their bill, Gigi reached for her purse.

"Absolutely not," Harrison said. They both knew this wasn't a date, although it sure felt like one to him.

Harrison paid with a credit card, leaving a generous tip. "I'll walk you to your car."

She nodded, and they left the bar.

The last time they'd parted, she'd given him a hug. He suspected they'd end the evening the same way. Just a friendly, parting embrace that meant they'd lowered their guards long enough to become more than attorney and client.

When they reached her BMW, she glanced up at him, her pretty brown eyes so vulnerable, so…

Without a conscious thought, he brushed his thumb across her cheek. When her lips parted, all his best intentions went by the wayside, and he lowered his mouth to hers.

Chapter Six

As Harrison's lips touched hers, his arms slipped around her waist, and Gigi leaned into his embrace. His mouth, soft yet demanding, worked its magic on her. His sweet taste and arousing scent darn near turned her knees to rubber and her brain to mush.

They continued to make out like a couple of teenagers on a hormonal high. And, had she been young and stupid, as she'd once been, she might have suggested a drive out to Lovers Lane. But they weren't teenagers. Nor were they lovers. And this kiss, the public display…

This was crazy.

She drew back and placed a splayed hand on his broad, muscular chest, felt his warmth, as well as his quickly beating heart. Hers was pounding, too.

"We can't do this." She stepped back.

"I know." He raked a hand through his dark hair,

which he usually wore neat and styled, and mussed it in a boyishly, endearing way. "I'm sorry. I, uh, shouldn't have done that. It's just that…"

"I know." She tucked a strand of hair behind her ear. "Too much, too fast, too soon. Right?"

"And inappropriate," he said, his tone low, and his gaze on hers. "But we've definitely got chemistry." His lips formed the hint of a smile, then he glanced away.

And that's what she found more than a little problematic. She lifted her fingers to her lips, which were still tingling from the heated kiss. "Tell you what. Let's pretend it never happened." She reached out her hand. Not that she'd forget. "Deal?"

He shrugged. "Okay. Still friends?"

"Sure. And just friends." Yet as her fingers slid around his hand, a burst of heat shot up her skin like fireworks.

Harrison let out a deep sigh.

Gigi reached for the BMW's door handle and forced a professional smile. "No matter what becomes of our business relationship—or our friendship—I'd really like to work with your mother. Just let her know I'll be expecting her call. And looking forward to it."

"Thanks. The two of you did hit it off Friday night."

"That's right," Gigi said. "And for the record, if you hadn't been at the Chatelaine Bar and Grill, and I'd run into your parents on my own, I would have still enjoyed meeting them."

She climbed into the driver's seat and took one last look at him, then noticed his expression—it was one she couldn't read. One she was afraid to decipher.

She gave him a playful salute that was meant to lighten the memory of what they'd just done. "See you around, Counselor."

"Not unless I see you first." He closed her door, then returned her mock salute, pointing an index finger to his brow.

Gigi couldn't make any promises when it came to her handsome attorney and *her* ability to separate business and pleasure, but at least she'd escaped with both her heart and her ego unscathed tonight.

There went a class act. Harrison, his arms folded across his chest, his weight shifted to one hip, watched Gigi drive away. They might have downplayed the kiss they'd shared, but it had been hot and arousing. More so than he'd even imagined.

Apparently, his impulsive urge to take her in his arms hadn't screwed things up. Only, now that he'd experienced the sparks between them, he'd be careful. It wouldn't happen again. It couldn't. There was too much at stake. He couldn't blow his first, big professional opportunity because he couldn't control his urges. What was he? Sixteen again? A late bloomer wishing he had a date with the prom queen?

A romance with Gigi Fortune was just as hopeless. There was no chance in hell that anything real and lasting would develop between them. They had too many differences—cultural, social and financial.

Paul Rodriguez, an army buddy of his, and a fellow officer, had had a whirlwind romance with a trust-fund baby and married her a month later. And they hadn't been able to overcome the odds. To make matters worse, the woman had an ironclad trust fund, and Paul walked away with nothing but a broken heart and a ruined military career.

Harrison suspected a family like the Fortunes would have a damn good trust drawn up, too. Not that he gave a hoot about money. But the Fortunes were powerful and could ruin him before he even got a chance to start his civilian career.

Once he got into the driver's seat of his own vehicle, he flipped on the interior light, reached into his pocket and pulled out the business card Gigi had given him. He studied it for a moment, then set it on the dashboard. He took a picture with his cell phone and texted the image to his mom.

Thank God, he hadn't blown things with Gigi. Over the years, off and on, his mother had suffered bouts of depression. And now that she'd retired, he didn't want to see her slide into another blue funk because she'd lost the daily connection with her coworkers. Mama needed a new focus, new friends. And he hoped that Gigi could help make that happen.

After sending the photo, he typed out a follow-up text. Gigi wants you to call her.

He hit Send, then started the engine, backed out of the parking space and headed home. But the forbidden kiss was still on his mind. He wasn't sure how he could look at her again without thinking about it. He'd been able to dismiss it tonight, but what he couldn't so easily dismiss was his growing attraction to his client and his desire to hold her in his arms and kiss her again.

"Enough," he said out loud. He and Gigi were treading on an inappropriate client relationship, something that could cause him to lose the connection to her or her brother…and the family business.

Besides, he didn't know how that kiss had affected her. The way she'd kissed him back, seeking his tongue as it sought hers, implied that it had been just as hot and arousing for her as it had been for him. But he doubted she was in the market for a fling. And anything more than that wasn't the least bit likely. Besides, he had a more important plan to see through—a civilian career to build.

A ding sounded from his phone, indicating an incoming text. Rather than ask Siri to read it to him, he made the short drive to his home. Once inside his garage, he shut off the engine, reached for his cell and read his mother's response. That is so sweet. I really like her.

He texted back. She's looking forward to talking to you and wants to meet in person.

He'd no more than gotten out of his car and closed the garage door when his cell phone rang and his mother's picture lit up the scene. "Hi, Mama."

"The case you're working on for her must be a big one."

"Yep. The sort of opportunity a new civilian lawyer dreams about." Harrison knew his mother better than anyone. And no matter how she tried to masquerade her line of questioning, he knew what she was trying to do.

"Did you have dinner with her? Take her to a nice place?"

He grinned. The Flying Pig wasn't romantic, yet look

how the evening had turned out. "We did meet for a drink this evening."

"Hmm."

How could one woman pack so many implied words into a simple sound?

"Stop, Mama. I've told you and Papa this before. I'm her attorney, and she's my client. We might be easing toward a friendship, but that's all. End of story."

If his mother had her doubts, she kept them to herself. And that's just what Harrison intended to do. Keep his doubts and his budding feelings to himself.

He'd have to start by forgetting that kiss.

Although he wasn't so sure how easy that would be.

Virtual phone calls via the computer screen were helpful, but Gigi always preferred to have face-to-face meetings whenever possible, especially when the woman was a new client. And in this particular case, Gigi was looking forward to seeing Sylvia Vasquez in person—and at her home in Chatelaine—even if it meant another two-hour drive from Corpus Christi less than a week later.

A few minutes before two o'clock on Friday, the appointed time for their first meeting, Gigi turned onto Daffodil Court, a tree-lined street in a quiet neighborhood. She continued to the address she'd been given and parked in front of a brown stucco house with beige trim. Before reaching for the black leather briefcase and her purse, which sat on the passenger seat, she studied the home where she suspected Harrison had grown up.

A white picket fence enclosed a well-manicured and

freshly mowed lawn. A hearty variety of blue, white and lavender hydrangeas grew under a big bay window, while bright yellow and orange marigolds lined the walkway that led to the front door. There wasn't anything fancy or out of the ordinary about the residence, yet she got a warm, cozy feeling just looking at it and admiring the work of someone who clearly enjoyed gardening. Nevertheless, she couldn't sit here all day.

She unlatched the front gate, let herself into the yard and followed the walkway to the front door, where two potted geraniums flanked a brightly colored welcome mat. She rang the bell, and a dog—a small yappy one, it seemed—let out a volley of warning barks. Sylvia shushed it, then opened the door with a wriggling Yorkie in her arms and greeted Gigi with a bright-eyed smile.

"Thanks for agreeing to meet with me," the newly retired woman said, stepping aside to let Gigi in the house.

"Who's this little guy?" Gigi asked.

"This is Chewie, which is short for Chewbacca. She gets a little too protective at times, but she's very friendly."

Gigi gave the scruffy little dog a scratch behind the ear and got an appreciative lick on her hand. "It's nice to meet you, Chewie."

"Do you like dogs?" Sylvia asked.

"I do, although I don't have any pets." Gigi had considered getting a cat, but she'd never gotten around to it.

Sylvia placed the little dog on the floor and let it scamper off. "Can I get you something to drink? Coffee, iced tea, water…?"

"Thank you. Iced tea, please."

Sylvia led her through a comfortable living room, the walls painted a soft blue, to the small dining area that shared the same space. An antique hutch displayed a variety of china and crystal. The sort of things that many of her retired clients had a hard time letting go of when they downsized, even though their kids didn't want it. But there was something special about Sylvia's collection, most of which looked like antiques, possibly hand-me-downs, but were probably not worth anywhere near as much as the priceless art and statues that had graced her parents' home...and reminded her of a museum.

"Please. Have a seat," Sylvia said. "I'll be right back with the iced tea."

"No worries." Gigi pulled out a chair and, before scooting it close to the oval table, put her briefcase on her lap, opened it and withdrew a file containing several forms, a pen and a pad of paper. Then she closed the case and placed it and her purse on the chair next to her.

Once she was prepared for the meeting and seated properly, she scanned the dining area, wanting to get to know Sylvia Vasquez better. On the nearest wall, a large picture of Harrison looking sharp in his dress blues hung beside the hutch, his ceremonial sword at his side. Maybe, if she was lucky, she'd gain a little insight into Counselor Vasquez himself.

Sylvia returned with a tray carrying two glasses of iced tea, a couple of coasters, napkins and a sugar bowl and spoon. After serving Gigi and herself, she set the tray on the table.

"I never considered a life coach before," Sylvia admitted, "so I have no idea what to expect."

"Let's just chat for a while," Gigi said. "Tell me about your childhood, your educational path, your dreams along the way...and whatever else comes to mind."

Sylvia took a sip of her tea. "I don't know where to start. My parents were missionaries, and I was born in Guadalajara. I have dual citizenship and a passport I've only used once. Nearly thirty-five years ago, when I went to my aunt's funeral in Montreal."

"I'm sorry. Were you close?"

"Yes. She was a wonderful aunt. I wish Harrison had gotten to know her, but she died before he started preschool."

"You mentioned last Friday night that you'd like to go to Paris. You certainly have time to travel now."

"Yes, I know. But Andres is very committed to his ESL classes, and then there's his bad knee. So I don't think we can go anytime soon. But in all honesty, I'm a homebody at heart. I enjoy puttering around the house and working in the garden."

"Your front yard is lovely."

"Thanks. Yet I don't want to spend the next ten or twenty years at home, either." Sylvia let out a soft sigh. "I'm afraid I'm just too boring. And not client material."

Gigi reached across the table and placed her hand over Sylvia's. "That's not true. Together, you and I are going to find the perfect direction and project for you."

"I hope you're right."

"Tell me. Was there ever anything you were passionate about as a kid?"

Sylvia glanced down at the table and fingered the edge of her napkin, her brow furrowed. A couple of beats later, she looked up. "You know, as a child and a young teenager, there was one thing I really wanted to do, but it wasn't possible then. And I doubt that it's feasible now."

"What's that?"

"I wanted to be an artist. I'd spend hours at a time with whatever I could get my hands on—finger paint, colored pencils, crayons, felt pens... Art of any kind never failed to lift my spirits. It filled my days. But then, when it was time to choose a college and find a career, well, I wanted to eat, so I went to nursing school. After that, I got a wonderful job...and a loving husband. Then, after a while, a precious baby boy. I'm afraid there just wasn't time for it any longer."

"There's time now," Gigi said. "You could take art classes, join a quilting club, take up knitting... The sky's the limit."

"That would appeal to me. And it would fill my days." She paused, clearly troubled about something. "But..."

"But what?" Sylvia asked.

"Well, it sounds a little...self-centered, I suppose. I'm used to taking care of others—at home and at the hospital. Pursuing art at this point in my life might be fulfilling, but it wouldn't be helpful to anyone other than me."

"Aw, but that's where you're wrong. What about art therapy? With your background and possibly a class or two, you could provide an important benefit to people in nursing homes, rehab facilities and many other places. You'd also work with a variety of age groups—

children, teenagers, adults, the elderly. And being bi-lingual is a plus."

Sylvia's eyes brightened. "I'd never even considered doing something like that. I'll have to do some research, but that certainly sounds like something that would allow me to use my background to help people while satisfying that artistic bug."

"And that's just one of many things you could do in this new season of your life. I'm going to email you a questionnaire to complete over the next few days. I'll come back next week, on Saturday morning, if that works for you. And we can go over it together. How does that sound?"

"Wonderful," she said. "You know, when Harrison suggested that I call you, I was a little hesitant. I thought talking to a coach about something that should be easy to figure out myself was a little…frivolous. But I'm so glad you came. I have a good feeling about this."

"So do I. And it's not frivolous. You have a lot to offer." Gigi smiled. "I'm glad you were open—and that you're hopeful."

"I am now. Can I offer you some chocolate-chip cookies? I made them earlier today."

Gigi tried not to snack between meals, but she wasn't about to turn down home-baked cookies. Or to pass an opportunity to continue their chat on a more personal level. "That sounds good. I'd love one."

While Sylvia snatched the empty tray and pitcher, and hurried to the kitchen, Gigi made another scan of the Vasquez dining room, her gaze again landing on the military picture of Harrison. She'd learned a bit about Sylvia this afternoon, but nothing of her son. That shouldn't be surprising, since Gigi wasn't here to talk about him. But it was a bit disappointing. A romance wasn't in their future, but that didn't mean she didn't want to know more about him.

Sylvia returned with a refilled pitcher of iced tea to replenish their glasses and a large platter of cookies— too many to eat in one sitting. "I hope you like these. They're Harrison's favorites."

Aw, good. A natural opening. Gigi reached for a cookie and took a bite. "Hmm. These are delicious. No wonder Harrison likes them."

Sylvia beamed. "Thank you. It was my mother's recipe, and I added my own touch." She winked. "But it's a secret ingredient, so don't ask."

Gigi laughed. "Did you bake for Harrison when he was a little boy?"

"Every chance I could. Andres and I had wanted a child for a long time, but I had a difficult time conceiving. We'd just about given up having a baby of our own, and imagine how happy we were when he came along."

"Lucky baby," Gigi said.

"Lucky us." Sylvia reached for a cookie. "Andres and I wanted to spend as much time with him as we could, so I cut my workdays back and took twelve-hour shifts on the weekends. That way, we rarely needed a babysitter. And then, when he went to school, I added a third day."

"Did he enjoy school? I assume he did well."

"Yes, he loved to learn, and he was exceptionally

bright. He made us so proud. But school wasn't always easy for him."

"Why?" Gigi reached for a second cookie.

"When he was in junior high school, he was bullied."

Gigi's heart cramped at the thought. "I can't imagine why."

"He was small for his age and didn't hit a growth spurt until he was a senior in high school. But Jason Walker, the star football player, a big kid who was a year behind him—because he had to repeat a grade, I might add—resented Harrison for being smart."

"Seriously?" Gigi knew that some jocks could be mean and tease kids who weren't athletic. "Just for being bright?"

"Jason was a slow learner, but he was big, bulky and strong. I think that his size and stature was the only thing that made him feel good about himself, so he used to pick on Harrison. When Jason bloodied his nose, then threw him into the dumpster behind the cafeteria, Andres and I'd had enough. We'd talked to the principal on several occasions, but Jason didn't seem to care how many detentions he got. And Harrison rarely complained. He said it would only make things worse."

"That's cruel."

"Yes, it was. And it broke our hearts. But something changed in high school, and Jason backed off. We were never sure why, but we were relieved. Anyway, Harrison never let it deter him from excelling in his studies."

Harrison had been a tough, determined little boy. And, no doubt, that strength and focus had seen him through the military and positioned him well for his civilian life.

"Fortunately," Sylvia added, "things got better during the summer before Harrison's senior year. He finally began to grow and put on weight. I always think that was one of the reasons he joined the army. Of course, he also liked the idea of the military paying for college and law school."

"You must be very proud of him."

"Oh, we are. He was always a good boy, but he's an exceptional man."

Sylvia and Andres were biased, of course. Most parents would be. Her own parents, Delphine and Phillip, crossed her mind. They'd always said they were proud at the appropriate milestones, like graduations and report cards, and she didn't doubt them. But she hadn't always felt it. And she wasn't so sure that Reeve had fully felt it, either.

There were times when she'd wondered if she and Reeve had been items on their parents' to-do list.

"Did you know that, when Andres has his surgery, Harrison volunteered to teach his ESL classes?"

"No, I didn't know that. I imagine that'll keep Harrison busy, especially if he has to drive back and forth to Chatelaine every Friday night."

Sylvia smiled. "He's always been that way—going above and beyond. Unlike most of his high-school classmates, he had ambition. He got to the top of his class by hard work, so he's never taken his job or his life for granted. Extra credit, extra projects."

Gigi had learned a lot about Harrison Vasquez this

afternoon, but what she really wanted to know was whether he'd had any serious relationships. Sylvia hadn't mentioned anything about that, and Gigi knew better than to ask. She didn't want Sylvia to think Gigi had a romantic interest in her son. Even if she couldn't completely deny that she did.

"Well," Gigi said, "this has been very enlightening. Thank you for the tea and cookies."

"You're most welcome. I'm feeling better about my retirement already, even if I don't have a solid game plan in mind."

Gigi slipped her supplies back into her briefcase. "But you have a direction, at least one to consider."

As Sylvia walked Gigi to the door, they agreed to meet again next Saturday. Admittedly, Gigi was looking forward to it—maybe more so than Sylvia. She felt a closeness to the woman she'd never felt with her own mother.

When they reached the front door, Sylvia opened it. But before Gigi could walk out, Sylvia embraced her with another hug. This time, it wasn't unexpected, and it warmed her to the core.

Thirty minutes later, after arriving at the hotel, her cell phone rang. It was Harrison.

"I can't thank you enough for meeting with my mom today. She was almost giddy with excitement. I haven't seen her like that since I told her I was retiring from the army and moving back to Texas."

"You said you saw her. Are you in town?"

"I just arrived. I must have missed you. My mother said you'd just left."

"You're back in Chatelaine? That's two weekends in a row."

"I hadn't planned to be here, but my dad wants to introduce me to his students tomorrow. Anyway, this might be late notice, but I'd like to take you out to dinner—tonight, if you're not making the drive back to Corpus Christi. Or if you are, then maybe one night later this week."

She didn't respond right away. She probably ought to remind him of the decision they'd made to keep their relationship a business one. But for some damn reason, she didn't care what they'd decided. Dinner with Harrison Vasquez sounded like a great idea.

"I'm in the area," she said. "I'm staying at the LC Club tonight. I plan to drive home tomorrow morning."

"If you don't have plans this evening, I'll pick you up at seven."

She didn't have any plans at all, but she had a feeling a few ideas would crop up while she got dressed for dinner and waited for Harrison to pick her up.

Chapter Seven

Harrison and Gigi enjoyed a candlelit dinner at The Silver Spoon, a nice steak house that had been aptly named after the nearby Chatelaine Silver Mine and—Harrison assumed—the enormous wealth of the family who owned it. He suspected the restaurant was just another one of the many Fortune ventures.

After dinner, they stopped by the Snowman's Creamery, which had opened last year. Then they took a walk down the shoreline, each eating an ice-cream cone. Tiki lights lit their way, casting a romantic ambiance more reminiscent of Kaanapali Beach in Maui than a lake in Texas.

"I don't usually order dessert," Gigi said.

Harrison stifled a smile. She was already two-for-two when it came to having dinner with him. He glanced at her figure, tall and regal. Perfect.

She lifted the cone to her mouth and used her tongue to catch the drips. Damn. She made eating ice cream sexy.

As they strolled along, he studied the way her blond waves tumbled over her shoulders, the way she closed her eyes when she savored the taste of the cold vanilla treat, the way she ran the tip of her tongue across her lips.

His blood stirred, and while he was determined not to get carried away again, he couldn't shake the memory of the sweet crème-brûlée flavor of her kiss.

Shake it off, man. Shake it off.

There'd been a good reason to keep their platonic relationship from drifting into a romantic one, but, at the moment, it seemed to have slipped his mind.

Still, he tore his gaze away from her and came up with a safe, generic topic to keep his brain on track.

"Do you play golf?" he asked.

She glanced up, the cone in her hand tilted slightly. As her lips parted, his libido perked up.

So much for keeping his mind on a nonsexual track.

"Yes," she said. "I play, but not as often as I'd like to."

"Same here. It's hard to find the time, but at least I'm trying to make the effort. The firm has a corporate membership at the Hillside Country Club, so I have a a home course, but I haven't managed to play a round yet."

"Hillside is a great club. They offer a variety of special events—trivia night, comedy hour, music on the patio most Friday afternoons."

"I take it you're a member," he said.

She nodded. "I have been for years, but I've got the same problem you do—clearing my schedule."

"Maybe I should get us a tee time next weekend. That way, we'll be forced to play a round." Wrong choice of words, he realized as his mind went to a double meaning—*forced to play around*. He hoped she didn't get the wrong idea. "If you know what I mean."

"You're probably right. I tell my clients that it's important to find a good balance between life and work." She took another lick of her cone. "But if you love what you do, then it's not really work, is it?"

She had a point. "I can't say that I love everything about practicing law, but I take pride in my work when I'm able to help my clients."

"I feel the same way."

"It's not as if I have any real reason to rush home at night or be there on weekends," he added. "I don't have a wife or kids, so my time is my own. I tend to work."

They continued to walk in silence, past a park bench inviting people to take a seat and rest a while, to enjoy the view of the flickering tiki lights reflecting on the water. For a moment, he felt the emptiness of his life, of the condo he called home. Nothing fancy. Just four walls, the usual furniture enhanced by a case of books, an elliptical and a television. Or so it seemed, now that he thought about it.

"Do people ever ask you why you're not married?" she asked.

"Other than my parents?" They exchanged a smile. "Not really. Do they ask you?"

"More often than I like." She tossed the last of her

cone into a trash can. "You're lucky you're a man. It's different for women. There's this expectation that we should marry and have families, and we have a ticking clock to deal with. But that life has more options for men."

Harrison disagreed. "That's not really true. I'd probably have more leverage at the firm if I was a family man. But I'd never marry just to fit someone else's image of what I should be."

"I got the feeling that your parents would like to have grandchildren. Do they ever pressure you?"

"I'll admit that they've broached the subject at times, usually around the holidays—Thanksgiving and Christmas. But I told them I might never get married. I'm sure that was disappointing to them, but they realize it's my decision."

"Why are you opposed to marriage?" she asked. "Not that it matters. Just wondering."

"I thought about it a time or two." One time in particular. With Sherrilyn. "A few years ago, I met a single mom who was…pretty special. And I really liked her kids. Two little boys who were six and eight."

"What happened?" she asked.

He didn't usually talk about it. "She, uh… Well, her ex-husband came back in the picture, and she decided to give their relationship another try. For the sake of the kids. And I understood."

It still hurt, though. And it made him think that maybe he wasn't cut out for marriage and family. Not everyone had the kind of love his mom and dad shared. He'd noticed that growing up, too.

"How about your parents?" he asked, hoping to steer the conversation away from him. "Do they ever question you about marriage, grandkids?"

An awkward hush rose up between them until Gigi said, "My parents don't seem to be the least bit interested in having grandchildren. At least, they've never pressured me to get married again."

Harrison's mother had mentioned that Gigi was divorced, but when he'd quizzed her about the reason, she didn't know the particulars.

"What's holding you back?" he asked. "A broken heart? Disillusionment?"

"I'd rather not talk about it."

"Fair enough." He hadn't meant to get too personal. Maybe he should suggest that they turn around and head back to the hotel.

"I'm sorry, Harrison." Her steps slowed to a stop, and he paused, too. "That probably sounded as if I've been scarred by it. I've actually moved on and learned from the mistakes I made, the consequences of taking the easy way out."

He wasn't sure what she meant by that, and he didn't want to press, but he was more than curious. "Everyone makes mistakes. It's part of life."

She looked out at the lake for a beat, then turned to him with a sigh. "I was seventeen and a senior in high school when I met Anson at a championship football game. And I'll admit there was more than a spark of attraction. But Anson came from a blue-collar family."

Had that been the problem? A red flag?

"He was handsome, bright and had his whole life

mapped out for him. He was going to law school, would eventually run for public office and then land a seat in the U.S. Senate."

"Impressive."

"Yeah. Sure."

So she clearly didn't admire her ex-husband's goals.

"I was young. And stupid. Opposites might attract, but the differences should have been daunting."

He didn't doubt it. They were probably mismatched socially, as well as financially. "I doubt you were ever stupid. Maybe just naive."

"Maybe. My trust fund supported us both and paid for Anson's Ivy League college and law school."

Apparently, by her snarky tone, that hadn't gone well. But Harrison knew better than to comment.

"I fell into the proverbial role of a 'trust fund baby,' even if it didn't feel right. But like I said, I was young and dumb—"

"Naive," he corrected.

She shrugged. "I fell into a domestic role. I was a good wife and didn't mind letting Anson's star shine. I enjoyed decorating our house and trying new gourmet recipes, being on a ton of charitable committees, while Anson worked hard. He was away from home a lot, so when I wasn't representing the Fortune family at charity events, I spent my free time playing golf and tennis. Thinking about that now, I realize I'd become my mother."

So she wasn't a golf novice.

Her shoulder brushed against his arm, and he felt the strongest compulsion to reach out, to take her hand in his. To offer sympathy or compassion or friendship. But she might not appreciate the gesture. Not now, while she was reliving what had to be painful memories.

"After Anson passed the bar, his connection to my family and my money helped him land a position at a prestigious law firm, where he put in long hours. I'd hoped to start a family, but he'd always tell me it wasn't the right time."

Harrison sensed what happened next was going to be ugly.

"One evening, ten years into our marriage, Anson was working late—again. I decided to surprise him and bring him dinner. But the surprise was on me when I opened his office door and found him having sex with one of the paralegals."

Harrison had no idea what to say, other than "The bastard. I'm sorry."

"Me, too. When I told him I wanted a divorce, he was more concerned about how the split would affect his political career. And if he'd get alimony."

"So you divorced him."

"Of course. And thanks to my father's insistence on a prenuptial agreement, there wasn't a lot to fight about. And as soon as it was final, he married the paralegal, who was already pregnant with his child."

"Ouch."

No wonder she was gun-shy and defensive when it came to people wanting to take advantage of her because of her last name.

"The divorce shattered me. I'd always done everything expected of me, everything right. But I'd failed, and everything had turned out wrong."

Harrison took her hand and pulled her around to face him. "Thank you for sharing that. I know it couldn't have been easy. But Anson was a jerk. And you deserved so much more."

He spotted vulnerability in her eyes. Something she'd tried her best to hide from him...and the world, no doubt.

Without any forethought, Harrison offered her a compassionate hug. She returned his embrace, but for some crazy reason, neither of them took a step back. Her fragrance, which smelled like exotic flowers, taunted him.

Finally, she eased away, but when she gazed up at him, he was toast. He pulled her back into his arms and kissed her with a longing he hadn't expected. She leaned into him, and he intensified the kiss, his tongue seeking hers, sweeping, dipping and tasting.

It had been so long since he'd felt this kind of flash fire, this heated urgency, that nothing else seemed to matter. At least, not until an older couple strode toward them, walking hand in hand.

Harrison's brain kicked into gear and he pulled away. "I'm sorry. That was out of line. You're my client."

She gazed up at him with an expression he found difficult to read. Was it regret? Disappointment? Was she about to chastise him for the indiscretion?

"What are you sorry about?" she asked. "That you kissed me? Because I was there, and I didn't object. I hope you aren't using that client baloney as an excuse."

"No." That was only one of them. But he wasn't about to bring up their many differences. He might have a nice financial portfolio, one that might impress a lot of women, if that was his style. But he didn't have the kind of money the Fortunes had. And he needed his position at the law firm. He didn't want to screw it up. "I could be fired by my firm if they found out."

"I won't tell." She placed her hand on his arm and her touch burned through his shirt to his skin. Her eyes signaled she might be open to a walk on the wild side, and it took all his strength to resist, but he had to because... Damn. He might be highly successful and well-respected, but he was grounded in reality. Getting involved with Gigi Fortune was far too risky.

For now, he'd just continue to be haunted by thoughts of her. Hot thoughts of her, he decided, watching her lick her lips.

He slid back, away from her touch. "Your case won't last forever," he said, injecting a little hope. "Let's table this discussion."

She looked a bit surprised, but then nodded. "That's probably a good idea." They began walking toward the hotel. "But keep in mind, Counselor, I'm not opposed to another dinner. Or maybe a game of golf."

"I look forward to it." Although something told him dinner and golf might not be enough. Still, he'd hold his act together, at least until the end of this case. But that might be easier said than done.

After the way things ended on that shoreline walk last night, Gigi had returned to her suite on the top floor, but she hadn't slept a wink. When she wasn't reliving that heated kiss she and Harrison had shared, she was rehashing the conversation that had followed.

I'm sorry. That was out of line. You're my client.

Gigi hadn't been able to get a read on his troubled expression, which had bothered her at the time—and now, even more so.

What are you sorry about? she'd asked. *That you kissed me?*

He'd told her no. He was concerned about getting fired. At that point, she should've nodded and let the conversation end organically. But, oh, no. She had to go and complicate the situation by saying she wouldn't tell. And that might have given him the idea that she wasn't opposed to more than just dinner and golf.

What if he had wanted to take her up on it?

She might have invited him up to her hotel room, something one or both of them would've regretted in the morning. But he'd rejected her.

Did he see her as a bold trust-fund baby toying it up with the staff?

Agh… She punched her pillow, then planted her face into it.

Just after dawn, she'd finally given up on sleep and packed up her things. She took a shower, downed a cup of coffee and a serving of yogurt sprinkled with blueberries and granola, then checked out of the hotel and headed back to Corpus Christi.

She was only an hour away from home when her cell phone rang. The display on the dash told her Harrison was calling.

Her tummy inverted, and her heart turned a somersault. Dang. What did he want? She nearly let it roll to voice mail on principle alone. But curiosity wouldn't let her. "Hi, Harrison. What's up?"

"I thought I'd make a tee time for Sunday afternoon. Are you still up for a round of golf?"

The question stunned her. "Seriously?"

"Sure. Do you have other plans?"

Not a single thing, but… "Aren't you concerned about getting fired for fraternizing with your client at the country club?"

"Playing golf wouldn't be out of line. It'd be sanctioned as a client meeting."

She bit her lip. Could she restrain herself? Not make a fool of herself? Again?

He paused for a couple of beats. "Look. We agreed getting romantically involved isn't a good idea, no matter how strong the chemistry is between us. But that doesn't mean we can't socialize. And I can't think of a better way to do that than being outdoors in the fresh air and sunshine. And hey, if it makes you feel better, we'll call this a business meeting and discuss the case in broad terms, although I don't have anything new to tell you, other than Mariana has found a reputable lab that will run her second DNA test."

Gigi supposed she'd have to be tested, too, but she'd prefer to use a different lab.

"So what do you say?" he prodded. "How about we play for five dollars a side? And winner buys drinks in the clubhouse."

Not only was he tempting her better judgment, but now he was also taunting her competitive spirit.

"Fine. Brace yourself for a little friendly competition. Text me the tee time."

He laughed. "You got it."

Gigi never shied away from a challenge, but something told her that getting involved with Harrison Vasquez—even socially—could put her at a big disadvantage. She wasn't used to navigating a friendship when her hormones, which had steered her wrong in the past, insisted their relationship was meant to be so much more than that.

As they were finishing the back nine of the valley course at Hillside Country Club, she wasn't about to prove herself right. They were evenly matched so far, and tied.

The sun beat down on them, but a soft breeze rustled the trees, keeping them from overheating. He began to inch ahead, which surprised her. How did he have the time or—dare she think it—the money to get so good at a sport that took a lot more skill and practice than an observer might think?

"Did you play a lot in the military?" she asked.

"Yeah. One of the perks of multiple deployments. It allowed me to play at a lot of different courses in the world. How'd you get so good at the game?"

"Oh, you know. Played a lot over the years." And took a ton of lessons, which wasn't giving her the edge she needed right now.

"This is one of the nicest courses I've ever played," he said, "if not the best."

Harrison wasn't a scratch golfer, and neither was she. But he could hold his own against one—and she could, too. Reeve had always commended her for shooting better when she was under pressure. Still, by the time she and Harrison reached the seventeenth green, she was only up by one, and Harrison had begun to get on her nerves.

He was making it look too damn easy as he prepared to chip his ball onto the green, his dark eyes concentrating on the sloping hill while avoiding the pond. His well-defined arms glistened with perspiration from the afternoon sun, yet somehow his hair looked neat and perfect. He swung, and as his luck would have it, the ball landed just a few feet shy of the hole.

Dang it. If he made the putt, he'd make a birdie. And her best hope was to keep it tied. If he'd tossed her a smirk or been anything other than a good sport, she might have made a snarky comment. As it was, she had to just do her best. She got herself positioned, but out of the corner of her eye, she saw him chug a water bottle. "Hey, you mind? I'm trying to play here. And you're way too distracting."

"Am I?"

He certainly was, with that sexy grin, that square-cut jaw and his polo shirt rippling across his broad chest and flat belly. "Will you step aside, please?"

"Sorry." He leaned against the golf cart.

As if that helped.

She focused. Swung. The ball raced past the cup and

didn't begin to slow down until it was a couple of feet past the hole. Then it continued to roll all the way to the pond, freaking out a mother duck and her six ducklings. "I hate this game!"

"That's because you're losing, and I get the feeling you don't lose very often."

She stomped back to the cart, put her club in the bag, then nodded at him. "Move over. I'm driving."

Cool as can be, he circled the cart and got in. "Have at it."

She was mad, and for no real reason. It was a really bad idea to floor the gas pedal, but she did it, anyway, and zipped up the slope toward the eighteenth tee. When she saw a discarded club directly in front of them, she swerved to the right and nearly ran them off the cart path and into the rough.

"Whoa," Harrison said. "Slow down."

"Sorry." She blew out a sigh. She would have to birdie out for a chance to keep this competitive.

As if sensing that she was reaching a breaking point that would completely throw the game in his favor, he didn't seem to revel in it. Instead, he reached out and placed his hand on her shoulder. "Don't worry. I've seen your talent. You've got this, Gigi."

Her jaw dropped momentarily, but she recovered as quickly as she could. Instead of being her opponent, he was behaving like a teammate.

Who did that? Certainly, not any of the men she knew.

Something changed. Between them? Or in her? She

wasn't sure what was going on, but she was softening toward him.

Not a good idea, girl.

The last time she'd felt this sexually attracted to a man, things had gone badly. And she wasn't just talking about Anson, her no-good, scheming, cheating ex. She'd cared about Michael Devlin, too. Who would've guessed that her first significant other in years would prove to be a charming liar, too?

Needless to say, the last thing she needed was another disappointing crush. Or worse, another broken heart.

As Harrison made the last putt—and put the final nail in the coffin—he turned to her and smiled. "We'll have to do this again."

"I'll practice first."

He laughed. "I don't doubt that. You're a real competitor, Gigi. It's been a pleasure playing with you."

"Thanks. Believe it or not, I'd like to play again."

They got back into the cart, and Harrison drove to the pro shop.

Gigi lifted her visor and combed her fingers through her hair. Perspiration glimmered off her throat, something he found endearingly sexy. Then she reached into her pocket and whipped out a five dollar bill. "Here's your winnings, now where's my drink?"

Harrison tucked that bill into his pocket with a grin, knowing it wouldn't even cover the tip for the bar bill. Once he parked the cart, they were met by Ken Gregory, the head pro. Harrison recognized him from his photo on the club website. Ken, whose name seemed most appropriate, reminded Harrison of a Ken doll, all blond and tanned, and dressed to the hilt in his country-club finest.

"Ms. Fortune," the slim, fair-haired man said. "It's been a while. It's good to see you. We like to see our Founders Club members enjoying themselves."

"Thanks, Ken." She offered him a polite smile, then placed her fingertips on Harrison's knee. "This is Harrison Vasquez, a friend of mine. He's a new member."

Harrison reached over, and the two men shook hands.

"Vasquez?" Ken furrowed his brow as he watched them get out of the cart. "I don't recall the name. You must have joined recently."

"Last month," Harrison said. "I'm an associate member. My law firm, Bentley, Donovan and Tyler, has the corporate account."

"Oh." Ken nodded. "That makes sense. If you need help with your game, I hope you'll book a lesson." He focused his big blue eyes on Gigi, although Harrison could hardly blame him. The woman was stunning, even with her hair a bit windswept, her cheeks flushed. "How'd you play, Ms. Fortune?"

"I lost to the counselor here, but I can't complain. It's a beautiful day. And it felt great to be outdoors. And on the bright side, I don't have to buy drinks."

"I haven't seen you for a while," Ken said. "Been out of town?"

"Just busy."

"Well, now that you're back into the swing of it, I'm here to give you some pointers."

Harrison just bet he was. He knew a tomcat on the prowl when he saw one. He watched Ken stroll away toward a group of attractive women.

"Come on," Gigi said. "Let's sit on the patio and have that drink."

Harrison followed her toward the clubhouse, feeling more uneasy about his roots than he'd felt in the past twenty years. And that didn't sit well with him.

He played a decent game of golf and dressed in the proper, respectable country-club attire. But as an associate member, he obviously didn't carry the same clout as one of the Founders—especially the beautiful Gigi Fortune.

But heck. He was ex-military. JAG, no less. He wasn't ashamed of his background. Maybe just a bit insecure of how he fit in with these upper-crust folks.

Minutes later, they were seated on the patio. While they waited for the waitress to bring them their drinks— a Corona with lime for him and a glass of merlot for her—she said, "I'm going to call your mom and set up time to meet her in Chatelaine on Wednesday."

Harrison sat up. "You're going to be in town in the middle of the week?"

"Originally, we'd planned to meet on Saturday, but I rescheduled with her this morning. My producer will be there, and I'm going to tape my final podcast with her company before her start-up company becomes part of FortuneMedia."

"You don't want to work with the family company?"

"Not particularly."

Harrison didn't mean to pry, but if he was going to represent the Fortune siblings, it might be helpful to understand the family dynamics. "I sensed some tension between you and Reeve when we first met at my office."

She lifted her wineglass and took a sip. "We used to be close, but not so much these days."

"Is there a reason for it?"

She pondered the question for so long that he suspected she wasn't going to answer it. Then she gave a slight shrug. "My parents loved me and Reeve, but they had busy lives and hired nannies to look after us. We didn't think anything of it. A lot of our friends had similar childhoods. But when we were teenagers, my dad took a special interest in Reeve and began to groom him to take over Fortune Metals. That was a brutal surprise. I'd always assumed, as the firstborn, that I'd be involved in the family business. When I was seventeen and broached the subject—and the unfairness of it all—my father told me that I'd be more helpful if I represented the family in our philanthropic interests."

"And that disappointed you?"

"It hurt *and* disappointed me." She shrugged. "It didn't help when Reeve told me that I was more like our parents than he was, particularly my mother, saying I was self-centered and lacked heartfelt affection. And that's not true. I'm more like my great-grandfather."

"Do you resent your brother?"

"I suppose I do."

"Why?"

"For not believing in me. Not supporting me." She stared into her wine, lifted the glass and swished the merlot around. Then she took a sip. "But he probably resents me, too."

"You? Why?"

"I got to follow my passion, even if it was misguided. And he was pushed without any other options into running the family business. I think that's why he started diversifying."

That was good to know, Harrison thought. But it wasn't going to be easy working with them if there wasn't family harmony. "Maybe you should sit down with Reeve and have a heart-to-heart."

"You might be right. But not today. And not right away." She brushed her hand across the table, as if sweeping at imaginary crumbs. "I'm sorry for venting. I don't usually do that."

Her vulnerability had cropped up again, and it made her seem even more approachable. In spite of her money and social status, she hurt like the rest of the world. "Maybe you should vent more often."

She scoffed. "I doubt it. I've learned the hard way that venting isn't always safe. Or helpful."

"Then you've vented to the wrong people."

She arched an eyebrow. "Am I supposed to believe you're not one of them?"

"I can't tell you what to believe. But I'm safe. And trustworthy."

A slow grin slid across her face. "So you say. But a lawyer saying 'trust me' doesn't instill confidence."

"I hear you. But in time, you're going to come to realize it's true. My clients can trust me. And so can my friends." He placed his hand over hers. Rather than pull back, she wrapped her fingers around his.

"Okay," she said. "Maybe."

Energy passed between them. Deep. Stirring. And at an extraordinarily intimate level. He was about to ask when he could see her again, but then the Ken-doll approached, holding bright red visors with the club logo in his hand.

Gigi pulled her hand away from Harrison's and slipped it into her lap, leaving his fingers feeling cool and empty.

Ken plopped down in the empty chair. "Hey, you two. Got these awesome club visors for you. On the house, of course."

"Great," Harrison said. Just what he'd always wanted. A hat that would remind him of the day the golf pro ruined his next play.

Still, that wouldn't stop him from asking Gigi out on an actual date—and not one that could be explained away as a business meeting. He'd seen a softer side to her. Under that confident, lovely exterior lay a wounded soul, and he was drawn to her even more. There would be other opportunities for him to see her.

But he wasn't a fool. The woman didn't need another player in her life, another parasite hoping to secure a bright future. He'd take it slow and prove himself, wait for her to say "Proceed, Counselor."

Harrison wasn't naive, either. He doubted Gigi would

ever consent to anything other than an attorney-client relationship. And he couldn't blame her for that.

He knew who'd been born with the proverbial silver spoon—and who hadn't.

Chapter Eight

Gigi paced the living room, angry that Harrison hadn't called her. Not that he owed her anything. But she'd been out of sorts ever since they'd played golf on Sunday.

She stopped in the center of the room, then shook it off. She strode to the garage, then took an empty acrylic drinking glass from the kitchen and returned to the living room. She laid the glass on its side and practiced putting—just in case Harrison did call and suggest they play another round at Hillside.

The first two shots breezed past the glass, one of which rolled under the sofa. She blew out a sigh and slapped one hand on her hip as the other gripped the putter.

Okay. She could certainly use the practice, but there was no way she'd take a freakin' lesson. Not from Ken.

The last time she'd run into him at the pro shop, he'd asked why he hadn't seen her lately, and she'd made a stupid and embarrassing Freudian slip. *My schedule's been very erotic lately.*

He'd lifted his brow, and his lips quirked into an assumptive grin.

Erratic! She'd blurted out the word to correct the mistake. But he'd laughed, and then later that same day, when she'd seen him in the club dining room, he seemed to think they had a private joke, which they most certainly did not.

Ken actually thought that she'd go out with him—at least, he'd been about to broach the subject when she steered the conversation in another direction. He was so not her type. And too cocky for his own good.

Funny how she'd once thought the same thing about Harrison. But she now realized she'd been wrong, especially considering the kindness he'd shown her after the game, the way he'd listened—truly listened to her. He seemed to get her like no one else ever had.

Other than Grampy, of course. Her great-grandfather had known she could have taken over the CEO position at Fortune Metals. He would have encouraged her to go to college right after high school. And he would have insisted that her father give her and Reeve equal respect and responsibilities.

But Grampy was gone. And she'd yet to find anyone else who'd loved her the way he had, or who'd wholeheartedly listened to her as if her thoughts and feelings had great value.

Except for Harrison. Was he someone she could trust? She wanted to believe that he was.

She'd expected him to call after they'd left Hillside Country Club, but he hadn't, which was disappointing, but at least he'd sent a text, thanking her for the game. But she'd hoped for...

No, she hadn't expected anything else and wouldn't let silly what-ifs weigh her down. So she kept herself busy on Monday, calling clients, scheduling meetings and responding to never-ending emails.

On Wednesday morning, she drove to Chatelaine to tape another podcast and to meet with Sylvia Vasquez at her home. She'd no more than passed the Harv's New BBQ sign when Diana Dawson, who was producing today's podcast, called.

Gigi answered. "Diana, I'm almost at the station. How's my favorite mentee and producer?"

"Good, thanks. Are you all set for the taping?"

"Yes. In fact, I'll be arriving in about fifteen minutes."

"Good. You're coming early. That'll give us a chance to reminisce about the fun we've had taping your podcasts...and for me to give you an update."

When Gigi arrived at the Stellar Productions headquarters, a quaint old building Grampy had loved so much that he'd purchased it, she entered the front door and found Diana waiting for her.

"I can't believe this is the last time you'll be working with me," Diana said.

"Um, yeah. About that..." Something Harrison had said on Sunday had caused Gigi to reconsider her hard-line stance against her brother and FortuneMedia. Did it really matter to her that Diana was selling Stellar Productions, and if FortuneMedia was now printed on her business card? "I've been thinking it over. If you'll be staying on after the stock purchase, I'd like to continue working with you. I can't think of anyone else I'd rather have produce my podcasts."

"Thanks, Gigi. I'm so glad to hear that. But just so you know, this will be the last time we'll be taping at our studio in Chatelaine. The decision was made to raze the building to the ground."

"What?" Gigi's didn't need to ask who'd made the decision to knock down the building that housed Stellar Productions. That quaint old structure reflected almost everything Gigi loved about Chatelaine. Besides, Grampy had bought the building with the idea of turning it into something worthwhile—possibly a bed-and-breakfast or even a place for the Chatelaine Historical Society to create a museum. "Pray tell, whose idea was it to demolish the building?"

"Do you know Julia Chalmers?" Diana asked.

Gigi's brow furrowed as she tried to place the name, but no, she wasn't familiar with the woman. "Who is she?"

"She's the facilities director at Fortune Metals. And if you can believe this, she compared our company headquarters to a sow's ear and told your brother he'd be better off tearing it down rather than wasting the money it would take to rehab it."

Gigi took a deep breath, and her hands gripped the front door as if she alone could hold the building together and somehow change that plan. But that would be easier said than done. Her only option was to throw a fit and object to the corporate decision, but she doubted that would do any good. When Grampy purchased the property, he'd put it in their Fortune family trust, which Reeve controlled. And unfortunately, it seemed that whenever she and her brother were at odds, he always came out ahead.

After taping her podcast, having an espresso with Diana and climbing into her car, Gigi did her best to shake the dark cloud that been hanging over her since she'd learned that Reeve planned to demolish the building where Stellar Productions was headquartered. But she couldn't. Her brother, once again, had made another unilateral decision. You'd think that since Gigi had been the one who helped secure Diana's lease that Reeve would have had the decency to run the idea by her.

She took one last look at the building that reminded her of Grampy. How many times had she stood at the oversize windows with him and gazed out at the street? He'd even taken her with him to choose the soft green color for the interior walls.

"This old house is twice my age," he'd said. "But like me, it still has value."

That was as true today as it was then. And she'd be damned if she'd allow her brother to tear down the building without objecting—loudly.

As she pulled away from the curb and headed to her next appointment, she turned on the radio, which helped to improve her mood a little, but it wasn't until she arrived in front of the Vasquez house on Daffodil Court that her thoughts shifted to more pleasant ones.

Andres was on the sidewalk, with Chewie at his side. He was talking to a lanky teenage boy with a lawnmower. Sylvia had mentioned that her husband enjoyed working in the yard. Gigi assumed he was training the teenager to take over his chores while he recovered from knee surgery.

When Andres spotted her arrival, he brightened and gave her a friendly wave.

She smiled, then reached across the console and grabbed her briefcase and purse. Once she got out of her car, she approached the white picket fence.

Andres met her at the gate. "Good afternoon. Sylvia is looking forward to your meeting today."

"I am, too." Gigi wanted something new and—hopefully—exciting to think about.

Andres limped along the walkway while Chewie pranced at his feet. Gigi followed behind.

"Don't worry," Andres said, as he opened the front door for Gigi. "I'm not sticking around. I'm taking Chewie to the groomer. And after that, I've got plenty of errands to keep me busy while you ladies chat."

Once they'd entered the house, Andres called out, "Sylvia! Gigi's here!"

Moments later, Sylvia met them in the living room, with its cozy, eclectic mix of antique and vintage pieces, including colorful throw rugs that covered the polished hardwood floor.

"Can I get you something to drink?" Sylvia asked

Gigi. "Coffee, iced tea, water? I even have citrus-flavored soda."

"Water will be fine. Thank you."

"Well," Andres said, "if you'll excuse me, I'll leave so you two can get started."

Once he'd left and shut the door, Sylvia led Gigi to the small dining area where they'd sat last time, then she went to retrieve their drinks.

Before sitting at the table, Gigi withdrew from her briefcase the completed questionnaire Sylvia had returned, as well as a couple of handouts she thought would be helpful. Then she set the briefcase on the floor and took a seat.

Sylvia returned carrying a tray with a platter of brownies, two dessert plates, napkins and glasses filled with ice and water.

"Those look yummy," Gigi said. "You must love to bake."

"I do, but after Harrison moved out, I didn't bake very often. I tried to cut back on our sweets. But lately I've found myself whipping up goodies because I have so much time on my hands."

"That's where I come in." Gigi gave her a warm smile. "Let's go over those questions you answered and see if we can come up with some new ways to spend your free time."

Thirty minutes later, Sylvia's new season in life had a plan and a worthwhile purpose.

"Thank you for printing out the information on the art-therapy workshops. I'll have to drive an hour or more to get to most of them, but maybe, if I take the one offered in Corpus Christi, I can spend the night with Harrison." Sylvia let out a sigh. "But it'll have to wait until the fall session. I'll need to stay close to home while Andres recovers from his surgery."

"Actually, if you'd like, you can start with the online classes." Gigi sorted through the handouts. She slid the one she'd been looking for across the table to Sylvia. "Here's a list of the ones offered virtually. So you're not limited to those that are within driving distance."

"This is great. Thank you. You young people are so smart. I'm afraid I'm still old-school."

"You're sharp. So you'll catch on before you know it."

Sylvia reached for the platter of brownies and offered one to Gigi. "Do you mind if I ask you a question?"

"Go right ahead."

"What made you want to become a life coach?"

Gigi placed one of the chocolatey treats on her dessert plate. "It's a long story."

"I have all day." Sylvia took a brownie for herself. "I'm retired, remember?"

Gigi couldn't help but smile. Nor could she ignore the question when Sylvia had been more than open with her. "I made a lot of mistakes when I was younger. And I'd been disappointed by…" Did she really want to be that honest?

"Well," she continued, "let's just say my family dynamics didn't allow me to consider anything other than becoming a socialite. I hate to admit it, but I was the proverbial trust-fund baby."

Sylvia reached out and placed her hand over Gigi's.

"You're so much more than that. I can't imagine anyone placing you in that kind of box."

Well, her parents had. And so had Anson, who'd taken advantage of everything Gigi and her trust fund could provide. "I try very hard to prove people wrong. But it still hurts."

Sylvia gazed at her with eyes that cared, that healed. And it made her tear up. Dang it.

"What still hurts?"

For the life of her, Gigi couldn't hold it back any longer. "I'd always thought that I'd have an important role to play with Fortune Metals, but I was completely passed over. Ignored. Disregarded."

"I'm sorry, honey. That wasn't right. I hope you can let that go."

Gigi huffed and pressed back into her chair. "It was just so unfair."

"I get that. And believe me, everyone, at one time or another, has been treated badly or unfairly. What doesn't kill us often makes us stronger. But holding onto the past and brooding about it won't change it. Sometimes we have to tell ourselves, 'So what if that happened? Now what?'"

Now what indeed. Gigi had moved on with her life, and forged a successful career. But she hadn't been able to forget the disappointment. She looked at Harrison's mom. "You're right."

Sylvia patted Gigi's hand. "I find it interesting that a rearview mirror is very small, but the windshield is big and wide. You don't want to miss the present because you're looking at the past."

Pow. Right to the heart of the issue.

"Eat your brownie," Sylvia said. "Give yourself a moment to savor the here and now."

"Amazing," Gigi said. "I've been trying to encourage you to a second career in art therapy. And now you're encouraging me. Maybe you should be a life coach."

"It's easy to see someone else's problems," Sylvia said. "And much easier to offer advice than it is to take it."

"True."

Once they'd finished their treats, Gigi reached for her purse and briefcase.

"I'll walk you to the door," Sylvia said. "Thanks so much for coming. You've given me a lot to think about."

Gigi pointed at her. "And *do*, right? Check into those online classes."

"I will. Hopefully you have a lot to consider, too."

"You're right. I do." The older woman had recognized Gigi's self-torment about what should've been. And she'd made a valid point to just let it go, something Gigi would have to do if she really wanted to move on in life.

Sylvia opened the front door. "Thanks, Gigi."

"You're more than welcome. And thank *you* for the sound advice. I'll touch base with you next week, but call me if you want to talk sooner."

"Will do." Sylvia followed Gigi to her car. "Your parents must be very proud of you. I know that I am."

Her kindness, her validation and the sincerity in her eyes caused Gigi's heart to swell and her eyes to mist. Then Sylvia gave her a heartfelt embrace that warmed her from the inside out. Gigi found it hard to respond with words. Anything she came up with was sure to fall short of the sentiment she was feeling right now.

Instead, she nodded, mouthed a thank-you, then slid behind the wheel. As she started the ignition, she gave Harrison's sweet mother a wave.

Did Harrison have any idea how lucky he was? Or how much Gigi envied him?

Once she was on the road, her phone rang. This time, it was Harrison. Her heart soared as she took the call.

"How'd the meeting with my mother go?" he asked.

"It went well. I think your mom has a good idea about what she wants to do with her time, but I'll let her tell you more about it."

"Okay," he said. "Are you coming home this evening? Or are you staying over at the LC Club?"

She usually spent the night rather than make the long drive back to Corpus Christi, but it sounded as if he had something in mind. "I haven't decided. Why? What's up?"

"I thought we could have dinner together—possibly at the country club. It's prime-rib night."

"In that case, I'll come back. I'll text you when I get home."

"Good. I'll make reservations for seven. Will that work?"

"Sure."

"I'd be happy to pick you up," he said.

She paused. "Is this a date, Counselor?"

"Not unless you'd like it to be."

She considered the consequences. But not real hard. "Let's play it by ear."

"Then I'll pick you up at seven."

It might be wiser to meet him there, but if truth be told, she wanted it to be a date. And she couldn't wait to get home and choose just the right outfit to wear.

She just hoped that she—or rather *they*—wouldn't regret it later.

Taking Gigi out to dinner was akin to playing with fire, but Harrison hadn't been able to get her off his mind since they'd played golf last Sunday. Maybe. Nope. Further back than that. Since he met her at his office. And in spite of the risk, he couldn't seem to stay away.

He stopped at the gate to Lone Star Estates, hoping she'd already told the guard she was expecting him. She had. The gate opened, and he drove to her house. He parked at the curb, then strode to the front door and rang the bell. Should he have brought flowers?

No. Too much, too soon.

Moments later, when she answered the door, she took his breath away. Her hair was swept up into a stylishly messy topknot, her makeup damn near perfect—red lipstick, mascara highlighting her thick lashes. But it was the glimmer in those big brown eyes and her dazzling smile that struck him hard enough to rattle his brains. And damn. She was wearing a form-fitting red dress with a slit that revealed her thigh, and pointed gold shoes with the highest heels he'd ever seen.

The entire package poked a stick at his libido.

"You look…radiant," he said.

"Thank you." She gave him a once-over and grinned. "So do you, Counselor."

"I was going to take you to the club, but I realized we could run into one of the other attorneys at my firm. So I made reservations at Donovan's. I hope that's okay with you."

"That's perfect. And definitely a better idea."

She turned to reach for her purse, a designer clutch, and her stiletto heel slid on the floor tile. She wobbled, her ankle turned and she gasped as she grabbed onto the door handle to steady herself.

"You okay?" he asked. "Need some help?"

"I, uh…" She glanced down at the killer heels, one of which she'd raised off the floor. "I twisted my ankle."

"Pretty shoes."

"Yes, they are. And still brand-new. I'd been saving them for a special occasion."

He tossed her a grin. "You think I'm special?" That thought shouldn't excite him so much. It wasn't like he was a teenager, for goodness sake.

Her cheeks flushed. "When I was twenty-five, I could have run through the airport to catch a flight in these shoes, but now that I, um, never get carded, I don't usually wear spike heels, so I'm a little rusty. And to be completely honest, I'm not so sure I can walk." She winced as she rotated her ankle, only to stop midway. "It's not broken, but it hurts."

"How can I help?"

"I think I'm beyond that on many levels." She laughed

it off, but as she hobbled closer to the door, he reached out to steady her.

"Whoa. You sure you're all right?"

"Thanks, Harrison. But darn it, this isn't going to work. I'm sorry, but I'm going to have to cancel and get some ice on this."

There was no way he'd leave her now. "Listen, you're right. Let's get some ice on that ankle, but you have to eat. What do you have in your fridge?"

"Just a hodgepodge of stuff—veggies, yogurt, coffee creamer. Cheese maybe. Why?"

"I'll make us dinner."

"Seriously? Do you know how to cook?"

"I didn't get to be thirty-eight years old, living on my own, without knowing my way around a kitchen. Why don't you take a seat on the sofa. I'll whip something up."

"Better yet," she said, "if you help me, I'd rather sit on one of the barstools at the counter and watch you."

"Now you're talking." He stepped into the foyer and slipped an arm around her. "You have an ice pack in the freezer?"

"Ah, no."

"Frozen peas?"

"Yes, I think so. I have veggies of some kind."

"Good, that'll work. Let's proceed first with rest, ice, compression and elevation."

"Sure, doc."

"If I help, can you make it to the sofa first so I can take a look at that ankle?"

"Can you file a court case?"

"Funny." He grinned.

He helped her to the sofa, and she carefully took a seat. But as she turned toward him and lifted her bad leg to extend it on the middle cushion, her dress slid up her thigh, revealing red lace panties, and he sucked in a breath.

Suddenly, he was out of his element—gentlemanly speaking. On the other hand, overwhelming sexual attraction insisted that he knew exactly how to proceed.

Chapter Nine

Gigi sat on the sofa, one arm draped over the armrest, her injured leg extended and supported by the cushion, as Harrison slipped off her spike heel and carefully removed it.

"I feel like Cinderella in reverse," she said.

"Which makes me Prince Charming." He gently ran his hand over her foot, checking out her swollen ankle, but his touch felt more like a sensual caress.

At this rate, they both might decide to skip dinner.

Damn, the man was gorgeous. "Are you sure you were with JAG in the army and not a medic?"

He glanced up and smiled. His dark eyes were so warm, she could jump right into them.

"Yep. JAG all the way. But we all had first-aid training." He reached for her good foot and slipped off that shoe as well, leaving her barefoot. And tingling all over.

"I don't think you did any serious damage, but you

shouldn't put any weight on it. You mind if I carry you to the kitchen?"

"I'm not an invalid," she said, although she'd like to be held, carried.

"I know you're not. But I don't want you to make your ankle worse."

She'd like to feel better, too. And, hopefully, by the time dinner was over, she would.

"All right," she said, her voice coming out a little squeaky. "Go ahead and carry me."

He looked around. "I know where your home office is, but where is your kitchen?"

She pointed to the arched doorway, and he scooped her into his arms with very little effort. With each step he took, she breathed in his sea breeze scent, absorbed the warmth of his body and felt the flexing biceps in his arms.

He pulled out one of the barstools facing the kitchen counter and carefully set her on it. Then he adjusted another so she could rest her bad ankle on the seat cushion. "Before I start snooping around your fridge and pantry, I'll get those frozen peas and fix an ice pack for you."

"Thank you."

As Harrison proceeded to the Sub-Zero refrigerator and opened the freezer section, Gigi couldn't help but admire him. As gorgeous as he was when facing her, his backside was just as appealing.

After he'd prepared the frozen package and wrapped it in a dish cloth, he carefully placed it on her ankle, holding it at just the right angle. His free hand rested on her calf. Dang. She'd never known how hot frozen peas could be.

"Have you got this now?" he asked.

Not really. "Yes, I've got it."

He nodded, released the makeshift ice pack, then strode to the refrigerator and opened the door. He scanned the nearly empty shelves. "Hmm. No eggs? Just yogurt and a honeydew melon that's seen better days?"

"I haven't gone shopping yet."

"Apparently." He shut the Sub-Zero and walked into the pantry. Gigi could have said, "Don't bother." But she didn't. She knew all he'd find there was oatmeal and a box of Swiss chocolates one of her clients gave her. Maybe some pasta.

He slowly closed the pantry door and laughed. "I'm a pretty decent cook...when I've got something to work with."

"I warned you."

"How about Uber Eats?"

Gigi tossed him a smile. "Sure. That'll work."

"So what's your preference? Italian, Chinese, Tex-Mex?"

"I haven't had Chinese in a while."

"You got it. I'll place an order for the Peking Palace on Main. What are you craving?"

Besides him? *Stop that!* "I'll have the chicken chow mein—light on the chicken and heavy on the veggies."

After Harrison placed the order and set his phone on the marble countertop, he looked at her. "In the meantime, do you have any wine?"

"Always."

"Good to know."

"Wouldn't be without it." She pointed to a small wine cooler in the corner of the kitchen. "Take your pick, and

I'll have whatever you're having. There's also a wine cellar just beyond the dining room if you don't see what you like."

His gaze began at her eyes, lingered over her lips, down to her breasts, and then back to her eyes. "I see what I like."

She blushed. "Okay." She did, too.

Forty-five minutes later, they opened a second bottle of wine. When the delivery guy arrived with the food, Harrison met him at the door, then returned to the kitchen.

"We can eat on the patio," Gigi said, finding the remote that turned on the lights and spa. "It's nice out there."

"That sounds good to me." Harrison opened the slider, then lifted her in his arms and carried her to a glass-topped table with cushioned chairs. He arranged for her to prop her leg on the chair next to her. She could have told him that the ice pack—or maybe just the wine—had taken the edge off the pain and reduced the swelling, but she liked having him carry her.

"Be right back," he said. "Don't go anywhere."

"How could I without you to carry me?"

He chuckled and went back inside the house.

While she waited, she took in her backyard. The white twinkly lights that adorned the trees and a waning moon provided a romantic ambiance she couldn't have planned if she'd tried. Water from the hot tub overflowed into the pool and added a soft, relaxing background sound. And the scent of night blooming jasmine filled the air.

Harrison returned and set the table—plates, napkins, a variety of Chinese dishes still in the takeout boxes.

They each filled their plates.

"You have a nice backyard," Harrison said, as he tore open his chopsticks. "Do you use it often?"

"Not as often as I'd like. I think the gardener spends more time out here than I do. And the guy who works for my pool service."

"Such a shame to waste it."

She stared into her chow mein, realizing she did take all this for granted. She'd been to the house where he'd grown up. He probably only had a community pool somewhere.

They ate and chatted about nothing important. Baseball. Rodeos. Favorite foods and the fact that they both loved popular movies from the eighties. Gigi couldn't help stealing occasional glances at him and watching him handle those chopsticks as if he'd learned to use them as a child.

He reached for the wine bottle. "Are you ready for a refill?"

She already had a good buzz. "I think I'd better hold off for a while."

"Then how about a fortune cookie?" He reached into the empty bag, withdrew two of them and handed one to her.

"Perfect." She opened the cellophane wrap, broke the cookie and withdrew her fortune.

"What's it say?" he asked. "And you have to add, 'in bed' after you read it."

"What?"

"You never heard of that game? It's a little childish, but it's good for laughs." He ripped open his fortune cookie and chuckled. "A pleasant surprise awaits you. In bed."

She laughed. "You're right. That's silly. But I'll play along." She scanned her fortune, and her cheeks heated.

"Go on."

Okay. She was a good sport. Right? "Now is the time to pursue that love interest." She took a deep breath, then added, "In bed."

Their gazes met. And, oh, man. The look on his face was locked and loaded, but in a sexual way. If she'd been a lady in Victorian times, she'd pull out the fan from her reticule and use it to cool her face.

He coughed and broke eye contact. "Told you, it was childish." He nodded at her elevated foot. "Hey, how's your ankle?"

She rotated it slowly. It was tender, but it didn't hurt too badly. "Actually, it's feeling a little better now. I might be able to put some weight on it."

"Good. But don't push too hard to get back on your feet." He fingered the slip of paper in his hand, and his lips quirked in a crooked grin. "I like holding on to a fortune."

Her tummy did a zing. "I'll bet you do." She smiled, then lowered her elevated foot and placed it on the patio floor. "I'll give it a try."

She hobbled over to the double chaise lounge and sat on the edge. "Yeah, it still hurts a little, but at least I can walk." She looked at him. She shouldn't ask this, but she did. "Would you mind feeling my ankle again? Do you think the swelling has gone down?"

"Sure." He got up from his seat at the patio table,

made the short walk to the padded chaise, sat beside her and took her foot into his hands.

She closed her eyes, enjoying the feel of his fingers running over her skin.

"Yeah, I think it's better. Icing it helped." He scanned her patio and the waterfall created by the hot tub flowing into the pool generating a light mist. "It's a nice evening to swim. You ever do that? Swim at night?"

Never. In fact, she didn't usually find the time to swim during the day. But, hey… "I'm game if you are."

"I didn't bring my suit."

She poked her foot at his thigh. His taut, muscular thigh. "You could skinny-dip." She arched an eyebrow, and her lips tweaked into a grin.

He sucked in a breath as his gaze traveled from her face to her ankle and back up. "Really? Just strip down, in your backyard?"

"The block wall provides plenty of privacy. Besides, I'd love to see that."

"Sounds like a challenge."

She smiled.

He unbuttoned his shirt. "I dare you to join me."

She'd never done anything like that in her life. And she might be making a big, wine-buzzed mistake, but she never backed down from a challenge. In fact, she thrived on them. "You're on, Counselor." She turned her back to him. "Unzip me."

Unzip me.

Damn. She was serious.

She swung herself to a seated position, her back to him. "You know how, right?"

Yeah. It was just like riding a bike. Harrison swallowed. Hard. Then he slid the zipper down her back, past her red, lacy bra strap and down to her hips, where he could see the edge of her matching panties.

An erection stirred. But, hell, what guy wouldn't have a hard-on right now?

She got to her feet, let the dress fall to her ankles, then slowly turned to him. "Now it's your turn."

He rose and unhooked his belt, but damn. His hands trembled and he fumbled around. This woman had him rattled.

She tossed him a playful grin. "Need any help?"

He lifted his hands in surrender. "Be my guest."

She pulled the buckle until the belt passed through the loops and dropped it on the chaise. Then she nodded at the waistband of his trousers. "Should I?"

"You're doing a great job so far. Don't stop now."

She unbuttoned his pants, then slowly lowered the zipper. He suspected she'd felt his erection through his trousers, yet all the while, her gaze never left his.

This was too much. He pulled her into his arms and began a slow path of kisses, starting at her lips, down her throat, between her breasts, which were a lot fuller than he'd imagined. He tugged his teeth on the lacy edge of her bra.

"You're good at this," she said, her voice breathy and sultry. She damn near melted in his arms.

"You have no idea how badly I want you," he said, his voice soft yet ragged.

"I want you, too."

A moment of clarity broke through his haze of passion, and he stopped. "But I don't have protection. No condom."

"I'm on the pill. Not that I've been sexually active, it's just that—"

He placed his finger against her lips. "No need to explain." Screw the swim. He kissed her again, and he was lost in a swirl of heat and desire that, if he wasn't careful, he'd drown in.

"Are you sure you want to do this?" he asked. "Because if you're having second thoughts, I'll respect that."

"Right now, I can't think of anything I'd rather do. Here, on that lounge chair, in the hot tub, in the house." She smiled at him. "No regrets, Counselor. How about you?"

"None whatsoever."

He shed his pants. As he reached for his briefs, she unhooked her bra and tossed it to the side. Then she slid her skimpy red panties over her hips, down her legs and kicked them to the side.

He'd thought Gigi Fortune was beautiful when dressed in a business suit or a red sexy dress. But neither outfit could compare to the one she'd been born with.

He joined her on the double chaise, where they continued to kiss, to taste and to stroke each other until they were both crazed with the need to finish what they'd started.

He undid her tight bun and let her hair fan out around her shoulders. Never had he been so turned on, so enamored.

"Counselor," she said, "don't make me wait."

She didn't have to ask twice. He rose up and over her luscious, naked body. She spread her legs, and he entered her slowly at first, relishing the slick feel of her innermost parts. As he moved in and out, desire took over, and he increased the pace. With each thrust, she arched up to meet him.

As they continued to make love, any reservations he had disappeared. He suspected hers had, too.

When she reached a peak, she cried out, and he released along with her. They came together in a sexual explosion he'd never forget.

As the last waves of their climax ebbed, he held her close, barely breathing, afraid to speak and break the spell she'd cast over him.

Had she suspected the evening would turn out this way?

He certainly hadn't. Not like this. But he'd been tortured by thoughts of her for weeks, and he figured that she felt the same way.

He rolled to the side, taking her with him.

She smiled and placed a hand on his chest. "We probably should talk about where we go from here."

He wanted to object, to tell her to let it wait until morning…or next week. Or better yet, why talk about it at all? But Harrison hadn't gotten to where he was by avoiding tough conversations. "Why don't we take it one day at a time? And see where this goes?"

"So you don't see this as a one-time thing?"

"Not unless you do. Want that, I mean." *Please, say you don't. Not yet.*

She snuggled up against him and whispered, "Do you know what I'd really like to do?"

He was almost afraid to ask. "What's that?"

"I'd like to take a swim, shower and then top off our lovemaking by eating ice cream in bed—right out of the carton."

He laughed. "I like the way you think."

She brushed a kiss on his brow, then slowly got up from the chaise. "Ready for that swim now?"

"I am. But are you?" He looked down at her ankle.

"I won't be making any fancy dives off the board, if that's what you mean. But if it's too much, I'll sit it out on the steps in the shallow end."

"Do you want me to carry you?" Harrison asked.

"I think I can make it on my own." She took a step with her good foot, then, taking it easy with the bad one, she carefully made her way to the deep end. "So far, so good. But I won't be playing water polo."

He sat there and watched her walk in all her beautiful, naked glory. Assured, yet not cocky. With her back to him, she dove into the pool.

No way would he sit this out. He made his way to the edge of the pool, then dove in after her. Underwater, her long hair trailed behind her, like a mermaid on a mission.

Thoughts of Lady Gaga's sensual song from the most recent version of *A Star is Born* crossed his mind, the lyrics too true to deny. It was clear that he and Gigi were far from the shallow end now.

Gigi had no more than come up for air in waist-deep water when she saw Harrison dive into the deep end. He'd rocked his business suit and he'd cut a fine figure on the golf course. But neither image could compare to the gorgeous hunk naked. Tanned skin, broad shoulders, taut abs… Talk about a guy with raw masculinity.

He popped up right in front of her. Water glistened on his dark hair and his tanned skin.

"See?" He scrubbed a hand over his wet face. "Isn't this fun?"

It was sure to be even more fun if they played around like a couple of silly kids.

"You bring out the wild child in me," she said.

"Oh, yeah?" He flashed a boyish grin. "I like that."

"I just bet you do." She could suggest they play a wicked game of Marco Polo. But she wasn't going to make it hard for him to find her.

A long strand of hair tickled the side of her face. She brushed it aside to no avail.

Harrison reached out and tucked it behind her ear. His palm lingered on her jaw, and his wet thumb stroked her cheek. Then he tilted her face upward and brushed her lips with his.

She slipped her arms around his waist and they kissed, long and deep. Had she ever been kissed so thoroughly?

Gigi had never had a moonlight kiss in a pool before this, had never even imagined one. She let out a whimper, then rubbed against him, letting him know what she wanted. And she felt his erection stir.

He tore his mouth from hers, yet he didn't pull away. "Believe it or not, I'm ready for round two."

"Sounds good to me, but we'll have more room to enjoy each other if we go into the house."

"I'm not going to let you walk that far." He scooped

her into his arms, climbed out of the pool and strode across the patio to the open sliding door. "You'll have to point the way to your bedroom."

She knew she could walk on her own, but heck. How many times in a girl's life did a hunk carry her into sweet bliss?

"Down the hall. Second door on the left."

Chapter Ten

It was nearing midnight, and well before the so-called witching hour, but after a wonderfully wild night of lovemaking, Harrison was already bewitched. He loved the way they'd spent the evening and could almost imagine himself falling for the woman beside him.

No, that wasn't happening. Nor was it a good idea. A romantic relationship with Gigi Fortune wasn't likely to end well. But right this minute, as he and Gigi sat amid the rumpled sheets in her bed, eating ice cream out of two separate pint-size cartons—strawberry in hers and espresso in his—he wasn't looking forward to ending it any time soon.

He paused for a beat, lowering his spoon, and savored the amazing and alluring sight of the beautiful woman who'd turned him inside out. Her hair, a blond mass of damp curls, framed her face as she dug into her strawberry Ben and Jerry's.

"Hmm," she said, "I love ice cream."

He'd always liked it, too, but now, more than ever.

Either way, they were going to have to face the "now what?" question, and he dreaded it. For some crazy reason, he wasn't looking forward to calling it a night, or trying to backpedal on a relationship that had moved eons beyond friendship.

He dipped his spoon into his own carton. "Is this espresso ice cream decaffeinated?"

Her expression morphed from a well-loved and sexually sated grin to one of surprise. "I never thought to check. Why?"

He winked and grinned. "It's just that I have to go to the office early tomorrow." He glanced at the clock on the bureau. "Or rather, today. And I need some sleep."

There. She could either invite him to sleep over, or he'd make a gracious exit.

"You're welcome to stay the night, if you'd like to. I have an extra toothbrush, although I suspect you'll need to stop at your place before heading to the office. I'm not sure what state our poolside clothes are in—probably not starched and pressed and ready to go."

"That's true. I can't go back to the office wearing the same clothes I wore yesterday."

"Just for the record, I think you look dashing, just the way you are now."

He laughed. "If I show up as naked as a jaybird, I'll have to look for a new job—and without a severance package or a reference." He sucked in a breath. *Here goes.* "I'm not sorry about what we're doing, but it's best if we keep our relationship under wraps."

She stuck her spoon into the ice-cream carton and

her mood sobered. "Look. I know that's a big concern of yours. I mean, you getting fired or called to task for being romantically involved with a client. But, assuming we continue seeing each other..." She paused but didn't look at him.

"I want to. If you do, that is." He held his breath.

Her grin said it all. "I won't tell anyone. This is just between the two of us."

"Good. I think it's best, at least until I finish your case."

"You got it." She reached out to shake on it, her fingers cold from holding the ice cream, and he brought her hand to his lips and kissed each knuckle.

"Appreciate it."

He also appreciated everything about *her*. Such class. So dignified, even after their romp. Kind and considerate, too. Man, she was the perfect woman. She could have her pick of any billionaire running in her social circle. What was she doing with him?

"Since you need to rest," she said, "let's get rid of these cartons, turn out the lights and get some sleep."

"You got it." But falling asleep wasn't going to be easy. Not when he was cuddled against his new, exciting and creative lover. This—whatever *this* was—might not last forever, but that was okay. He'd come to believe marriage wasn't in the cards for him, especially after Sherrilyn went back to her ex-husband. But maybe that was because he'd yet to meet the right woman. And if such a woman was out there—somewhere—she wasn't likely to be a Fortune heiress. But for now, they were perfectly matched, and he was happy. Not to mention, thoroughly sated.

* * *

Gigi had had romantic relationships in the past, but most of them fizzled out soon after they started.

But that wasn't happening with Harrison. Instead of dwindling, the passion and heat only seemed to grow stronger. She suspected that was due to the whole we've-got-a-secret thing, which added an exciting, clandestine aura to their nightly get-togethers.

They'd been meeting at her house for the last two weeks so they could maintain a low profile. Why risk being seen in public?

So dinner on her patio and skinny-dipping became their nightly routine, followed by delightful hours of making love. Harrison didn't usually stay over. "No need to give your neighbors any reason to gossip," he'd said. And while she enjoyed waking up in his arms, she'd been okay with him slipping off at midnight.

For the most part, their conversations had remained fairly generic, although Gigi wanted to know a lot more about him. She had plenty of questions about his childhood, his military career…and admittedly, his previous relationships, especially the one he'd had with the single mom who'd been "pretty special." But since she kept her past to herself, she figured she owed him the same respect.

Fortunately, their sexual escapades hadn't interfered with her day-to-day work. In fact, wasting time by on-line shopping had taken a back seat to getting things done, and she seemed to be even more productive and creative than usual.

Nevertheless, her feelings for the handsome Latino

attorney were growing. She suspected his feelings for her were, too, but she wasn't sure. And that was bothersome.

Maybe it was a case of too much, too fast, too soon. Only trouble was, she couldn't seem to get enough of him. And it wasn't just an addiction to pleasure. Even without saying a word, Harrison made her feel cherished in a way no other man had.

She continued to coach his mother, even though the older woman had a pretty solid game plan for the future. If Sylvia suspected anything about Gigi's relationship with her son, she didn't mention it. And the two women seemed to have grown close.

Last week, as Andres's knee surgery date neared, Sylvia had said, "I'm worried."

"About what?"

"What if something goes wrong?"

"Your husband will be in good hands," Gigi told her. "Knee replacement is a very common, routine surgery."

"I know." Sylvia all but rolled her eyes. "And the surgeon is highly respected. But there can be complications—blood clots, infection, nerve damage and any number of rare things. And my heart refuses to listen to my head. I've loved that man for so many years that I don't know what I'd ever do without him."

Had they been talking face-to-face, Gigi would have reached out and touched her hand, tried to ease her worries. As it was, they were meeting virtually, with miles between them. "How long have you been married, Sylvia?"

"It'll be forty-six years next Valentine's Day."

"Wow. That's great. I hate to admit it, but my marriage only lasted ten years, although the love died long before that."

"The trick," Sylvia said, "is to marry the right man."

That was a no-brainer, but mistakes happened. Sometimes hormones got in the way of reason.

"How do you know when you've found the right one?" Gigi asked.

Sylvia shrugged. "All I know is that it starts with friendship, humor and trust."

Gigi mentally checked each of those boxes where Harrison was concerned. Could he be her Mr. Right?

"And you'd better be good friends," Sylvia added, "because the sparks often fizzle as the estrogen level drops."

Gigi bit back a smile. When it came to Harrison, her estrogen train was still running at high speed.

On Monday morning, around eleven thirty, Sylvia called to let Gigi know Andres was out of surgery and doing well. "The surgeon said everything went textbook-perfect. And he's been moved to Recovery."

"That's great news. Do you need anything? Can I help in any way?"

"No, honey, but thank you. Harrison is here with us now. He's going to stick around this week and work remotely."

Gigi knew that. She and Harrison had discussed his plans yesterday afternoon, right before he left for Chatelaine.

"I'm glad your son is there," Gigi said. "Keep me

posted. If you don't mind, I might stop by to visit after Andres is released from the hospital."

"We'd both love to see you," Sylvia added.

Love. Such a nice word. Gigi hadn't heard it used nearly enough.

She'd clear her calendar on Friday, allowing Andres to get home and settled in. But she kept that plan to herself. She often got slammed with appointments at the end of the week, and rescheduling wasn't always easy.

"I'll do my best, but no promises," Gigi said before ending the call.

Still, things worked out nicely. On Thursday evening, Gigi checked into the hotel at the LC Club. After a light breakfast at The Silver Spoon on Friday morning, she picked up the to-go order she'd placed last night so Sylvia wouldn't need to spend too much time in the kitchen. Then she stopped by a nearby florist and purchased a bouquet of yellow roses.

Twenty minutes later, she walked to the Vasquezes' front door, flowers in one hand and a large white shopping bag bearing The Silver Spoon logo in the other.

Sylvia's car was parked in the driveway, but Gigi didn't see any sign of Harrison.

Rather than ring the doorbell and possibly disturb Andres, she set the bag near the welcome mat and knocked.

Moments later, Sylvia answered, immediately brightening when she spotted Gigi on the porch. "I'm so glad you came. Here. Let me help." Sylvia reached for the flowers. She took a sniff. "Oh. These sure smell good."

"I brought some to-go meals," Gigi said, reaching

for the bag. "I thought you might like a break from cooking."

"That was sweet of you. Let's put the food in the refrigerator."

As Gigi followed Sylvia into the kitchen, the bag in hand, she asked, "How's the patient doing?"

"He can be a little grumpy at times, and he doesn't like the idea of weeks of physical therapy, but other than that, he's healing and getting stronger. Right now, he's lying in bed, watching television with Chewie." Sylvia set the vase on the counter, then Gigi helped her put away the food—*insalata mista*, grilled chicken breasts with a lemon-garlic sauce and sautéed zucchini.

Sylvia looked into the plastic container that held cannoli for dessert. "Oh, my. What a feast—and a treat. I hope you'll stay for lunch."

"I can probably do that."

Sylvia picked up the vase of roses. "Come with me. Andres will be happy to see you."

Gigi followed Harrison's mother down the hall, the sounds of a televised sporting event growing louder.

Sylvia led Gigi into the couple's bedroom, where Andres was propped up in bed, his leg elevated with pillows. He held the remote in his hand, while he watched a soccer game on a wall-mounted TV. A snoozing Chewie was curled up beside him.

"Look who's here," Sylvia said.

The moment Harrison's father spotted Gigi, he muted the volume. "Good morning! What a nice surprise. Are those flowers for me?"

"I thought you could use a lift. And a little color to brighten your day."

"Seeing you brightened my day." Andres beamed. "And the roses are an added bonus. Men don't usually get flowers. In fact, this is the first time for me."

Gigi made a quick scan of the modest but cozy bedroom, with its lilac-print bedspread and white-eyelet sheets. Several family photographs adorned the chest of drawers, and a colorful framed needlepoint hung on the wall. It read, Do Unto Others As You Would Have Them Do Unto You.

Sylvia pointed to the chair nearest the bed. "Have a seat, Gigi. If you'll excuse me for a moment, it's time for Andres to take another pain pill."

Gigi and Harrison's father made small talk until Sylvia returned with the pill and a glass of water.

Andres took his medication, then leaned back against the pillows that had been stacked to prop him up. Little Chewie stretched and yawned. Then she got to her feet and gave Andres a nudge with her nose.

"Syl," Andres said, "I think Chewie wants a potty break."

"I'll take her outside." Sylvia scooped up the little dog in her arms. "But I can see your eyes getting heavy. We should probably leave you alone so you can rest."

Andres nodded. "That's probably a good idea. Thanks for coming to visit this old man, honey."

The sweetness of his tone touched Gigi's heart. "My pleasure." She followed Sylvia out of the bedroom and walked with her to the door that led to the backyard.

So this was what it looked like to have a long, loving

marriage. Gigi suspected her parents only stayed together for financial reasons. Love of the checkbook, rather than the mate.

After opening the slider, Sylvia set Chewie on the lawn. The furry little pup looked more like a brown dust mop than a dog. Then she dashed off to do her doggie business.

"Where's Harrison?" Gigi asked.

"He's running some errands for Andres, and then he plans to stop by and see a friend from high school."

"That's nice." Gigi was glad he was still in town. "Can I ask you a question?"

"Of course, you can."

"You'd mentioned that, as a kid, Harrison had been bullied in school, which was too bad. But in spite of an obstacle like that, he went on to join the army, go to college and become an attorney."

"I think he was able to achieve so much because of the bullying. He learned to use his words instead of his fists. After all, that's the only way he could win against those *burros*."

"As a parent, it must have been hard for you and Andres to see him suffer."

"Yes, it was heartbreaking at times. But it was also rewarding to watch him overcome it, although his efforts didn't work very well on Jason Walker. Nevertheless, Harrison was smart enough to turn the other bullies into his bodyguards, and they kept Jason off his case for the remainder of his time at Chatelaine High."

"I'm sure that's a skill he uses as an attorney."

"Harrison's a great negotiator and can get along

with just about anyone." Sylvia chuckled. "Not that he's perfect, mind you. He used to have a temper, but he's learned to tamp it down these days. And he can be stubborn to a fault when he thinks he's right. One of his JAG buddies once told me that Harrison has been known to cut down an opponent with words, as if the opponent was a creeping thistle and he was a Weedwacker. That might be true, but Harrison also has a good heart."

Many mothers were biased when it came to their children. And Gigi was reminded of something Grampy had once said: "Every old crow thinks her baby's white as snow."

That might be true in some cases, but not when it came to Delphine Fortune. Gigi's mom had never been all that involved in Gigi's high-school education, except for shopping for just the right dress for one of the country-club cotillions.

But Sylvia wasn't like Gigi's mom. She clearly adored and admired her son. But she also could call them as she saw them.

"I have a question for you," Sylvia said. "Have you taken a special interest in my son?"

Uh-oh. Had Gigi inadvertently given her that idea? Had she been that obvious? She doubted that Harrison had said anything, although the family seemed especially close.

"I take a special interest in all of my clients," Gigi said. "And in their families."

Sylvia nodded sagely, but there was a twinkle in her eyes.

The front door opened, then closed.

Harrison was home. Good. Gigi would let him field any further questions his parents might have. She was good at putting on a false front, but she couldn't flat-out lie to Sylvia.

There was definitely something going on between her and Harrison, but she'd be damned if she knew what to call it.

Harrison entered the kitchen holding a bag of groceries. He smiled, but the look in his dark eyes told her he wasn't pleased.

Uh-oh. Gigi hoped he wasn't going into Weedwacker mode.

Harrison had spotted Gigi's car parked in front of his parents' house, so he'd realized she was here, but when he'd entered the house and heard her visiting with his mom in the kitchen, heard their soft laughter, a niggle of apprehension had run along his spine.

He carried the groceries into the kitchen, where the two women sat at the table, chatting like old friends—leaning toward each other as if sharing a family secret. Gigi, as lovely as ever, her long wavy hair tumbling over her shoulders, had on a pair of black slacks and a green silky top, blending with the kitchen's springtime decor as if she belonged there. But the blending stopped there. She looked out of place.

The diamond studs were real, the purse resting beside her feet wasn't a knock off. And there was something else, too. The unseen. The aura of old money. No, she *was* definitely out of place. And she'd just catapulted herself into his family life, not to mention that she was giving his mother the wrong idea.

Harrison placed the bags on the counter. "I didn't expect to see you here, Gigi."

She looked up at him and smiled, but as she read his expression, that smile faded. "I stopped by to see your dad and to check in on your mom."

He nodded, as if that was reasonable. But it wasn't. If Gigi and Harrison weren't sexually involved, would she still have made the two-hour drive to visit a client's recovering spouse?

He doubted it. And his mother wasn't stupid. She had to suspect something more was going on between them, something he hadn't wanted her to know yet—if ever. Hell, the last thing he wanted to do was get his parents' hopes up. Or to have them make any announcements to their friends or neighbors.

"Gigi brought roses for your father," Mama said. "And food from that fancy restaurant at Lake Chatelaine."

"That was thoughtful," he said, although he wasn't happy that Gigi had taken it upon herself to get so involved with his parents. Or to spring a visit on them without telling him. That wasn't cool. He didn't want to drag his folks into his sex life, especially when he knew they were pushing him to find that special someone.

Sure, he thoroughly enjoyed his relationship with Gigi, but they were so different from each other, whatever they had wasn't likely to last. And whether Gigi realized it or not, she was toying with his parents' emotions. Hell, at times, he wondered if she was playing with his, as well.

But he'd entered the relationship with both eyes open and the knowledge that things could end as quickly as it began.

But his parents didn't know that. And he didn't want to see them hurt or disappointed when Gigi tired of him and went on about her life.

"Well," Gigi said, her expression sober, her demeanor stiff. "I don't want to overstay my welcome. So I'd better go."

She'd overstepped by inserting herself into his family as if she belonged there. And while he didn't mean to hurt her feelings, it was for the best if she left.

"Thanks for dropping by." he said.

"Don't be silly, Harrison. Gigi is staying for lunch. She brought plenty for all of us."

Gigi glanced first at Harrison, then at his mother and slowly shook her head. "No, Sylvia. I ate a late breakfast. Besides, it's a long drive home."

"I'll walk you to the car," Harrison said. "I'd like to talk to you about the case." He had nothing new to report but it was a convenient excuse to see her out. And to try and smooth things over.

She nodded. "Okay."

"Back in a second, Mama."

His mother waved them off with a smile. "You kids take your time."

Once they were in the front yard, Gigi turned to him and folded her arms across his chest. "You're clearly not happy to see me here."

He ran a hand through his hair. "Don't get my parents involved with us."

"I'm not. Your mother is my client. I care about her. And your father."

"I'm glad to hear that." And he hoped it was true. "It's complicated with my folks, and I don't want them getting their hopes up about us." And he sure didn't need all the poking and prodding that was going to follow once he went back into the house.

"I thought it would be a nice surprise," she said. "I'm sorry if you think I overstepped."

"I was surprised, alright." He opened her car door and she slipped in. "Be more judicious next time, okay? We agreed to keep this relationship between us. And I don't want my parents getting involved in my personal life."

"Right. We wouldn't want that." She looked at him as if he'd knocked her completely off stride, then quickly recovered. "You got it, Counselor." Her voice low and her tone dejected. She kept her eyes focused ahead as she climbed behind the wheel, lowered the driver's window and pushed the button to start her car.

Crap. He'd wanted to get his point across, but he hadn't meant to hurt her feelings. Why was everything so complicated with Gigi?

He leaned forward, resting his arm on the open window and catching a whiff of her alluring fragrance. "I'm sorry if I came off too strong, but I'd like you to be a little more careful in the future where my parents are concerned."

"Yes, I will." She gave him a half-hearted Boy Scout salute.

Double crap. He stepped back. She was in the wrong,

but apparently she didn't see it that way. And his apology had fallen short. He hadn't meant to chase her away. He had to bring this back around, let her know he still wanted her. And wanted her bad.

"I'll be tied up here until Saturday night, but are you up for a round of golf this Sunday?" he asked. "Back in town?"

She looked a bit crestfallen, then she quickly recovered. "Sure, why not? I always enjoy a little friendly competition."

"Same as before?" he asked. "Five dollars a side?"

"No, let's raise the stakes. Five dollars a hole and loser buys drinks in the clubhouse."

"You're on. I'll text you our tee time," he said.

She stared at him as she pulled the car door closed. Then she backed out of the driveway, leaving him to watch her go. She wasn't happy, but she'd agreed to a game of golf.

Still, something told him, between her showing up without telling him and him calling her out on it, they'd just taken a serious step forward. For better or worse, that just raised the stakes. And he wasn't just talking about their golf game.

Chapter Eleven

On Sunday afternoon, Gigi met Harrison at the Hillside Country Club for their "friendly" round of golf. Admittedly, she shouldn't have sprung the surprise visit to his parents on him. She wasn't sure what she'd expected when he walked in, but not what she got. He'd made her feel as unwelcome as a nosey neighbor with head lice. She'd wanted to let him have it, but not in front of Sylvia, who'd become much more than a client.

So what if she had both a business and personal relationship with his mother? And, for cripe's sake, he was the one who'd set that up in the first place.

While they played, he tried to make pleasant conversation. "It's a nice day," he'd said when they started out.

"Yes, it is."

"Nice shot," he'd told her after she chipped out of the sand on the second hole.

"Thank you," she'd said, keeping her responses at a minimum.

Finally, before they teed off on number three, he said, "I'm sorry for being harsh on Friday."

She turned to look at him, her expression flat. "You were an ass. And I haven't quite forgiven you yet."

"But you're here," he said.

Yes she was. Because, as angry as she was, as hurt as she'd been, she wasn't ready to end things. At least, not yet.

After Harrison sank his last putt on the eighteenth hole, losing the match by three strokes, he said, "You played well today. And you won. Have you been practicing?"

Putting into a plastic cup in the living room didn't count. "I'm not a novice. And I'm a competitor, remember?"

"You won't get an argument from me. Looks like I owe you a drink."

"Are you sure you want to pay up here?" she asked, having a difficult time tamping down a snarky tone. "Aren't you afraid you'll run into one of the other attorneys in your firm?"

"Playing a round of golf with a client isn't a problem."

"But *playing around* with a client is?"

Harrison blew out a sigh. "I told you I was sorry for being short with you on Friday." He glanced to his right, then to his left, as if making sure no one was looking or listening. "I admit I may have overreacted at my parents' home. I care about you. And I really enjoy being with you. Our relationship is… Okay, it's special. And under normal circumstances, it's not one I'd want to hide. But we agreed to keep it under wraps for the time being."

That was true. And she understood why he wouldn't want word to get back to the law firm. "I don't know why you just couldn't be honest with your parents and let them know we're…you know, dating."

"Because if I told them that, they'd be planning our wedding and picking out their grandkids' names. It's not the right time, Gigi. That's all. Can we please put Friday behind us and move on?"

"I suppose so." But she suspected that "move on" in his mind meant moving from the country club and spending the rest of the evening at her house, where he didn't like leaving his car parked out front.

"Okay," she said. "I forgive you. Just for the record, I enjoy being with you, too. And you're right. Neither your firm nor my brother should find out about our dating until you finish the case."

But there was no way she'd invite him home with her tonight—on principle alone. Was their relationship special? Or was she just a booty call?

"Should I pick up a couple of steaks?" he asked. "Or maybe fish or chicken? We could grill tonight."

Yep. Booty call. And while she was down for sex, she deserved better than that.

"I'm sorry," she said. "Maybe tomorrow or later in the week?"

How was that for showing him she wasn't pinning her hopes on more than a temporary, sexual fling?

He appeared to be taken aback, but he shrugged. "Sure."

They got back in the cart and returned it to the cart barn.

"Good round, Ms. Fortune? Mr. Vasquez?" one of the attendants asked.

"We had fun," Harrison said.

"I'll take your clubs to the storage locker," the young man said.

They both thanked the attendant before walking to the patio, where they found a table for two overlooking the pond near the eighteenth green—one of the toughest holes on the course.

A waitress, a middle-aged redhead with a jovial smile, stopped by the table to get their orders. Gigi asked for a glass of ice water to curb her thirst and a mojito, which sounded refreshing.

"I'll have the same," Harrison said.

While they waited for their drinks, a man approached their table. "Harrison. Good to see you here. I'm glad you're using the firm's membership." The fiftysomething, balding golfer turned to Gigi and smiled. "You look very familiar. Do I know you?"

Gigi decided to yield to the counselor sitting across from her.

"This is one of our clients," Harrison said. "Gigi, I'd like you to meet Stanley Tyler, a partner in the firm."

Stanley reached out a hand. "Your name sounds familiar." Recognition lit his face. "Of course, Gigi Fortune."

She merely shook his hand and said, "Nice to meet you."

Stanley nodded to Harrison. "See you at our monthly staff meeting on Monday." As the waitress returned with their drinks, the lawyer took his leave, but not before Gigi detected a smirk on his face.

"Here you go," the waitress said. "May I get you anything else, Ms. Fortune? Shall I keep your tab open?"

Apparently, the bartender or another club employee had filled in the waitress on the name of one of the Founders members. Before Gigi could respond, Harrison said, "We're fine for now. And I'll be picking up the tab."

You bet he would. Gigi had played her heart out on the course, and she'd enjoyed taking him down a notch.

But that didn't mean she wanted to see him get in trouble at work. "You okay?"

"Why wouldn't I be?"

"Your coworker?"

"One of the partners I have to answer to." He brushed it off. "But, nah. Not a problem."

Harrison might have brushed off the awkward meeting, but he wasn't happy about it.

Apologizing and setting things right with Gigi were the least of his problems. He was in big trouble. And not just because Stan had spotted them at the club.

He didn't like the idea that Gigi might be putting on the brakes. In truth, he was at risk of falling heart-overhead for her, and if he did, that wasn't going to work out well. Not in the long run. He used paper cups, while hers were crystal.

But what did that matter? He'd lived thirty-eight

years without having a lasting relationship. And he'd weathered a disappointing breakup without any lasting scars. What made him think this one was going to last or end differently?

Okay, this relationship was different. But that's because he'd never dated anyone who'd come from an ultrawealthy background.

He sighed. Okay, it was more than that. No woman had ever stirred him the way Gigi did.

They sipped their drinks and looked out at the golf course, not speaking. But they continued to steal glances at each other. This was awkward, and he hated that.

A woman in her late forties, with more than one face-lift under her belt, approached the table. She tried to smile gracefully, but she couldn't hide that fishlike mouth and that taut, stretched skin.

"Gigi Fortune! As I live and breathe. You're back in the swing of things…so it seems. Our Thursday-morning ladies group just lost a member. Would you possibly be interested in joining us again?"

"That sounds fun," Gigi said, "but I'm afraid I can't, Claire. I've got a busy schedule these days."

"Oh, that little podcast thing you do? And working with clueless women?"

Gigi's fingers tightened around her drink; she was clearly pissed. "Yes. That. So I'm busy, which is why I don't get out here too often."

The woman turned to Harrison and gave him a once-over. "I don't blame you for stealing a little time away with this handsome man."

In spite of her rudeness, Harrison offered her a friendly smile.

"I haven't seen you around." She extended a bejeweled hand that had to hinder her golf game, while her diamond tennis bracelet glinted in the sun. "Claire Delacourt."

"I'm a fairly new member," he said as he shook her hand. "Harrison Vasquez."

She tilted her head, brow furrowed. "Vasquez, you say? Hmm. My housekeeper has the same last name. Isabella Vasquez? Any relation?"

Harrison stiffened inwardly, but shrugged. Obviously she thought every Latino in the area was related. Then again, maybe she was suggesting that *his kind* didn't belong at the club unless they had a job to do, like serving, gardening, washing dishes. Never mind that he was conversing with a Fortune.

He put on his charming smile, albeit one that was fake, and answered the snooty woman. "Sorry, not related. But Delacourt…? Any relation to Carl Delacourt and the Ponzi scheme that rocked San Antonio a couple of decades ago?"

Claire's eyes widened, then she let out a nervous laugh. "Of course not. But nice meeting you." She turned on her heel and hurried toward the open door leading to the clubhouse.

Harrison shot a glance at Gigi and feigned ignorance. "Did I say something wrong?"

Gigi laughed. "That was her uncle. Well played, Counselor, because I was about to throw my drink in her face."

Harrison liked that Gigi was going to stand up for him. In fact, he had to admit he liked everything about her.

"That woman is a complete snob," Gigi said. "And she's nosier than anyone you'll ever meet."

"Well, thanks for having my back."

"That's what friends are for."

Yet the word *friend*, especially out of her mouth, didn't sit well with him. But he didn't dare say anything. Not when they seemed to be drifting back to peaceful banter.

And not before giving her time to reconsider and ask him to bring those steaks to her house tonight after all.

Once they reached the parking lot, Harrison walked Gigi to her car, where he brushed a quick kiss on her cheek. And he didn't even scan the area to make sure no one had seen him. Was that smart? She probably should take some comfort in that, but... Needless to say, their relationship was complicated. And right now, it was awkward at best.

"Good night," he said. "I'll talk to you later."

He didn't say when, and she didn't ask, even though it was killing her to know what the future would bring— and what was happening between them.

She opened the car door and slipped behind the wheel. "Be safe."

He nodded. "You, too."

She wasn't sure why those parting words had rolled off her tongue. It seemed that Harrison was very adept at keeping himself safe...from emotional entanglements. Up until now, she'd done the same. But she'd lowered her guard with Harrison, and she feared they'd entered a relationship that was bound to end because he wasn't willing to go deeper than the water in a wading pool. She just hoped that she'd be able to shake her feelings for him when it was finally over.

After arriving home, she went to her home office to check her messages. A new client had called while she was out. She took note of the name and phone number. Normally, she didn't return calls on the weekend, but she made an exception today. She could use a distraction.

So she called Monica Jeffers and made an appointment to meet via Zoom on Tuesday afternoon.

Then she listened to the next message, but when she heard the now-familiar voice, she stiffened.

"Hello, Gigi! This is Mariana Sanchez calling. Like I told your attorney...nice guy, by the way. She laughed. *Anyway, I took that second DNA test. I don't have the results yet, but there shouldn't be any surprises. I'd really like to meet with you. Please call me."*

Gigi continued to stare at the phone long after the beep sounded and the recording ended. And her stomach twisted.

My *nice* attorney, huh?

What in the hell had Harrison told her? He was supposed to chase her off, not become her new best friend.

Gigi had half a notion to call him, but she dialed Reeve's number first.

"Hi, Gigi," her brother said. "What's up?"

"Mariana Sanchez called again. She claims to have

taken a second DNA test, and she's pushing to meet with me before the results are in. That makes me think she's trying to put the squeeze on me...or us."

"Seriously? Have you told Harrison?"

"Not yet. I wanted to talk to you first. I'd like Harrison to offer her cash to just go away and leave us alone. Do you think fifty thousand would do the trick?"

"Maybe," Reeve said, "I hope so."

"Good. I'm on it. I'll let you know how things pan out."

She hit End, then called Harrison.

"Hey," he said, "I was hoping I'd hear from you tonight."

"Mariana Sanchez called me again," she said. "And my brother and I want you to offer her fifty grand to go away."

Well. That was blunt and very Fortune-like.

At first, Harrison had assumed Gigi was calling because she'd had a change of heart and canceled whatever plans she may have had tonight and wanted him to stop by after all. But apparently dinner on her patio and some more skinny-dipping were still out.

"What all did Mariana say?" he asked, turning the conversation more professional.

"Just that the DNA results are pending, but she's eager to meet with me, anyway."

"I have time to go back to Rambling Rose on Wednesday," he said. "Unless you want me to go sooner."

"As far as I'm concerned, you can't go soon enough. I have a real uneasy feeling about that woman."

"Why? Did she sound threatening on the call?" As far as Harrison could tell, Mariana was just a harmless older lady.

"I don't know. I didn't feel threatened, but I just don't like that woman contacting me."

"Block her number, then. And alright, I'll drive out there late Monday afternoon, but I might not get there until evening."

"That's fine with me. I'll write a check. You can stop by the house on your way out of town and pick it up. That way you can hand it to her when you make the deal."

"Let's hold off on that. Let me talk to her first."

Gigi sighed. "You can talk with her first, but I want you to have the check in hand. I want this ended. Now."

Harrison sucked in a breath. She was putting an end to them, too. He could sense it, feel it. She was running away. That might be the right thing to do, but he really wasn't ready to call it quits. And the fact that everything was crumbling around him hurt more than he cared to admit. But he had to suck it up. Shut down the personal feelings and get back to business.

He cleared his throat. "If you insist."

"I do. And I want you to give me a call as soon as you've talked to her."

"It'll probably be late."

"I don't care about that."

"Will do, then," he said.

The call ended as abruptly as it started.

On Monday evening, Harrison met with Mariana at a small coffee shop in Rambling Rose, where they sat at a table outside, away from other patrons. The older woman seemed both happy and nervous to see him.

"I'm not sure why Gigi doesn't want to at least talk to me. It's just that…" She sucked in breath. "Listen, Mr. Vasquez, I'm happy with my life in Rambling Rose. I'm respected and have a successful business. I'm not looking to do anything other than meet the relatives I didn't know I had."

Everything he'd learned about her pointed to that fact.

"You see," she added, "I was an only child, raised by a single mother, who passed away a few years ago. I have no siblings, no cousins, no other real family. If I came across as pushy, it's just that I was so happy to learn that I have… Well, that I'm not alone in this world."

Harrison couldn't help but believe the woman. And sympathize with her. But he had a job to do. "Gigi and Reeve would like me to offer you a check."

"What for?" She furrowed her brow. "I don't need anything."

The way she looked at him, the sincerity in her eyes, made him feel like a jerk for just doing his job. "They'd rather not have a relationship with you."

Tears welled in her eyes, and she nodded. "Okay. I get the picture."

He had the strongest compulsion to place his hand on hers, but he resisted. "If they don't want to meet me, that's fine. They don't need to give me any money. I have plenty of my own. But I hope they'll go through with the testing. We're all related to Walter Fortune."

Then she got to her feet, leaving her coffee on the table, and walked away.

After their meeting Harrison decided it was best to see Gigi in person. He called when he reached the guarded gate. She gave them permission to let him in, and by the time he rang her doorbell, it was nearly eleven o'clock.

Gigi opened the door and instead of a greeting or saying "hello," she said, "I hope you came to give me good news. Did she accept our offer?"

Since she didn't invite him in, he stood on her porch like a member of a trade or a professional lawyer... and like an ex-lover. "No, she didn't. And I have to tell you, Gigi, I don't think she means any harm. I truly believe she just wants a personal connection with you and Reeve. She isn't looking for a payoff."

"Have you even checked into the guy I told you about, Lincoln Fortune Maloney? I don't know anything about him, but I'd bet a dollar to a doughnut that Mariana caught wind of the Maloneys' windfall and decided to land some wealth of her own."

"I followed up on that while I was in Rambling Rose. Lincoln is a descendant of Walter's brother, Wendell. Mariana claims to be Walter's grandchild. The second DNA test will give us an answer. But my gut says that test will prove positive. And that Mariana just wants to get to know you."

"I don't *want* a relationship with that woman." Gigi appeared to be angry, but he suspected it was actually panic he saw in her eyes. "I don't believe that's all she wants. Everyone has their price. Offer her more money."

"Look, Gigi. I'm telling you it's not about the money. I think it's about family, a relationship." How could he get her to understand what he'd come to see in Mariana's eyes, to hear in her voice? "You say you don't want that, but you seem to want it with *my* family. With *my* parents."

She blinked and her shoulders stiffened. "You're way off the mark, Counselor."

"Am I? You don't want anything from my parents but friendship. Why do you think Mariana is any different? Because I don't think it is."

"How *dare* you say that."

"Say what? All I did was offer an opinion, like any good attorney should do. Just meet with Mariana and hear her out."

"No freaking way. And your so-called opinion went well and beyond in this case. You have one job. Just offer her money and make her go away."

"You're not going to buy her off, Gigi. Face it. Your money can't give you a pass this time."

"Is that what you think is going on in my head? That I only need to whip out my wallet and life is peachy? Problem solved?"

"Damn, Gigi. I don't think that, but that's how you're acting."

She chuffed. "You don't understand what it's like to be a Fortune. After all, how could you?"

"You're right," he snapped. "I don't know what it's like. And you have no idea what it's like to belong to a caring family." Before he could say "Let's talk about this in the morning, after we've both cooled off," she slammed the door in his face.

Beyond angry and frustrated, Harrison walked back to his Audi. Granted, he'd seen the end coming. He and Gigi were worlds apart socially, financially and culturally. In her eyes, he'd always be beneath her. And he'd be damned if he'd try to convince her otherwise.

Chapter Twelve

After Harrison left last night, Gigi had wanted to scream in frustration at Mariana Sanchez…and at Harrison for being on the verge of dumping her. She walked into her home office, her private fortress of solitude, and took a seat at the desk that had once belonged to Grampy.

One day, when she'd been about eleven or twelve, he'd stopped by the family home in Corpus Christi to visit and found her seated on the overstuffed sofa in the formal living room, teary-eyed, bottom lip quivering, arms folded across her chest.

He immediately sat beside her, his expression sympathetic. "What's the matter, sweet girl?"

She'd sniffled. "Reeve has a friend over, and they're playing *Super Mario Kart*. I wanted to have a turn, but they wouldn't let me and told me to leave them alone."

Grampy slipped an arm around her, and she leaned into him. "I'm sorry they hurt your feelings, sweetie. I hope you didn't cry in front of them."

"No, I left the room."

"Good. Don't let anyone see your tears. It makes you look vulnerable. Take the power position and do your crying in private. Now, what say we blow this place and get some ice cream downtown?"

Gigi would never forget the warmth of his embrace or his scent—Old Spice cologne, a trace of pipe tobacco and the lemon drops he'd always favored. Nor would she forget the advice he'd given her that day.

And that's what she'd done last night. She hadn't shed a tear in front of Harrison. It wasn't until he'd backed out of the driveway that the first teardrop fell.

So much for the promise she'd made herself—to never let a man make her cry again.

She'd been in such a state of anger and frustration that she'd decided to wait until morning to call Reeve and report Mariana's refusal of the deal and to discuss raising the offer.

It was nearly eight o'clock, and she'd just taken a sip of her first cup of coffee, when her brother called her.

She snatched the cell phone off the kitchen counter and answered. "Hey, I was just going to call you."

"What in the hell is going on?" Reeve snapped, his tone brisk and sharp. He was clearly pissed about something.

"What are you talking about?" she asked. "I've kept you abreast of everything going on with Mariana Sanchez." Except for the latest twist that had come to her attention last night. But she intended to discuss it now.

"I'm talking about you and our lawyer," Reeve said. "Are you sleeping with him?"

A zing gripped her stomach. *Not at the moment*, she was tempted to say, but a response like that wasn't going to go over very well. "Where'd you get that idea?"

"Let's just say I heard it from a friend of a friend. You were seen holding hands at Lake Chatelaine one evening and a couple of times at Hillside Country Club."

"Harrison and I went out a couple of times," she admitted. "No big deal. And besides, it's none of your business." On top of that, whatever they had seemed to be fizzling out, just like any other relationship she'd had since her divorce.

"Well, dating Vasquez is a big deal and it *is* my business. *Our* business. Our family. And for the record, I have another case right now and was about to put him on retainer. But now I don't trust him."

At that, Gigi felt compelled to jump to Harrison's defense, if not her own. "Why don't you trust him?"

"Come on, Gigi. First we've got Mariana Sanchez trying to weasel her way into the family and drain some cash off for herself. And now the guy who's supposed to be defending us from that woman is doing the same thing."

The accusation stung like jalapeno juice on an open wound. And not because there was any truth to it. Her brother was more or less telling her that she couldn't attract a man like Harrison without a boatload of money. That may have been true about Anson, but...

Was that actually true about Harrison?

"You're wrong," she said, doubt still fluttering with her heart and ego. "Harrison and I had a couple of laughs. That's it." If anything, Harrison was backing off—at least, from her. Rejecting her for being what he considered a spoiled little rich girl. But Gigi wasn't going to share any vulnerability with her brother, which would surely come back and bite her in the butt.

Reeve chuffed. "Your relationship with Harrison is completely inappropriate."

There was some truth to that. They had crossed a line, but it was inappropriate for another reason. How could she and Harrison reconcile the vast differences in their backgrounds?

"Look, Reeve. We aren't seeing each other any longer. It's over. No big deal. And it never was."

"Don't be naive. He's our lawyer. And it was completely inappropriate and unprofessional for him to romance his client."

Gigi knew that. She and Harrison both knew that. And that's what had added to the hot nights. "Our time together didn't affect his ability to work the case. So don't get your panties in a wad."

"Sounds like that social climber got into your panties—or at least tried to."

Now that wasn't true. She'd been the instigator, but that was none of her brother's business. "Harrison might be a lot of things, but he's not that. And keep your nose out of my private life."

"Keep *your* private life out of our business. That's

why Dad didn't want you running Fortune Metals. You're not savvy enough."

The painful comment hit hard and deep. "This conversation is over, Reeve." Then she ended the call. Her only regret was that she'd been on a cell phone and hadn't been able to slam down the receiver, hard enough for him to realize just how angry she was.

She left her full cup of coffee on the counter and walked to the shower, where she let the water wash away her tears.

Yesterday, after several long-winded meetings at the firm, a two-hour drive to Rambling Rose, that meeting with Mariana Sanchez, another long-ass drive home, followed by that blow-up at Gigi's house, Harrison had tossed and turned all night. Just after dawn, he'd finally given up. He took a shower and got dressed for the day.

He drove through Starbucks and ordered a venti cup of his favorite morning brew, then headed to the office. Unfortunately, as much as he hated to admit it, he couldn't shake his frustration with Gigi. And he didn't want their short-lived romance to be over. But she'd made it clear that it was, which was just as well. Trying to fit into her world was tiring. He didn't belong, and they both knew it. Maybe that was the real reason he'd insisted on having a secret fling, although when they were together, laughing at a joke, sharing details about their day, eating on the patio, swimming in the raw and making love… Well, it hadn't felt like a casual affair.

Still, he'd have to talk to her again, and not just about the case. He never liked ending an affair on bad terms.

He parked in his assigned space at Brighton Towers, then took the elevator to the eighth floor. He strode to the office, opened the glass door to the lobby and stopped at the reception desk, where Jessica, the receptionist, had just ended a call.

"Good morning." He offered the middle-aged redhead a friendly smile, one that suggested he didn't have a care in the world, which wasn't the case.

"Harrison," Jessica said, "Mr. Bentley would like to see you."

The head of the firm. His boss. The big cheese himself. Harrison wondered what that was about. He also had an uneasy feeling. "Is he free now?"

"I believe so." Jessica picked up the black telephone receiver and pushed the intercom button. A couple of beats later, she said, "Mr. Bentley, Mr. Vasquez just arrived. Are you free now?" She nodded. "Okay, I'll tell him." She hung up the receiver. "He said to send you in."

"Thanks." Harrison made the walk down the hall to his boss' office and knocked lightly on the door.

"Enter," Paul Bentley said.

Once inside the massive office, with its imposing dark wood furniture and wall-size window that provided a stunning view of downtown Corpus Christi, his boss said, "This won't take long, but have a seat."

Harrison slipped into the leather chair in front of Bentley's desk. "What's up?"

"I'm removing you from the Fortune case. Your services are no longer needed."

Seriously? Those words nearly knocked the wind out of him. How...? Then an idea struck.

"Did Mr. Tyler have anything to do with that decision?" he asked. Stanley Tyler had seen them together at the Hillside Country Club. Had he surmised an inappropriate relationship was going on between them?

"No, the decision was made at the client's request." Bentley cleared his throat. "I assume you know why. And I certainly have a hunch, but I don't want details. In fact, I suspect it's better if I don't know them."

Seriously? Gigi had fired him? He'd known she was angry last night, but he hadn't expected her to be vindictive. It felt as if his heart had done a free fall to the floor.

Harrison took a long breath, then slowly let it out. He was almost afraid to ask the next question, but he had to know. "What effect does this have on my standing at the firm?"

"None. At least, not unless another client drops you for similar reasons. Look, son. You have a bright future ahead of you. I'll chalk this up to you being new to the civilian sector. But watch yourself. Don't jeopardize your reputation."

He counted relief among his many emotions. "I'll make sure it doesn't happen again, sir."

"Like I said, you haven't lost your job. But I'd like you to take the next few days off. Use the time to think about what went wrong with the Fortune case—and figure out how not to let it happen again."

There's no way in hell his heart was going to overrule his head again. And as much as he'd like to blame it on hormones and lust, his heart had definitely taken the lead.

"Alright, then," Bentley said. "That's all I have to say about that. George Pullman is taking over the Fortune case, and you're taking over the one he was working on. The brief is already on your desk. But don't worry about it until you get back to work on Thursday. The court case has been postponed two weeks."

"Thank you, sir." Harrison rose, pushed back the chair and let himself out of the office. His steps slowed in the hallway as he realized what had just happened. He'd lucked out, he supposed, because it could have been so much worse. And all because he'd let Gigi Fortune sweep him off his feet.

Sure, it had been fun and exciting. But now the threat of losing his position at the firm hung over his head.

The decision was made at the client's request.

He could have questioned his boss further, but what good would that have done? It would have only led to self-incrimination. Besides, it was obvious that Gigi had made the call.

How could she have done that to him? He'd heard the adage about a woman scorned, but had he made her that angry?

As he continued down the hall toward his office, his anger melted, and reason returned. Their relationship was a tangled mess of hits and misses. Their emotions were sure to spill over to the case. That's when mistakes were made…and cases were lost.

He pushed open his office door. Fine. He knew why she had him fired from the case. She just could have respected him enough to talk to him instead of stabbing his career in the back.

Just after one o'clock on Tuesday, Gigi finished the initial Zoom meeting with Monica Jeffers, her newest client. Monica lived in a modest neighborhood in Corpus Christi, and she'd just lost a promising job. She'd gotten a nice severance package, but since she was nearing retirement age, she had some decisions to make about where she wanted to go from here.

As was her custom, Gigi considered her clients and dressed accordingly. She believed it helped if the woman saw her as someone like herself, someone she could relate to and trust.

For this particular meeting, Gigi had worn her hair in a single braid that hung down her back, applied just enough makeup to look nice on the screen and put on a simple white blouse and a pair of her most comfortable jeans. Not that her pants or running shoes would show.

Initially, Monica had been downtrodden. "Who's going to hire a fifty-nine-year-old woman who looks like me? Fat. Scraggly, graying hair."

"You stop that thinking right now," Gigi had replied. "You're incredibly talented and experienced. We'll figure out what your next move will be."

After that, the meeting had gone exceptionally well, and both she and Monica were sure Gigi could help. She made a few notes in Monica's file, then walked to the kitchen to fix a tuna salad for lunch. Just as she opened a can of solid white albacore, her doorbell gonged. She wasn't expecting visitors, and she hadn't gotten a call from the guardhouse, so she assumed it was the gardener or a neighbor. She quickly rinsed and dried her hands. Then she went to the foyer to see what her visitor needed.

When she opened the door and spotted Harrison on

the stoop, his presence took her aback, especially since he wasn't wearing that familiar smile. Nor even a hint of one.

She didn't need to ask how he'd gotten past the front gate because she'd put him on the permanent guest list. She'd once enjoyed having him show up at various times unannounced, but not today. Not when he still bore some of the same animosity he'd had last night.

Still, she stepped aside, wishing she'd known he was coming. She might have put on more makeup or changed out of the comfy jeans. Which was silly. What was she thinking? Was she trying to win him back again? "I wasn't expecting you, but come on in. We need to talk."

"That's not necessary. Besides, I'm not sure how much help that would be at this point." He handed her a manila envelope, and she took it.

She studied the envelope then gazed at him. "What's this?"

"The original emails and letters Mariana sent you. George Pullman's secretary made copies, so I thought I'd return them."

"George Pullman? Who's he?"

"The new attorney assigned to your case."

Gigi gasped. "What are you talking about? I don't understand."

He scoffed. "Hey. I played with fire, and I got burned. I knew I was crossing a line, so I don't blame you for wanting to move in a different direction. I just wish you would've come to me first. Going above my head and to the senior partner in the firm wasn't cool. I thought I was more than just your lawyer."

She was stunned. And, more so, confused. "I didn't talk to anyone at your firm."

"Whatever. I need to go." Harrison turned and started to walk away.

"Wait." She left the porch and followed him. "I have no idea what you're talking about."

"Oh, come on. Give me a break. Don't play this game." He slowly shook his head. "I get why you had me removed from your case. Once our relationship hit the rocks, our disagreements were sure to spill over into our professional relationship. And that could possibly taint the case. You did the right thing, but just the wrong way."

The accusation—both harsh and false—completely blindsided her. "I... I'd never... Harrison, I didn't call your firm. I swear I didn't have you removed from the case. Reeve must have made that call."

Harrison crossed his arms. "You're casting blame on your brother? I thought you took the lead on this case."

"I did. But apparently, Reeve heard rumors, and he—"

Harrison raised his palm again, not letting her finish. "Stop. Don't try to justify how you handled this."

"I didn't..." Her heart pounded so hard it rattled her chest, and she couldn't complete her defense.

He turned toward his car. "See ya."

As annoyed as she'd been last night, as gobsmacked as she was now, she couldn't just stand here and let him go. "Wait." She continued to his car. "Will you just listen?"

When he opened the driver's door, he said, "It's okay, Gigi. I'm okay."

"But if someone talked to the senior partner, it must have been Reeve."

"Right." Harrison slowly shook his head. "But why would he do that? You took over weeks ago, and I haven't talked to him since."

"Someone saw us together and told him. I had no reason to have you dropped from the case."

"You had reason. Love affairs don't usually end well, and someone always comes away unhappy. Or vindictive. I get that. All I'm saying is that you shouldn't have gone behind my back. If you would have told me you wanted me off the case, I would have agreed and put in the request for a change of counsel myself. Instead, I got called on the carpet and dismissed by my boss. And I didn't appreciate that."

As he climbed behind the wheel and reached for the door handle, he paused and gazed at her. "You know, I really liked you, Gigi. And I'm sorry it had to end this way. Even though we had some good times, we both know moving on is for the best. Good luck with your case." Then he closed the door and started the engine.

As Gigi watched him drive away, her shock and confusion turned to anger. And she wasn't sure who angered her the most—Harrison or Reeve. She felt like throttling Harrison because he wouldn't hear her out. But Reeve had steamrolled over her once again.

She wasn't going to take it quietly, either. First she would clear her calendar for the rest of the day. Then she was going to drive to the Fortune Metals office and confront her brother.

Some things couldn't be done over the phone. What she had to say could only be said to his face.

Thirty minutes later, without taking time to freshen up or change her clothes, Gigi careened into her reserved parking space at Fortune Metals, the one she rarely used. Then she marched into the spacious, glass-walled lobby as if she owned the place—and, theoretically, she did.

She strode right past the gaping receptionist. She took the elevator all the way to the top floor. Her plan was to barge right in and let Reeve have a piece of her mind, but he'd locked the blasted door. She knocked, but he didn't answer. He was gone? She swore under her breath, then took the elevator back to the lobby. Her anger had barely subsided.

When she reached the reception desk, she felt a bit sheepish. She'd seen the woman before and would have addressed her by name, but for the life of her, she couldn't remember it. Sadly, she'd rarely had reason to speak to her, which she regretted now.

"I'm sorry, but I seem to have forgotten your name."

"Sheila," the fortysomething woman said.

"I'm sorry for zipping past you earlier, Sheila." Gigi offered a faint but sincere smile. "But I was in a rush to see my brother." She also hadn't wanted Sheila to forewarn him of her arrival. "Do you have any idea where I can find him?"

"There was an issue at the Chatelaine office Mr.

Fortune had to take care of. So he drove out to Chatelaine early this morning. I'd be happy to tell him you stopped by, Ms. Fortune."

And ruin the element of surprise?

"No, that's not necessary. I'll give him a call later this evening, after he's put out the fire." She offered Sheila another smile, then left the building.

But there'd be no phone call tonight. Instead, Gigi slid behind the wheel of her Beamer and drove to the Chatelaine office.

And just as she did before, she bypassed the receptionist and marched right to her brother's private office. When she opened the door without knocking, Reeve looked up in surprise.

"How *could* you?" she asked, slamming the door behind her.

"Okay. I take it you talked to Harrison."

"Yes, and he thinks I'm the one who dropped him from the case."

"Gigi, you were taking the situation too lightly. I had to salvage the case before you and lover boy ruined everything. And you were in denial that you two had even done anything wrong."

"Maybe so. But you have no right getting involved in my personal life."

"Point taken. I may have overstepped, but hell, Gigi, you were screwing our lawyer. That's on you. Both of you. And it was totally unacceptable and unprofessional. Maybe you don't know any better, but Harrison should have."

"Just one minute, Reeve. Who are you to tell me I'm

at fault?" She blew out a huff and crossed her arms. "It's time we faced the truth, little brother. This isn't just about Harrison. It's about us—you and me—and you running over me every time I turn around."

"What are you talking about? I've been working my ass off to run the family business and look after your financial interests."

"My inheritance was locked into place well beyond the time you took over. And I have my own investments, on top of my personal income from Gigi's Journey, so it's time to climb off your high horse."

Reeve sat up a bit straighter, but he didn't back down. Nor did he respond. Maybe he wasn't sure how to handle her when she was furious. She clicked her tongue. "Let's back up. You knew I'd taken a personal interest in Stellar Productions, yet you never even had the courtesy to tell me you were going to buy it. And now, after your so-called 'improvements,' it's no longer the same company. And how dare you plan to tear down that quaint old house? That was Grampy's favorite place in Chatelaine." She shook her head in disgust. "What's wrong with you, Reeve? You were such a sweet kid."

"I grew up," he said. "And honestly, I didn't think you had, so I was protecting you. Like a good brother."

She stiffened. "Are you kidding me?" She hadn't expected the meeting to go well, but his attitude was too much. All the advice she'd ever given any of her mild-mannered clients rose to the surface.

If you don't take a stand for yourself, who else will? Don't forget, the squeaky wheel gets the grease.

"We're going to have a long-overdue talk, Reeve."

She pulled out the chair in front of his desk and plopped down. "It's time to open up a can of worms, because some things need to be said. And you're going to listen."

He studied her as if she'd grown ten extra feet, then he pushed aside a file he'd been reading, reached into his desk drawer, pulled out a bottle of rare scotch whiskey and set two glasses on the table. He poured two shots and pushed one toward her. "I'm listening."

"I don't know where to start."

"The beginning is a good place."

She downed the drink, and he poured her another. "Fine. You freaking abandoned me just when I needed your support."

His brow furrowed. "I did? How?"

Was he that clueless? "Grampy wanted *me* to run Fortune Metals. Don't you remember?"

He pulled at his collar. "Not really. If memory serves me correctly, he also said the same thing to me."

Yeah, right. She huffed. "Dad gave me the brush-off, and when I went to you for support and understanding, you ignored me. Did you do that on purpose?"

"Um. No."

She slapped the desk, then took the second shot. "So I was cut out of any business involvement and shuttled off to cotillion and charity balls."

"I had to do that stuff, too. And for the record, you weren't the only one who felt resentful. I'd barely gotten out of college, and suddenly the business was thrust on me."

"But at least you were encouraged to go to college."

"Weren't you?"

"No. I was so confused about where my place was in the family, that when Anson showed me some interest and respect, I fell for him. And I don't need to tell you what a big mistake that was."

"Yeah, Anson was a jerk."

She rolled her eyes. "You might have told me back then. Why did you let me marry him?"

"Let you? How was I supposed to stop that runaway train?"

"By being my brother."

He waited a beat, then nodded. "That's fair. I probably should have, but I was caught up in college applications at the time and didn't think you'd listen to your baby brother."

In truth, she probably wouldn't have. "I was really shattered after my divorce. And I felt so alone."

"You never told me."

"I didn't think you'd listen."

"And for what it's worth," he added, "after that big social extravaganza you and mom called a wedding, you focused all your attention on Anson—the ass—and I was left out in the cold."

He didn't go into any more detail than that, but she knew what he meant. Their parents hadn't been all that involved in their lives, and at one time, it seemed that they'd only had each other. But when she'd gotten married, Anson had become her main focus.

"I'm sorry," she said. "I didn't realize you might have needed me, too."

He shrugged. "Well, what's done is done."

Was it? She let out a sigh. "Believe it or not, I've missed the relationship we used to have."

He sat back in his desk chair, and his broad shoulders slumped. "Me, too. For what it's worth, I always looked up to you. So you weren't the only one who'd felt abandoned."

Sharing the truth, revealing her pain, nearly gutted her, but realizing he'd suffered, too, brought tears to her eyes.

Grampy's words came back to haunt her, to admonish her. *Don't let anyone see your tears. It makes you look vulnerable. Take the power position and do your crying in private.*

She looked up to the ceiling, trying her best to prevent her tears from overflowing. At least Reeve wasn't arguing with her now. Or defending himself.

"And you've been carrying all of that around with you ever since?" he asked. "How long has it been?"

"More than twenty years," she said.

Reeve raked a hand through his hair and sighed. "I really thought I was protecting you and taking care of you."

"You weren't. But now I realize you didn't know I needed you."

He nodded. "I didn't realize you cared about Fortune Metals or the family business."

"I've always cared. Grampy told me I'd run things one day, and I believed him and looked forward to being a part of things. But when dad started taking you aside and grooming you for the job and ignoring me, I grew resentful."

"I knew you were angry about something, but to be fair, Gigi, whenever I asked, you told me it was nothing."

She considered the comment, and dang, it rang true. "It's hard to admit jealousy and resentment."

"I guess so. But thanks for finally telling me now. I guess I've come across as a jerk at times."

She nodded, a slight smile tugging at her lips. "More times than not."

"Well, I'm sorry. And believe it or not, I miss being able to mess around with you—to joke and not have to worry that you'd take offense. You haven't exactly been a barrel of laughs, you know."

"I have to admit, I should have said something sooner."

"I wish you would have."

She nodded, then got to her feet. "I'd better go. That was a lot to dump on you at one time."

"You got that right. I need to wrap my head around all of it. But I promise to be more sensitive to your feelings from now on. And how about you promise to openly communicate with me? I promise I'll listen. At least, I'll try."

"You got a deal. Thanks."

"You want me to call the law firm and get Harrison back on the case?"

"I appreciate the offer, but no. Let it go."

He stood and walked her to the door. A hug might have been in order, but neither of them made a move.

That was okay. She wasn't ready to embrace him yet.

She was still struggling with what she'd revealed...and how it would affect her in the future.

Rather than drive home that night, Gigi checked into the hotel at the LC Club, exhausted and feeling as if her legs might not hold her upright. She needed to get something to eat.

She also needed to tell Sylvia that the coaching sessions had ended. Not only because she could no longer work with Harrison's mother, but also because Sylvia was well on her way to an exciting new season in her life. She feared the conversation might lead to one that was more personal. If it did, she wasn't sure what to say, although honesty did seem to be the best approach.

Under the circumstances, a Zoom session was probably in order. God only knew what Harrison would say if he learned she'd gone to his parents' house again without his permission. She wouldn't bother asking, though. He'd made it clear in no uncertain terms that he'd never approve of her contacting his parents again.

Still, she owed it to Sylvia to end their association in a professional manner. In person. And Harrison could squawk all he wanted. Sylvia might be his mother, but she was Gigi's client. And that was *her* business, not his.

If Harrison had been given an actual vacation day, he would have considered going to the country club, joining a group of strangers looking for a fourth and playing a round of golf. Although he would have chosen a course other than Hillside Country Club. He didn't want to risk running into Gigi or any of the snobbish people he'd come into contact with there.

As it was, he really didn't feel like doing much of anything.

I'd like you to take the next few days off, Bentley had said. *Use the time to think about what went wrong with the Fortune case—and figure out how not to let it happen again.*

Harrison didn't need to think about it. He knew exactly how it happened. He'd been charmed by his lovely client. Completely enamored of her. He'd gotten lost in her big brown eyes, her fragrant hair. Her soft skin. And his surging testosterone refused to listen to reason or common sense.

It hadn't been easy to walk away from a relationship he'd foolishly begun to think might last indefinitely, might make it to the altar. He stopped himself. He was not going there. Most marriages didn't last, anyway.

Except for his parents'.

Remembering them, he figured he probably should use the time to check on his dad. If he spent the night at his parents' house, he'd be able to give his mother a break. She might like to see a movie and have dinner with a friend. So after packing an overnight bag, he drove to Chatelaine.

There was no need to surprise them. Hell, he'd had more than enough surprises today to last the rest of his life. Besides, his mom might like a heads-up so she could make a few phone calls and line up her evening.

Once he was on the road, he called the home number, and his father answered.

"How's it going, Papa. Are you feeling any better?"

"Some. Yes. The pain isn't as bad, except when the physical therapist visits. The guy is brutal."

"I wanted to let you know that I'm coming home for a day or two. I had some time off and thought Mama might like to get out of the house for a while."

"It's a workweek," Papa said. "And you just started at the firm. Have they given you vacation time already?"

He had a point, which meant he wasn't quite buying that explanation, so Harrison tried another approach. "Actually, they took me off the Fortune case and told me to take a couple days off to clear my head before I dig in and prepare for an upcoming case, one that's pretty important to the firm."

"Hmm."

Okay, so his dad the high school teacher had gotten enough lame, teenage excuses over the years that he could spot one from miles away.

"Papa? You still there?"

"Yep. So what really happened? Or should I tell you what I think?"

"Shoot."

"You got involved with a client, which wouldn't be ethical. Or else, you came so damn close you decided to back off."

"Bingo." There was no point in denying it.

"For what it's worth, I can certainly see why. Gigi is a beautiful woman—inside and out."

She was definitely beautiful on the outside, but the jury was still out on her true character. "I'll admit, things between us took a romantic turn, Papa, but it's over now."

"If you're no longer on the case, tell me why it ended."

Harrison rarely kept things from his parents…unless he'd been in a war zone. And he kept his love life to himself, since he didn't want them dreaming up wedding plans. But Gigi was no longer in the picture, although with each passing minute, his regret built.

He revealed the story, skipping over the frolicking in the pool and in bed. But his dad had always been able to connect the dots.

"If she said she didn't get you fired," Papa said when Harrison finished, "I think you should believe her."

"I don't think so, but even if she was telling me the truth, it goes beyond that. We're so mismatched that it would never work out in the long run. In fact, I don't think I'll remain a member of the same country club. Every time I turned around, even if I didn't see her, I'd be reminded of her."

"I think you may be overreacting. I suspect your feelings are running deeper than you're used to."

He had a point.

"Listen, Papa. Once I get home and Mama takes off, we can talk more." The conversation wasn't one he wanted to have while driving. But, truth be told, he didn't want to have it at all, anywhere. Just talking about it hurt too much. So he'd probably suggest they watch ESPN.

"Drive carefully, son. I'll see you when you get here."

Harrison arrived on Daffodil Court an hour later, only to spot Gigi's BMW parked at the curb.

His gut clenched. What in the hell was she doing here? Dragging his parents into their fight? Sweet-talking them into believing her side of the story? Why would she bother?

Even if she hadn't told Bentley to remove him from the case, as she'd claimed, that didn't excuse her for butting into his family again.

Harrison parked behind her car, then strode to the front door—he was locked and loaded for a fight.

Chill, he reminded himself.

His phone buzzed, and he pulled it out of his pocket. Great. Reeve Fortune. What did he want?

"What's up, Reeve?"

"Listen. Gigi was here a while ago and she read me the riot act. I need to tell you something. I was the one who called Paul Bentley."

Harrison gaped. "What?"

"You heard right. I'm sorry. I went behind both your backs. In my defense, I was only trying to protect Gigi and my family's interests."

Crap. Harrison looked at Gigi's car. She'd been telling the truth. "Are you serious?"

"Yes. And before you think my sister is up to something, making me call you, she isn't. She doesn't know we're talking. I'm one-hundred-percent guilty about what went down at your firm."

Harrison ran a hand through his hair. He was at a loss for words.

Reeve cleared his throat. "How can I make it up to you?"

"I'll think of something. Thanks for telling me, though. In the end, you're a stand-up guy."

"So are you. And I'm sorry."

The call ended.

Harrison took a minute to calibrate what he'd just heard. He paced in a circle, the cell phone still in his hand. How could he have not listened to Gigi? She must think he was a first-class heel.

He'd just blown it with the one woman who'd lit him on fire, not just physically, but mentally and emotionally, too.

He blew out a sigh and pulled himself together. He was a sharp lawyer. He could find a way to make this right with Gigi, although he'd have to suck down a huge serving of humble pie.

Chapter Thirteen

Before Harrison could open the door, he heard a television sports announcer's voice growing louder. He entered the house and spotted Papa seated in the recliner, his legs extended.

"Where is she?" he asked.

"Gigi? She and your mother are talking privately in the kitchen. And I have to tell you, son, I think you're wrong about her."

"I know."

"She's a peach."

"I know." In fact, everything about her was admirable. And appealing. But that didn't make her marriage material for him—no matter what his parents thought. Unfortunately.

She would make a great wife for someone, a man who traveled in her circle, who had the kind of money her family had. And Harrison wasn't that man, as much as he might want to be.

He started for the kitchen, then lingered unseen, just outside the doorway. Gigi was sitting at the small table across from his mother, drinking a cup of coffee, the aroma mixing with her familiar floral scent. A plate of muffins sat in front of them, although they didn't appear to have been touched.

"I think Harrison made a few false assumptions about me the first day we met at his office, and he just can't seem to shake them. I wish he'd just listened to me. Let me have my say."

"My son can be a stubborn man when he thinks he's right," Mama said softly. "I'm sorry that, in this case, he was wrong."

Gigi, her blond hair woven into a braid that hung down her back, shrugged a single shoulder. "Nevertheless, it's over."

"Que lastima," Mama said. "That's too bad."

Harrison studied the wealthy socialite who could dazzle and assess a room with a single smile. Seated at the small oak table with his mother, she looked especially nice today—fresh, with her hair in a youthful style and only a hint of pink lip gloss on her face.

His insides stirred as he recalled her sweet mouth, how she tasted when he'd kissed her senseless. Her white button-down blouse showed a mere hint of her breasts. Between the hem of her blue jeans and her white sneakers, a bit of ankle peeked out.

She made cute and wholesome look sexy.

He cleared his throat, and both women shot a glance to the doorway.

"Harrison," Gigi said, her voice soft. "I didn't expect to see you here."

Obviously. And she'd come without giving him a heads-up.

She got to her feet. "Don't flip out and yell at me. I just stopped by to tell your mother that our life-coaching sessions are over. And I didn't think it was appropriate to tell her over the phone or through a computer screen. After…you know." She looked down at the floor, and his mother slowly shook her head.

When Gigi looked up, she added, "Don't worry, I'm leaving." She picked up her mug and carried it to the sink.

Mama shot him one of those I-thought-we-taught-you-better-than-this frowns he hadn't seen since his school days. Then she got to her feet, leaving her own cup on the table.

As Gigi turned away from the counter, Mama slipped her arms around her and gave her a warm hug.

"Thanks for everything," Mama told her. "You're a sweet, beautiful soul."

Gigi remained in the embrace, as if taking comfort in it. "I should be thanking you. I'll never forget you, Sylvia."

As the two women slowly—and reluctantly—drew apart, their eyes glistened with unshed tears. The heart-felt emotion filled the room, and it nearly shook Harrison to the core.

"Gigi," he said, "can we talk? Privately?"

She seemed to ponder the request, then shrugged. "Sure. Why not?"

They'd had some of their best conversations in an outdoor setting, so he opened the kitchen's sliding door. Once she'd stepped outside, he followed, then closed the door.

The backyard where he'd grown up, as nice as it was, couldn't compare to Gigi's. Papa had lovingly tended the roses and maintained a beautiful lawn, but he hadn't hired a landscape architect to design it or bring in exotic plants and flowers. And it lacked a custom-built swimming pool.

But his family home had heart. And so did the feeling he got from being here, alone with Gigi.

She crossed her arms. "I know you asked me not to visit your parents anymore, and I won't do it again. It's just that your mom…" She took a deep breath, then slowly let it out. "My mother didn't have a maternal bone in her body, and I found myself drawn to Sylvia, with her maternal warmth and understanding. She seemed more like a friend to me than a client, so I wanted to end our visits in a personal way. But I'll be going now." She turned on her heel.

That must have been really difficult for her to say, he realized. "Wait. That's not it."

She looked back at him. "Then what did you want to talk about?"

He sucked in a breath. "I just had a call from your brother."

"Reeve?" She looked surprised. "What did he want?"

"To set the record straight. He told me that he, and he alone, called my firm. And I know you didn't ask him to call me."

"I see. So now you believe me."

The look she gave him nearly lanced him to the quick. "I was wrong to accuse you. Can you forgive me?"

"I'm not sure if we can take back the things we said."

Harrison ran his hand through his hair. He'd been so puffed up and angry before, so defensive, but now it felt like the air had gone out of his tires. "I'm sorry for being harsh."

Again, Gigi shrugged. "I'm not going to lie. It hurt. Where did that attitude and behavior come from? Your parents are kind and thoughtful."

"I don't know." She was certainly leaving him with something to think about, although he doubted there was anything he could do to change things.

Gigi unfolded her arms. "You told me that you liked me. And I like you, too. And thanks to my brother, you now know I'm honest, right?"

Her words were like a jab to the heart. He nodded through the pain.

She continued. "I thought we had more than 'like' between us. But you're right. We're not a good match."

"I'm not sure that's entirely true, Gigi." He eased toward her, and she stepped back.

"I once asked your mother how a woman could tell when she'd met Mr. Right."

He lifted an eyebrow. This was going to hurt.

"She said it starts with friendship, humor and trust. We had the first two, but trust? You squeezed the toothpaste out of that tube."

"I'm sorry," he said. "If you're willing, I'd like to start over. As friends, of course. At least, at first. We've had a lot of fun and some special moments. I don't think we should throw all that away."

"Friends and fun—that's all well and good, but we're missing the most important ingredient. And since you can't trust me, I'd be foolish to trust you."

Then she walked back into the house, closing the slider behind her, leaving him on uneven ground. Leaving him to stew in his own stupid failure.

It would take a special man to be the partner she deserved. And, as much as he'd like to try, Harrison didn't think he could be that guy.

Finally, he returned to the house, where he found his parents together in the living room. They looked at him with disapproving glares. They were clearly disappointed in him.

"Is she gone?" he asked.

Both Mama and Papa nodded.

"I hate the idea of her driving back to Corpus Christi when she's upset," Harrison admitted.

With each tick-tock of the clock on the mantel, regret filled his chest.

"She's not going back to the city," Mama said. "She's getting a room at the LC Club hotel. Is it over between you two?"

"I think so."

"Do you want it to be?" Papa asked.

"Hell, no. But I blew it. She'll never trust me again."

"Oh, nonsense," Mama said. "Trust is earned, but I think most people deserve a do-over. Only one, mind you."

Harrison thought about that and hope fluttered in his chest. "You think so?"

Papa nodded. "One of these days, when you have more time to hang out here and feel sorry for yourself, I'll tell you the story about how I almost lost your mama over something stupid I did, but she gave me one last chance."

"After you begged, Andres. And the flowers and candy helped. So did the sincerity in your teary eyes." She looked at Harrison. "She's staying in town. Go to her. But plan something special or she'll just slam the door in your face."

"Right." Harrison would have to plan something special, but he needed to talk to her first. As he headed for the door, he said, "I have a key. So don't wait up for me."

"Good luck," Papa called.

As he stepped onto the porch, he overheard a giddy whisper.

His parents were clearly on Team Gigi. No surprise there.

He just hoped it wouldn't break their hearts when he gave it his best and last shot…and still screwed things up.

Gigi left the Vasquez home with her pride intact, but her heart was a mess. She pulled over a block away from GreatStore, but she wasn't planning to shop. She just needed a good cry, and what better place to hide her tears than inside her vehicle, under the protection of a shady oak tree.

She let out a sigh, then the tears dripped down her

cheeks. She rummaged through her purse for a packet of tissues, but came up empty. *Dang it.* No luck in the glove compartment, either, and it was so silly, but that made her cry even harder.

Why wasn't she prepared for the unexpected? Why did she make so many mistakes when it came to men? Why was she so misunderstood? First by Daddy, then Reeve. And now Harrison.

She let out a sob, and with no other way to wipe her tears and sniffles, she did the only thing she could—as gross and godawful as that was. She used her sleeve. And she sobbed even harder. Her mother, who'd always insisted upon being proper, would be appalled.

Gigi lifted her arm and swiped it under her nose again. *Take that, Delphine Fortune.*

After few more heaves and sobs, finally draining the well, she took a deep, shuddering breath, then wiped her face one more time with her sleeves, which were now damp.

Now that the waterworks were through, it was time to stop feeling sorry for herself and sort this out.

First the good part. She was pleased with the outcome of her confrontation with Reeve. Now they could mend past hurts and move forward on equal ground. And he'd been helpful today by calling Harrison and setting the record straight. Her brother was okay after all.

But not Harrison. She blinked back another tear, refusing to cry anymore.

At first, Harrison had shown her his sweet and thoughtful side, but she'd also seen how harsh he could be, how peevish. If Gigi had parents like Sylvia and Andres, she would have wanted to protect them, too. But by the way Harrison acted, it was as if he was afraid Gigi would somehow hurt them, and there was no way in the world she'd do anything like that.

She probably should have leveled with Harrison, just as she'd done with Reeve earlier today. She could have told him why some words and comments were triggers for her. Words and phrases that seemed to accuse her of relying on her family money to get by, or to suggest that she didn't need a career...or one that actually mattered. Because *she* mattered.

But not to Harrison. And for that reason, they'd never be lovers again.

She sniffled, then hardened her heart, at least to the consistency of gelatin. "Enough!" She'd shed enough tears over that man. It was time to move on. She started the ignition and let the car idle. She had to admit, losing Harrison—with good reason—left a hole in her chest. What could she do to make things better?

Ice cream. That would help.

She put the car in Drive, then headed to GreatStore, where she parked. She pulled down the visor and, using the mirror, gazed at her sorry reflection—her red, puffy eyes, her blotchy cheeks. What a mess. Thank goodness she hadn't been wearing mascara. She'd look like a raccoon.

She reached into her purse, and felt around until she found her sunglasses. Once she put them on, she checked her image again. Better, but certainly not perfect. Her wet sleeves were pretty gross, though. So she rolled them up.

The only saving grace was that in rushing to talk to her brother earlier she'd left without applying more makeup or taking time to put on a newer, more expensive blouse.

Ten minutes later, after consuming a double scoop of cherry ice cream in a sugar cone in her car, she headed to the hotel.

The cone was yummy and hit the spot in terms of taste and comfort food, but it didn't do a thing to mend her battered heart.

By the time Harrison arrived at the LC Club and pulled into the porte cochere, he'd barely shut off the engine when a valet approached with a welcoming smile. "Good afternoon, sir. Will you be checking in?"

"No. I'm just here to see a guest." Hopefully, she'd agree to see him.

He might not be able to convince Gigi he was sincerely sorry for being a hard-nosed jerk, but maybe he could make things better between them. They could run into each other—at the country club, at a restaurant or even at his office, should she need to visit George Pullman for some reason. Harrison didn't want things to remain awkward.

At least, that's what he told himself. In truth, he wanted to turn things around. He couldn't imagine not ever seeing her again, not sharing her bed, holding her close. And not having her in his life.

After leaving his key fob with the valet, he grabbed

the enormous bouquet of roses he'd bought as an olive branch, then strode to the front desk, where a young man wearing a crisp white shirt and black tie was standing behind the counter.

"May I help you?" he asked.

"I'm here to see Gigi Fortune. I'm not sure what room she's in, so would you be so kind and call her?"

"Ah, yes. Ms. Fortune. Of course. And your name?"

"Harrison Vasquez." A worrisome thought crossed his mind. What if she refused to see him?

The clerk typed in a few keystrokes and frowned. "I'm sorry, sir. Ms. Fortune hasn't checked in yet."

He felt a mix of relief and worry. Damn. She'd left a few minutes ahead of him, and it had taken a while for the florist to put together the bouquet. Maybe she stopped somewhere, too. Or had she driven back to Corpus Christi?

"Guess I beat her here," Harrison said. "If you don't mind, I'll take a seat in the lobby and wait for her."

"By all means, sir."

Harrison made his way past a large glass table in the center of the lobby that was adorned with a huge floral arrangement, and found a nearby chair. He set the bouquet on the smaller table beside him. She liked roses, right? What if she'd prefer another type of flower— orchids, maybe? That would make matters worse. It'd be just another example of how he didn't listen to her or understand her needs.

What was wrong with him? He was acting like an

insecure teenager, all tied up in emotional knots. But that's what Gigi did to him.

Ten minutes later, he was about to give her a call, when he spotted her walking in the door, her hair still woven in a single braid, designer sunglasses hiding her pretty brown eyes, white blouse with the sleeves rolled up and rocking a pair of faded jeans. While her clothing was simple and laid-back, it was the way she carried herself that claimed she belonged to the upper class—that and the large Louis Vuitton shoulder bag tucked under her arm.

He got to his feet and made his way toward her. "Gigi."

She turned, and her lips parted. "Harrison? What are you doing here?"

"We need to talk." He handed her the flowers.

Her expression softened a tad, then hardened. "We already did talk."

"There's a lot more I'd like to say. Can we please talk somewhere private? Maybe in your room—unless you'd prefer we do it someplace else."

She seemed to be considering it as she sniffed the roses. After a couple of beats, she said, "Wait here. I'll be back."

When she'd checked into the hotel and had the key, he followed her to the elevator. "Thanks, Gigi. I—"

"Don't talk. Not yet."

Okay, he thought. Their conversation was going to be on her terms all the way, and he was okay with that.

They took the elevator to the executive level on the

top floor, then she led him to her suite. She opened the door, and he followed her into a spacious room with an expansive view of the lake.

She dropped her purse and the flowers on the hall-way console. "Have a seat," she said, nodding toward the table in the middle of the room.

He pulled out a chair and sat down. She followed suit, plopping down across from him.

"Aren't you going to take off those sunglasses?"

"No," she said, "I'd rather not."

He cocked his head to the side. "Why not? We're inside."

She blew out a sigh, then raised them, revealing red, splotchy eyes.

Damn. She'd been crying. Because of him.

She slid the sunglasses back in place.

"Gigi, I'm sorry for jumping to conclusions. I made some false assumptions. In my heart, I knew you wouldn't have gone to your brother or to Mr. Bentley about me."

"I'm glad you finally realize that."

"I made you cry," he said, "and I feel terrible about that. Don't hide what I caused. Take off your glasses so I can see your beautiful eyes."

She slipped off the glasses and set them on the table. "I accept your apology, Harrison. There was some truth to what you said about buying people off. I wanted you to take a check to Mariana because that was my default setting. Throw money at the problem. I've seen it done all my life, and I've seen how it usually makes prob-lems go away."

"We can agree to disagree about how to handle Mariana," he said, "but don't let me off so easily. I should have believed you, especially since you've never given me reason not to. It's not your style to go behind my back to dump me from your legal case."

"You're right. It isn't." She played with her sunglasses, turning them over and over, as though she was doing the same with her thoughts. "And just so you know, I love your parents. They're awesome, and you're lucky to have them. I'd never do anything to hurt them or cause them any undue stress."

"I realize that now. They clearly adore you, and I was wrong to tell you to back away. And for the record, I hope someday you'll be able to love me, too."

Her gaze slowly lifted to his. "Love you? Like a dear friend?"

He slowly shook his head. "No, not like that. As hard as I fought it, and as much as I tried to convince myself that it was impossible to indulge those kinds of feelings for you…" He paused and sucked in a breath. *Get to the point, Counselor.* "I love, you, Gigi."

"Like a sister?" she asked.

"No, like my sweet, sexy lover. If you'll have me."

"Are you sure you want a snobby heiress with a silver spoon so deeply in her mouth that she'd need oral surgery to have it removed?"

He laughed. "Stop." Then he placed his right hand over his heart. "I absolutely love you. And I'd be willing to swear to that in court."

She broke into a smile. "I love you, too. And I've

known for a while. I was afraid to tell you. I had the feeling you didn't want me to get too attached, so I started pulling away. I was afraid you'd end our relationship before I was ready for that to happen. And I knew that I'd never want it to end."

"Good," he said, "because I'm ready to make a lifetime commitment to you…if you'll have me."

She let out a sigh that sounded like relief. "In a heartbeat."

As Harrison got to his feet, Gigi did, too. He opened his arms, and she stepped into his embrace. He kissed her softly, then deeply, and with all the love in his heart.

She drew away, a playful smile splashed across her face. "Let's go skinny-dipping."

"I'm game. As soon as—"

She placed her fingers over his lips, shushing him. "No. I want to do it now."

Surely she wasn't suggesting the hotel pool. Heck, all Harrison needed was to get arrested for indecent exposure. He'd get canned for sure. Nah. She couldn't mean that. "Let's check out of the hotel. I'll have the valet bring up our cars."

"No, Harrison. I can't wait."

He swallowed. Hard. How could she make something unlawful and naughty sound so damn appealing?

She grabbed him by the hand, then led him to the bathroom and pointed to the biggest bathtub he'd ever seen.

He should have known he could trust her to protect not only his heart, but also his reputation.

"I don't suppose you have any bubble bath," he said.

"I have anything you need."

More than that, she was everything he would ever need.

Gigi had never felt more loved, more relaxed, than she did right now, her naked back resting against Harrison's chest as they stretched out in the tub that took up a large part of the hotel bathroom.

She lifted her leg and, with her toes, flicked at the bubbles, sending a few of them upward.

Harrison stroked her arms. "You're amazing in bed, lady, but the things you do to me in water..." He let out a soft whistle.

"Don't you forget it." She wriggled her bottom against his lap, stirring another erection. "There's more where this came from."

"I'm counting on it." He swept aside her wet hair, then trailed kisses along her neck, taking time to tantalize the soft skin below her ear. His hands slid from her upper arms to her breasts, giving them each a loving caress.

"You're no slouch when it comes to lovers, Counselor. Can I put you on retainer?"

"For the rest of our lives," he whispered against her ear. "And it won't cost you a dime."

At that, Gigi pulled forward, the water sloshing over the edge of the tub. Then she turned to face the man she loved. Water from her breasts dripped onto his chest. His smile turned her inside out.

"Have I told you lately how much I love you?" she asked.

"Not nearly enough." Desire gleamed in his eyes. "I don't know about you, but I'm ready to go again."

"Me, too," she said. Then she slipped back into his arms, her breasts pressed against his chest, and kissed him thoroughly.

Something told her they wouldn't get much sleep tonight.

Chapter Fourteen

The next morning, while cuddled in bed after a beautiful night of lovemaking, Gigi splayed her hand on Harrison's broad torso, felt the steady rise and fall of his breathing, the warmth of his skin. She fingered the light scattering of chest hair, then arched up and kissed him.

"Mmm," he said, "I could get used to waking up like this."

"So could I. But I have to tell you something."

"More Fortune secrets?"

"The opposite. I don't want to keep us a secret anymore. I want the world to know that I love you. That we're together. An item, so to speak. But I'm worried about your position at the law firm."

"I've been thinking about that, too. But not for the reason you think. I wasn't let go by the firm, and honestly, now that I'm off the case, I don't think they'd give a hoot that we're together. In fact, they'd probably view it as a plus. They're big on family. But I'm not sure I want to stay there. I've been considering a move."

She sat up, jostling the mattress. "What kind of move? To another firm?"

"This is all in the simmering stage, so I'm still trying to make sense of it." He rolled to the side, facing her, his elbow supporting his upper body. "So if you can find the time, I might need a little life coaching myself."

She grinned. "I'm all yours, Harrison. In every sense of the word." She tapped her index finger on his brow. "What's going on in the beautiful brain of yours?" She ran her fingertip down his nose, and over his lips.

He nipped her finger with a gentle bite, stirring her desire all over again. "What would you say if I told you I'd like to work for a nonprofit?"

She hadn't seen that coming, but she'd fully support whatever he decided. "You'd be great at whatever role you choose. As I tell all my clients, you should do what fulfills you and makes you happy." She brushed a lock of hair from his brow. "What kind of nonprofit are you leaning toward?"

"That's where I might need your help. Maybe something to do with veterans and wounded warriors. I don't know."

"You don't know *yet*." A smile stretched across her face. "I'm more than happy to help you figure out your new role, Counselor."

"Speaking of roles," Harrison said, as he sat up in bed, "there's another one I'd like to take on. A *big* one."

"I'm all ears. What is it?"

"The role of a husband. If the woman I love will have me."

She reached for his hand and gave it a gentle, I-can-barely-contain-myself squeeze. "Are you *asking*?"

"I will. But there's something I have to do first." He placed a kiss upon her brow, then climbed out of bed. "I'm going to take a quick shower. Then I'm going to take off for a little while. Why don't you take a nap, then check out the room-service breakfast menu?"

"If you're thinking you need to buy a ring before proposing the question I'm so eager to hear, don't. I don't need a ring."

"Oh, you'll get one." He leaned over, cupped the back of her head and laid a kiss on her that made her toes curl. He stepped back and winked. "But not today."

Then he strutted to the bathroom in a well-earned victory march. He'd conquered her fears, her senses, her mind and her soul. She fell back with a sigh.

She rolled over at the sound of the shower. But what was he up to? What kind of surprise was he planning? She couldn't wait to find out what it was.

Five minutes later, Harrison was dressed in the jeans he'd worn last night, looking a bit rumpled...but as sexy as hell. He slipped into his shirt and turned to Gigi, who was still seated in bed, her legs crossed, the sheet pooled in her lap. "I shouldn't be too long."

Why was he being so mysterious? "You're really not going to tell me where you're going?"

He took a deep breath, then ran his hand through his damp hair as if she'd asked a question he found too difficult to answer.

She must have given him a sufficiently disappointed look because he finally said, "Okay, if you must know—and only because I want our relationship to be based on complete honesty and trust—I'm going to see your brother. You mentioned last night that he was staying in the area."

Her lips parted, and her brow furrowed. "Seriously? You're going to see my brother? I thought you patched things up with him."

He nodded. "We're good."

"Then why?"

"To ask for your hand."

Bam. Gigi thought she'd melt right there and then. She'd made some whoppers of mistakes in the past, but this cleaned the slate. "Harrison, we're adults. You don't need to do that." But it was charming and old-fashioned, and it made her love him even more.

"I know, but I don't want any objections to pop up during our nuptials." He sat beside her on the edge of the bed. "Have you any objections?"

"None, Counselor. Proceed with your case."

He kissed her and then headed out the door. Gigi sure hoped her brother wouldn't be a stick in the mud, although Reeve's disapproval wouldn't stop her from having the man she loved.

It would be nice to have his full support, though.

Last night, Gigi had mentioned that her brother was working late at the Chatelaine office and had planned to spend the night at his condo by the lake, a second home he rarely used, before he made the drive back to the city. And she'd been right. Harrison had confirmed it via text before he'd stepped into the shower.

As Harrison waited for the elevator, he whipped out his cell phone and called Reeve, who answered on the second ring.

"I'm headed to the hotel lobby," Harrison said. "Are you ready to have that coffee now?"

"Sure," Reeve said. "I need to get back to the city, but I've got time to talk, especially if we meet at that coffee shop at the far end of the lobby."

"Perfect. I'll see you there."

Five minutes later, the solidly built CEO of both Fortune Metals and FortuneMedia walked into the coffee shop, which was more like a miniature Starbucks wannabe, carrying a briefcase.

With light brown hair and blue eyes, Reeve Fortune bore a slight family resemblance. After greeting each other with a firm handshake, they both ordered large cups of black coffee, then they found a small café table just outside the perimeter of the three-sided shop.

Reeve set his briefcase on the floor beside his chair, then took a seat. "I have a good idea about what you want to talk about, but don't worry. I've already called Paul Bentley and told him to put you back on the case. I admitted that it was a complete misunderstanding, and that it was my fault, not yours. And if Bentley had a problem with my sister and you pursing a relationship, I'd walk."

"You said that? What did he say?"

"Not much."

Harrison had a feeling that Reeve wasn't often

wrong—and that he didn't like admitting it when he was. "Thanks. I appreciate that, but that wasn't necessary."

"Actually, it was. I want you back on the case." Reeve bent, reached into his briefcase and pulled out a large stack of files. After snapping the case shut, he plopped the file on the table, in front of Harrison. "Have a look at these."

Harrison briefly flipped through the paperwork, just to get a general idea of what Reeve was talking about, but it wasn't obvious, other than a bunch of Fortune names he hadn't encountered before. "What's this all about?"

"You're already familiar with the Mariana Sanchez case and her claim to be Walter Fortune's granddaughter."

Harrison nodded. The man Gigi called Grampy, the paternal figure she claimed would never step out on his wife.

"We were aware that Walter had a brother named Wendell, who'd passed away. But what we didn't know was that Walter and Wendell had two other brothers, Elias and Edgar."

"No way." How was that even possible? Didn't most families have a solid understanding of their roots?

"Yep. Elias and Edgar may be dead, but it's hard to say. They apparently vanished without a trace fifty years ago."

"Do you want me to try and locate them?" Harrison asked.

"Yes. I'd like to find out what happened to them, and

to make sure there aren't any other Fortunes coming out of the woodwork."

"Does Gigi know about this?" Harrison asked.

"Not yet. But she will. It just came to my attention. I've got business in the city, and I don't want to tell her over the phone. I thought I'd stop by her house this evening and tell her in person. So can you keep that under wraps until then?"

"Yes, of course." There was the segue Harrison had been waiting for. "I'll be there tonight. And that's what I'd wanted to talk to you about. As you know, I'm dating your sister, and it's pretty serious."

"I figured," Reeve said. "I'll admit that I wasn't happy about it when I heard rumors to that effect. I'm sorry for blowing up about it. I was just trying to protect my sister and our family interests."

"I don't blame you for wanting to look out for her, but she's a grown woman—bright and capable. She can look out for herself."

"I'm well aware of that—now, anyway." Reeve chuckled. "She let me know that in no uncertain terms when she charged into my office like a bull on a mission yesterday. I'll admit, though, I'd been underestimating her for years."

"Gigi and I should have been upfront with you about our relationship," Harrison acknowledged. "And that's why I wanted to meet with you."

Reeve shook his head. "Dude, it's all forgiven."

"Good." Harrison sucked in a breath. *Here goes.* "I plan on marrying your sister, and I'd like your blessing."

Reeve studied him for a moment longer, then reached

out his hand to shake on it. "Not that you need my approval, but you have it. Welcome to the family, Harrison."

"Just so you know, I love your sister with all my heart."

"I hope so."

"You have my word on that." Harrison tapped his finger on the stack of files. "And I'll always do my best to protect your family and business interests."

"I'd appreciate it. The last thing Gigi and I want to see is a slew of others, like Mariana Sanchez, trying to join our ranks." Reeve got to his feet and snatched the handle of his briefcase. "I'd like to stay, but I really need to get on the road."

"I understand." Harrison had a pressing commitment, too. He'd told Gigi he'd only be gone for a short time.

"Do you think Gigi would mind if brought over pizza and beer when I go see her tonight? I'm thinking it might take the edge off when I tell her about our rogue family members."

"I'm sure she'd like that—the pizza and beer, anyway."

"Good." Reeve paused for second and frowned. "I should tell you something. Gigi and I once had a close relationship—sharing jokes, teasing each other, that sort of thing. But after our father refused to train her and offer her a position at Fortune Metals, things went sideways. Dad pushed her aside, and Gigi and I have had a strained relationship ever since. She thinks I abandoned her when she needed me most. It wasn't intentional, but that doesn't make it better."

"Well, you're here now. That's what counts."

Reeve nodded. "I am. And, hopefully, we've gotten past that. So you might be seeing more of me in coming days."

Harrison reached out and shook Reeve's hand. "I hope so. Looking forward to it."

"By the way, you'll need to prepare yourself to become part of the Fortune family. We're not an easy bunch."

Harrison laughed. "I thrive on a challenge."

And he had a beautiful one upstairs that he needed to get back to.

Gigi had been delighted to hear her brother was going to stop by the house, especially since he'd given her and Harrison his blessing.

"All we need is the ring," he'd said, "then as far as I'm concerned we can start planning the wedding."

He was taking her shopping for a ring tomorrow, but she didn't need a diamond to show the world that she'd found the love of her life. Still, she'd like to have it on her finger when she and Harrison shared their good news with his parents.

She glanced at her watch. Reeve would be here any minute. It seemed like the old days, before their father had gotten an early retirement in his sights. So when the doorbell rang, she called out to Harrison, who was watching a ballgame on TV, "I've got it!"

She raced from the kitchen down the hall and swung

open the door. She smiled when she spotted Reeve on the stoop, his arms loaded down with two pizza boxes and a six-pack of beer.

"I wasn't sure if you still liked veggie pizza," he said as he entered the foyer. "So I picked up a meat-lovers special just in case."

"Yes, some things never change. I still love veggies." Gigi took the boxes and the beer from him. "I'll take this to the kitchen."

Moments later, she returned and found Harrison and Reeve in the living room, watching the game. Yep. Some things never changed. Texans loved their sports.

Reeve scanned the Southwest-style furnishings and the artwork on the walls. "I don't think I've been here since you remodeled. I like what you've done to the place. Fits the community better than that Grecian palace you bought."

"That was beyond horrid. Thanks. I knew this house had good bones."

"Are you ready for a beer?" Harrison asked.

"Sounds good."

"Gigi?"

"No thanks, I'm good." She watched him walk away and admired his form, her insides twitching and itching for him.

After Harrison left the room, Reeve muted the TV and filled in Gigi on the fact that Walter and Wendell had two brothers they hadn't been aware of.

"Oh, no. Are you sure?"

"I stopped by Bentley, Donovan and Tyler this afternoon and put Harrison on retainer. He should be able to get to the bottom of things."

"He accepted the case? He's been thinking about going in a new direction."

Reeve nodded. "He may still be planning a move, but he wants to look out for the family. He wasn't going to say anything to you until I did."

"Thank you for clearing his name," she said. "And for wanting him back on the team."

"Hey, he's one of us now. Or soon will be. And when I'm wrong, I admit it."

Not always, but she kept that comment to herself and turned to a more serious thought. "I've missed you, Reeve."

"Right back at you, although you'll probably get sick of having me around now."

"Never." They exchanged a nod that sealed the deal. It felt good to have a brother again—one that wasn't just in name only.

Harrison returned with two long-neck bottles of a new Austin IPA and handed one to Reeve, who thanked him then strode to the leather sofa and took a seat beside Gigi.

"It's out in the open," Reeve said. "She knows you're back on the case, Harrison, and I think she's happy about that."

"Good." Harrison kissed her cheek, then he picked up his beer and turned his attention to the game. "What's the score?"

"Rangers are down by two." Reeve tasted the beer and let out an approving smack of his lips. "By the way, sis, Alejandro Castaneda is stepping down from the Fortune Metals board of directors."

"That's too bad. He's dedicated his life to the company."

"He wants to do more traveling with his wife, sons and their kids," Reeve explained.

That was nice to hear—a man wanting to be with his family, and not just his wife. She wished she could say the same for their father.

"I'd like for you to take his place."

"Me?" Gigi didn't know what to say. That wasn't the kind of announcement she'd ever thought she'd hear from her brother. At least, not in recent years.

"Are you interested?" Reeve asked.

"Absolutely. Thanks for the consideration."

"I'm just sorry for not insisting that you be more involved with the mining operation years ago. It's long overdue."

She wanted to jump up and hug him, but she wasn't a giddy teenager any longer. Although, ever since Reeve had begun to make strides at healing their relationship, she suspected they'd both eventually slip back into the way things used to be. At least, she hoped so.

"You want to take time to think about it?" Reeve asked.

"I just did. And I accept." Feeling pleased and somewhat vindicated, she added, "I promise to do my best to live up to Alejandro's legacy."

"I know you will." Reeve took a long swig of his beer, then set the bottle on the coaster that rested on the lamp table. "And I'm opening up a new position at FortuneMedia, one that's right up your line of expertise."

She leaned forward, completely intrigued. "What's that?"

"I'd like to hire you as a resident career-development coach."

Talk about shocking the words right out of her. "Wow. I don't know what to say."

Reeve chuckled. "How about telling me you'll think about it?"

"I will. Definitely. But I have a lot going on right now, with several new clients, not to mention a wedding to plan."

"Take all the time you need. I don't want just anyone working with my employees." He winked, then reached for his beer and added, "Hey, where's that pizza? I'm hungry."

Some things never changed. Gigi chuckled. "On the kitchen counter. You know where it is. Make yourself at home."

Gigi turned to Harrison. "How do I say it in Spanish? *Mi casa es su casa?* Only in this case, I think it would be *nuestra casa es su casa*. Our house is your house. Yes?"

Harrison smiled. "Yes. *Nuestra* is right." He set his beer on a coaster, then got to his feet. "I'm glad your brother is making himself at home, but we'd better join him before he takes all the best slices."

As Reeve left the room, Gigi shot a glance at Harrison, who was grinning like the proverbial Cheshire Cat. "Did you know about all of this?"

"No, but I'm not surprised. I'm happy for you, Gigi. You'll do a great job juggling that position and wedding plans."

"Speaking of weddings," Reeve said, as he returned to the room with a plate piled high with the meaty pizza. He reached into his pocket and pulled out a small black velvet box and handed it to her.

"What's this?" Gigi asked, as she accepted it.

"It's our great-grandmother's wedding ring," Reeve said. "I don't know how I ended up with it. But it really should belong to you. I know how close you and Grampy used to be."

She carefully opened the lid, and when she spotted the polished diamond surrounded by red rubies, she sucked in a breath. Tears filled her eyes—tears she refused to hide from the two wonderful men in her life.

Harrison reached out his hand to her, and when she took it, he drew her to her feet and led her to the kitchen.

As she and Harrison entered the kitchen, she said, "I love you, Harrison. And, for the record, I've never been happier."

"I feel the same way. And I can't wait to make you my wife."

She gave him a warm, loving kiss. "Can I be with you when we tell your parents?"

"Absolutely. I wouldn't have it any other way. But from now on, I hope you'll refer to them as *our* parents."

Goodness. The unexpected gifts just kept on coming.

As they reached the pizza box on the counter, Harrison's steps slowed and he whispered, "How long do you think Reeve is going to stay?"

Gigi froze. Didn't Harrison like Reeve? Was he that eager to send him on his way?

"I don't know." A sense of uneasiness settled over her. Gosh, she and her brother had just reached a truce and understanding. "Why do you ask?"

"Don't get me wrong. Your brother's a great guy." Harrison shot her a grin that dimpled his cheeks and put a twinkle in his eyes. "I just think this is going to be the perfect night for a swim."

She brightened, knowing just what he meant. "I couldn't agree more. As soon as it's safe to shed our clothes, you've got a date."

A nightly date that would lead to a lifetime of marital bliss.

* * * * *

Look for the next installment of the new continuity
The Fortunes of Texas: Hitting the Jackpot

Don't miss
Fortune's Runaway Bride *by New York Times*
bestselling author Allison Leigh

On sale June 2023, wherever Harlequin
books and ebooks are sold.

And don't miss the previous titles in
The Fortunes of Texas: Hitting the Jackpot

A Fortune's Windfall
by USA TODAY bestselling author
Michelle Major

Fortune's Dream House
by Nina Crespo

Winning Her Fortune
by Heatherly Bell

Fortune's Fatherhood Dare
by Makenna Lee

Available now!

SPECIAL EXCERPT FROM

HHARLEQUIN® SPECIAL EDITION

She turned her back on love,
but her heart never forgot him.

Read on for a sneak preview of
Starting Over at Trevino Ranch
by Amy Woods.

Chapter One

"Dad would for sure disown me if he saw what I'm doing right now," Gina Heron muttered under her breath as she scrolled down the page on her laptop screen. She must have started and abandoned the application for unemployment benefits at least ten times since breakfast, and she still couldn't seem to manage looking at it for more than a few minutes at a time without that familiar queasiness kicking up again.

"Well," Gina's sister, Sophie, responded from her spot facing a nearby bookshelf, where she'd been organizing new travel titles for the last half hour. "Dad's not here, is he? So, I wouldn't worry too much about him judging you." Her tone was gentle.

"I know, I know," Gina said, rubbing her temples as she released a sigh. "But he always chided us to 'never take a handout' and in my head I've got a track on repeat of him saying, 'when things get hard, you've got to pull yourself up by your bootstraps.'" She crossed her arms for emphasis, just like Dad would have done.

Sophie put down the book she'd been holding and moved behind Gina, wrapping her arms around her sister's shoulders. "To that I would say, it's pretty damn hard to pull them up when you don't have any straps to speak of...not to mention boots."

Gina giggled softly, thankful for her older sibling's steadfast sense of humor.

"Besides," Sophie continued, squeezing Gina's shoulders before heading back to her work, "it's not a handout. It's *your* tax money, there for a rainy day when you need it." She picked up the next book from a box near her feet, briefly studying the cover. "And goodness knows you've had plenty of storms recently." Sophie paused. "I just wish I could afford to hire you myself. It would be so nice to have you working here with me—" she turned and gave Gina an apologetic look "—for actual pay, I mean."

Gina closed the laptop with a little more force than was probably necessary, earning a sideways glance from a customer browsing the shelf closest to her.

That was enough for one day. The application wasn't going anywhere, so she could continue staring at it tomorrow, hoping for some magic to happen so she wouldn't actually have to go through with completing it. Her sister was right, of course, and in her heart Gina knew she had no reason to feel ashamed for needing a little help until she got back on her feet, but a piece of her didn't want to admit defeat. Until she actually hit

Submit, Gina could keep pretending that her life hadn't suddenly erupted into a total mess.

Standing up to stretch, she glanced out the front window of Sophie's small-town Texas bookshop, Peach Leaf Pages. Late afternoon sun washed over the sidewalk, and passersby, clad in T-shirts and shorts for the warm spring day, carried to-go cups of tea and coffee and brown paper bags of goodies from the café next door as they browsed the decorated storefronts along Main Street. A vanilla latte sounded perfect, but Gina cleared all thoughts of delicious hypothetical treats from her mind as she headed to Sophie's closet-sized office in the back to use her sister's one-cup coffee maker instead, visions of dwindling bank account balances dancing in her head.

Today marked one month since Gina's latest teaching contract had ended, and she had yet to land another offer.

Since graduating with her master's over a decade ago, she had moved seamlessly from one teaching position to the next. Specializing in English as a Second Language instruction for professional adults, her skill set had always been in demand overseas, and she had never struggled to find work. She'd spent many happy years bouncing across Asia, enjoying the incredible people, food and cultures she encountered each time she took a new contract, all the while promising herself she'd find a more permanent position and settle down one day in the distant future.

She had never imagined that the timing wouldn't be her choice, that she'd be forced to stop moving against her will, before she was ready. But it seemed as though all of her colleagues with the placement agency had already found new positions or had chosen favorite locations to build lives. Meanwhile, Gina was stuck in her small hometown, treading water while her savings, and the little extra money she brought in from her tiny, word-of-mouth upholstery repair business, continued to decrease at an alarming rate.

Gina shook her head to clear away regret over a reality that no longer existed. She could keep her head in the clouds all day, but where would that get her? There was only one way to look at it now: at thirty-six, she would have to start all over again, and, having already achieved and lost her dream job, she had no idea how to do such a thing, or where to even begin. As thankful as she was that Sophie had been eager and happy to share her tiny space with her younger sister, Gina yearned desperately to regain her self-sufficiency.

"Oh, my gosh! I'm so sorry to hear that."

Gina turned abruptly at the worry in her sister's voice. A woman in her midsixties with cropped salt-and-pepper hair, sporting a stiff-looking back brace, grimaced in obvious pain as she spoke with Sophie, urgent tension in her voice.

"It's okay," the woman said, glancing woefully toward the children's section. "I'll heal in time, but I don't think I can sit through the reading today. I hate to leave you in the lurch like this, but I've got to get home and lie down. I'm due for meds soon and, until things get better, I'm having to take them like clockwork."

"Of course, Noreen," Sophie said, her words soothing as she followed the woman to the front of the store. "You should have just called, you poor thing. I would never have asked you to come in if I'd known you were in this condition. Dan must be worried sick."

Noreen waved a hand in dismissal. "Oh, he knows I'm a tough old bird. My back gives out every once in a while, so we know the ropes by now. The trouble is, I never know what's going to set the darn thing off. It'll be good as new before you know it, and I'll be back reading to the little ones."

"They'll miss you big time," Sophie said, holding the door open for the injured woman, who walked stiffly through, waving toward a sedan parked on the street just outside. The man in the vehicle—presumably her husband—got out of the driver's side and moved quickly to help his wife.

"There's Dan now," Noreen said. "Take care. My apologies again," she added with warm sincerity, hands clasped in front of her midsection. "I hope you can find somebody to take over."

"Oh, don't worry about us," Sophie called, smiling as Dan rushed over to take Noreen's hand. "You just concentrate on getting well."

As the couple got settled in their car and drove off, Sophie waved goodbye and closed the front door, setting off a pleasant chime of bells. She leaned against the solid oak and closed her eyes, pulling in a deep breath as if to center herself.

"They seem sweet," Gina mused, watching the car go.

"Yeah," Sophie agreed, opening her eyes as she stood

upright again. "They've been inseparable since they were kids."

A little shard of pain sliced through Gina. She had known a love like that once, long ago. Or at least she'd thought she had.

It became clear that Sophie's attempt to relieve her tension hadn't worked. She glanced in the distance over Gina's shoulder and bit her lip, worry filling her light brown eyes. Gina followed her gaze to the children's corner, a sweet alcove tucked in the space between two tall, blue-painted shelves full of picture and chapter books, adorned with cozy pillows, colorful carpet squares and sparkling strings of fairy lights.

"What's the matter?" Gina asked.

"Noreen was our children's reading hour volunteer." Sophie swallowed hard and looked down at her watch.

"So, you'll find another volunteer," Gina suggested. "Surely you've got a backup." But, as they'd been talking, Gina noticed that a few kids had started gathering on the carpets, their parents taking seats in a row of chairs set up just behind.

Sophie's head was moving slowly back and forth, and her teeth were making such a dent in her bottom lip that Gina worried she'd soon draw blood.

"So, I'm guessing…you don't have anyone else who can do it?"

"That's right," Sophie said, planting a hand against her forehead. "It's one of the million things on my to-do list that I keep thinking someday I'll have time for. Until you came to help out, it was about as long as Main Street, and it's getting shorter, but…"

"But you had a regular volunteer so that item wasn't at the top," Gina said, filling in with a growing sense of apprehension. She had an idea where this was going.

Sophie dove right in. "Come on, Gina, please?" She pulled up prayer hands in front of her pleading face.

"Um," Gina said, closing her own eyes so she wouldn't fall victim to her sister's huge, pleading, abandoned baby bunny ones, "I don't think I'm the right person for the job. You know I don't have much experience around kids." She swallowed anxiously.

"*Please*," Sophie said, the strain in her voice tugging hard at Gina's heartstrings. "You're a teacher, though. That's close enough, right?"

Gina stopped and dug in her heels, facing her sister as she steeled herself to be as firm as possible. "I teach business ESL *to adults*. Not exactly the same thing." She pulled her shoulders back, eyes darting about the shop as she desperately avoided meeting her sister's. "Now, if you'll excuse me, I believe I've got another round of job applications to fill out."

Sophie's expression softened. "Look. I know this is a little out of your wheelhouse. I wouldn't ask, but the kids are already here, and they'll be so disappointed if I cancel story hour."

Gina scanned the group of small humans as she considered her sister's request.

"Gina?" Sophie said quietly, reaching out to grasp her sister's arm.

"What?"

"It's just…you look nervous," Sophie said, a hint of a

giggle in her voice. "They're just children," she soothed. "They won't bite."

"You cannot guarantee that," Gina argued.

Sophie grimaced. "Well, you're right about that. But I can say they've never bitten Noreen, and that's something, right?"

Yeah, she looks sweet and all, but my sister can be pretty conniving, Gina thought.

Sophie assumed a serious expression and continued, "We're running out of time here, so are you going to help me or not? And, before you answer, remember whose couch you slept on last night."

Gina's mouth opened wide and her eyes narrowed. "Oh, that's low, Soph," she chided, clicking her tongue, even as she silently prepared to give in to the inevitable. She knew she couldn't leave her sister like this, not when there was a crowd gathered already and parents were starting to check the time impatiently.

Gina knew Sophie had put her heart, soul and years of saved-up dollars into her bookstore, and she'd worked her butt off to get it off the ground, even as nearly everyone around her said that brick-and-mortar book sales were a thing of the past. As she watched Sophie wring her hands, Gina knew what she had to do, and dammit she would do it.

"Fine," she said, her insides melting as Sophie's face lit up with gratitude, her pale cheeks regaining the color they'd lost. "But you owe me."

Sophie started to speak, probably to remind Gina again about the couch and the free roof over her head, but Gina stopped her.

"You owe me." She rolled her shoulders a few times and cracked her knuckles, preparing for the lions' den. "Two margaritas as soon as we close up. No negotiations. Take the deal or I'll walk." Gina fixed a steely gaze on her sister.

Sophie's lips trembled as though she might laugh. The nerve.

"I mean… I won't walk far, but, you know…back to the office to work on the books or something," Gina said, afraid she'd been a tad too harsh.

Only a tad, though.

"Deal," Sophie said, holding out her hand.

Gina shook it, very reluctantly, glaring additional death rays at her only sibling.

"Wonderful. Thank you so much!" Sophie bounced up and down. "By the way, the book is on the big chair in front of the kids." She snorted. "You'll be reading, *Tomorrow I'll be Brave*, by Jessica Hische."

A favorite of her sister's, Gina knew the book well, and the pertinence of its title, as well as the book's message that it's okay to be scared when trying new things, did not escape her. With a deep breath, she crossed her fingers and hoped she could live up to it.

No matter how hard he tried, Alex Trevino seemed doomed to fail when it came to getting his niece and nephew to their various activities on time.

He'd always taken pride in being early to events and appointments. As his *abuelo* taught him growing up: "on time equals late, and early equals on time"—advice he took seriously and continued to live by, and that had served him well for all of his thirty-seven years. Advice that seemed impossible to live up to when it came to kids.

His heart softened as he glanced in the rearview mirror at ten-year-old Eddie and six-year-old Carmen, wondering how it could possibly have taken so long to get them into his pickup. There must be some sort of time vortex when it came to children; it took twice as long to get them to accomplish anything as you thought it would, and even if you started getting ready early, the extra time somehow didn't add up the way it should, as if each minute flew by in only thirty seconds.

He must have made himself chuckle because Eddie asked, "What's so funny, Uncle Alex?"

Seeing no other vehicles on the sleepy ranch road, Alex turned quickly to smile at his nephew. The little boy had inherited the Trevino family's dark hair and eyes, and his mother's endearing dimples. "Oh, nothing much, bud." Alex turned back to face the road. "Are you guys excited about story hour?" he asked hopefully. He would do anything in his power to cheer them up these days.

"Meh," Eddie responded. "Story hour is for little kids, but I'll go because Carmen needs me to look out for her."

At this declaration, a lump formed in Alex's throat. It was a tender sentiment from a protective big brother, even if it was only half true. He knew for a fact that Eddie, an avid reader since age five, absolutely loved story hour, and really, any story he could hear, see, or get his hands on. That kid was going to become some kind of writer when he grew up. Alex would bet his family's ranch on it. On top of that, Eddie was just an all-around good kid, who had put his whole heart into looking after his little sister since their parents—Alex's older brother and sister-in-law—had lost their lives in a plane crash the year before.

Becoming Eddie and Carmen's guardian had been a whirlwind of lawyers, documents and packing up their things to move in with him, the tasks providing an escape from his own grief. Having gone from bachelor to caregiver overnight, Alex hadn't had a chance to deal with his own pain, and, while he'd been thankful for the distraction at the time, some days he wondered if he should spend some time finally processing everything that had happened, maybe even get some counseling… if he could ever find a spare moment.

Alex turned onto Main Street and located a parking spot near Peach Leaf Pages, then got out to help the kids from the back seat, taking a small hand in each of his. As the bell on the shop door chimed, announcing their arrival, Alex quickly noted that the children's area was already full, and the other kids were fully engrossed in the story.

So much for sneaking in without disruption.

He knew he shouldn't be surprised. Noreen Connelly, retired sixth-grade teacher—his, actually—was a stickler for punctuality, even when she wasn't on the clock, which meant this marked their third week of making a far more conspicuous entrance than he would have liked.

Oh well, Alex thought, guiding Eddie and Carmen

toward the reading circle, hoping there was still a spot left for each of them. Not much could be done about it now. As much as he'd like to, he couldn't turn back time any more than Cher could.

"Okay, guys," he said softly. "Let's be as quiet as possible so we don't interrupt the story."

He gently squeezed each child's hand and led the way.

"But how will we know what's going on?" Eddie asked quietly, mild frustration in his voice. "The new lady's already started reading."

"Yeah!" agreed Carmen, much, *much* less quietly than her brother, prompting an aggravated "Shhh!" from someone in the group.

Probably Kenneth, resident taskmaster. Aged five. Relentless enforcer of story hour etiquette, with a disapproving scowl that burned all the way to your toes.

Alex briefly closed his eyes, drawing in a breath. Okay, so maybe they needed to spend a little more time working on inside voices, at least before his niece started kindergarten the following year. He was definitely in support of a woman with a strong voice who knew how to use it…just…maybe not during story time.

"Carmen, sweetheart, let's try to whisper," Alex said, demonstrating. "And, Eddie, it's okay. We're only a few minutes behind. I'm sure you'll be able to catch up on the plot in no time."

He got his two settled with the other kids and moved farther back to find a seat among the other parents and guardians, who, thankfully, adjusted knees and purses to let him pass, probably having been in his shoes before. Maybe not as often as he had, but still.

Smiling gratefully, Alex finally slid into a chair of his own, just as something Eddie had said before caught his attention.

What *new lady*?

Noreen had been the only story hour volunteer every time Alex had brought Eddie and Carmen for the past several months, and as far as he knew, she had no desire to give up her position. The kids adored Mrs. Connelly. She did all the voices in the books, was so animated that Alex was certain she could have had an Oscar-worthy acting career if the teaching hadn't worked out, and she even used props and wore homemade, highly accurate character costumes. Likely there weren't many people lining up to take Noreen's place in the high energy, paycheckless endeavor. Plus kids that age were a tough crowd. Alex was pretty sure they could smell fear, and probably parental inadequacy too, which he had plenty of.

Taking *guardianship* of Eddie and Carmen had been an easy choice; he loved his niece and nephew and it was simply the right thing to do. He'd been in their lives from infancy, spending time with them at family events, never missing a single birthday or milestone, and babysitting when his brother and sister-in-law went on anniversary trips. Taking *care* of Eddie and Carmen, on the other hand...nothing had ever been more challenging.

Having wanted his own kids someday, Alex had never been naive enough to think that parenting would be an easy job, but he hadn't even remotely grasped how utterly *big* it was. Not just the day-to-day tasks involved in keeping two small humans alive, dressed and fed, and getting them to the places they needed to go, but the deeper stuff. The questions he couldn't answer. The philosophies he hadn't yet considered about how best to develop these two into good people, good citizens, good stewards of their gifts and resources who cared for their community and planet and…it was a *lot*.

He wasn't prepared, and he was slowly beginning to understand that maybe nobody was. Maybe nobody *could* be, not fully anyway.

In the meantime, he did the only thing he knew, which was to give his best moment by moment and hope it added up to something that would serve those kids well, because they'd sure as hell been through enough already.

A cheerful voice pulled his attention back to the present. Wait…there was something familiar about that voice. It set off a mosaic of memories—little pieces that didn't quite add up to anything solid, but made him feel a thousand hazy things at once. Spring rainstorms and a majestic show of lightning from the vantage of a barn loft; a summer day on a dock down at the reservoir, a beach towel for a picnic blanket; the high school football stadium, just before kickoff, a small hand in his and a soft voice encouraging him, easing the jitters that sometimes got so bad his stomach would hurt just before he had to go out on the field…

That voice. He'd recognize it anywhere.

And yet.

Alex looked up in disbelief. It couldn't be her. She

was gone—had been gone for years now. Not enough to make him forget, unfortunately, but enough to ease the hurt to a point that he'd been able to build a life that didn't include her.

It was then he noticed that the reading had stopped—in fact, all noise around him had ceased—and the entire row of parents, the kids on the carpet and the customers milling around the bookshelves…all had their eyes on him. Briefly, it crossed his mind that this level of unwanted attention should make him pretty damn uncomfortable, except that he couldn't really process any of it.

Not when Gina Heron, the love of his life, the same girl he hadn't seen in nearly two decades and had in fact never expected to see again, was staring straight at him.

"Um, excuse me, miss," interjected Kenneth the future hall monitor, pointer finger raised. "The story?"

Unable to take his eyes off her, Alex watched as Gina cleared her throat and forced her concentration back onto the slim chapter book that sat closed in front of her. Sliding from her lap as she startled, it took a dive and landed with a quiet *smack* at her feet, splitting the continued silence. She glanced down, not seeming to register what had happened until a little girl picked up the book, handed it back, patted her knee reassuringly and returned to a spot on the carpet.

Gina shook her head. "Thank you," she said to the little girl, eyes wide.

"Uh, okay," Gina said, thumbing through the pages until she found where she'd left off. "Let's continue."

Meeting Alex's gaze one more time before quickly pulling her eyes away, she picked up where she'd left off, her voice shaking a little from time to time until she regained her footing.

Alex closed his eyes and pinched his thigh, hard, through his worn jeans, but when he opened them back up, she was still there. Daring to look to his left and right, he was relieved to discover that he no longer captured the attention of everyone in the room. The parents around him had resumed reading emails on their cell phones and the shoppers were once again browsing, no longer curious about the sudden silence in the children's corner, and all was as it should be.

Except that Gina Heron, the woman he'd promised his heart to at age eight, the woman who'd turned down his marriage proposal after they'd planned a life together—the woman he'd tried with all his might and yet failed to stop loving—was apparently back in town. Add to this that not a single soul, not even Gina's sister, Sophie, who knew damn well that he and the kids showed up weekly for story hour, had thought to pass along this epic news.

To make matters worse, seeing her didn't just bring back all the bad stuff, all the heartache she'd caused. Looking at her now—that halo of untamable, curly gold hair, the almond-shaped light brown eyes that nothing slipped past, and those sweet soft curves he'd lost himself in so many times—it was easy to pretend that not a moment had been lost between them.

Too easy.

The room began to spin a little, and Alex's breath came in shallow spurts.

He couldn't just leave. It wouldn't be fair to the kids,

who needed routine and consistency and who looked forward to story hour. It would be selfish to disrupt their time just because he couldn't manage to get it together. All because of a woman he should have gotten over ages ago.

Chapter Two

I am going to kill you, Sophie Alice Heron, and scatter your remains in Marty Montalvo's chicken yard, Gina thought, seething, even as she wondered whether or not the lovably eccentric older guy still named his favorite fowl after country western singers. Her personal favorites had been Waylon Hennings, Dwight Yolkum and Tanya Clucker.

Focusing on the task at hand, she plastered on a smile for the kids. They didn't need to know that the person reading them a cute story harbored homicidal thoughts toward her older sister.

Her traitorous older sister.

How could Sophie not have told her that Alex might bring his kids to reading hour? How could Sophie not have told her that *Alex had kids*? He had to, because he was sitting back there in the parent chairs, staring down at the floor to avoid making eye contact with her.

For the love of all things holy, her sister owed her that much.

Alex had been the love of her life, and he had broken her heart. Even though she'd had to do it, leaving town, leaving him, after graduation had torn her to pieces, so many in fact that she'd almost failed at putting them back together. This information wasn't something her sister could have just forgotten, and as soon as these kids stopped staring at her, and the chapter was over... oh, she and Sophie would have words.

Just don't look at him and it will be easier, Gina told herself. She only had to get through this, and she could walk straight past the front desk and right up the narrow staircase at the back that led to her sister's apartment above the shop. It wasn't that hard.

Thanking the stars when she saw that the next page was only half-filled with words, the bottom portion a blank void of white space, Gina managed to finish the last bit of the story without having a panic attack or making a run for the door.

"And that's it for this week," she said, her voice so loud and unnaturally pleasant she was pretty sure she scared a few of the kids. "I'm sure...*someone* will be here next week to pick up where we've left off."

As the little ones began to disperse and reunite with their parents, her eyes darted around the bookstore to locate her sister, but her vision was cut off when a girl Gina guessed to be about six years old came up and stood before her, shifting from leg to leg.

Crap, Gina thought. She'd done her sisterly duty and filled in for the absentee story hour reader. Surely she didn't have to entertain follow-up questions. Kids always seemed to cut right to the chase, to ask the hardest questions—ones she, even as an adult, never quite knew how to answer.

"Miss?" the girl said, bouncing on her heels.

Gina closed her eyes to calm her racing heart, then opened them slowly.

"Yes?" she asked, meeting the little girl's eyes. They were umber in color and warm, set deep in a heart-shaped, tawny-beige face. As much as she didn't want to be, Gina surprised herself by responding to the kid's widening grin with one of her own. The girl gingerly placed a little hand on Gina's knee.

"I really liked how you read the story," she said, before turning on her heel and running straight for Alex.

Of course.

Gina's smile dissolved.

It was ridiculous not to have recognized those familiar features, even in another person's face. The hairs on the back of her neck stood as realization settled in. *Of course* Alex would have moved on, met someone else and started a life without her—a life that obviously included children.

What had she expected? That he would, what…wait for her? Really. She'd never given him any indication that she would come back and, in fact, hardheaded and stubborn at eighteen, she'd promised quite the opposite. It was a move that brought her sorrow nearly every day since. She'd made the decision to walk away from a lifetime with Alex; at the time it had seemed the right choice, at least to her young heart.

Growing up in Peach Leaf, with a distant, reluctant father had been difficult and isolating. Small towns weren't always friendships and potlucks and festivals. Sometimes it was loneliness, being surrounded by people who knew what was going on at home, who saw their dirty clothes and unkempt hair and knew how hard things were for her and Sophie, but who hadn't lifted a finger to help because it might have gotten messy.

Staying and building a life among the prying, judgmental eyes of her neighbors had never appealed to Gina, especially not when there was a great big world out there she wanted to explore. A life of travel and new experiences had called to her, and she hadn't been able—hadn't wanted—to resist.

Yes, there were moments here and there when she questioned her decision, but that's what life was: a series of choices. When you made one, there wasn't always the opportunity to turn back, and the years were too short to waste wondering what might have been. So, you moved on, and you did the best you could.

And yet here she was in the same room with him again, a place she never thought she'd be, and he was walking in her direction.

"Hey, Gina," Alex said softly, his expression guarded.

The simplest greeting, and yet it had the power to unravel her. The years of wondering whether she'd made the right move, of thinking about him every day whether she wanted to or not, of not being strong enough to throw out that old football jersey that followed her from one apartment to another no matter how far back she shoved it in a drawer…

Looking straight into his eyes, unable to find the right words to say, her heart would know him anywhere.

It was Alex. The Alex she'd loved so long ago.

Time had done little to change his features. He had the same deep brown eyes and tawny skin as the tiny girl who clung to his leg—though the sun had burnished his a shade darker—and the muscles under his shirt and faded jeans were hardened from ranch work.

He must have done what he'd promised, she thought, and taken over his family's decades-old business. It had been a point of contention between them all those years before, but she could see now that it appeared to suit him.

"Hi," she responded, her voice surprisingly steady considering the surge of complicated and confusing emotions swirling around in her brain.

Gina wished she'd never come back to this town, with its inescapable memories and history that had a grip on her. She knew she didn't want to spend her whole life in Peach Leaf. That's why she'd left all those years ago—to escape. At the same time, it was home, and everybody knew you could only run so far from it. And the biggest part of her history was standing right in front of her, pulling her back into a world she'd been so sure she wanted out of. So sure...

"So, you're the new storyteller?" Alex asked, studying her with an intensity she'd always found unsettling. He had known her so well for so long that the smallest change in her expression could tell him what she was thinking without a word spoken. It was both overwhelmingly comforting to be known that deeply, and disquieting because he was the one person she could never truly hide from.

"Ah, no. Definitely not," Gina answered. "I don't have much experience with kids."

"Odd way to spend an afternoon then, don't you

think?" Alex mused. His expression had softened and a corner of his lips ticked upward.

He was teasing her, she understood suddenly, inviting her to lighten the moment with him, and she was thankful for the gesture.

"Let's just say it wasn't exactly in my calendar," she said, grinning, her nerves loosening a little as she talked. "Sophie needed me to fill in for Mrs..."

"Connelly," Alex finished for her.

"Right," Gina said. "Noreen injured her back, so here I am."

"Sophie owes you one, doesn't she?" he asked, his lips splitting into a grin that reminded her why she'd been drawn to him in the first place.

Oh jeez. If she had any sense, she would walk straight out that door. Anything but stand there and watch those dimples start to get under her skin again. If she had any sense...

"You bet she does," Gina answered. And it was the last thing she could think of to say because, really, where would this end? What was the point of having a conversation at all, when she had no intention of digging up the past?

He was watching her again, little grooves at the corners of his intelligent brown eyes telling her he had at least some idea of her unspoken thoughts.

"Well," she said, "I've got to put this book away and get back to work."

His eyebrows perked up. "Oh, you're working for Sophie now?" Alex asked. "I know she's needed help for a while. This place gets so busy on the weekends. It's nice that you came back to town to do that for her," he said warmly, a hint of deeper interest underneath the polite, safe statement.

In lieu of explaining, Gina simply offered a resigned smile and pointed to the shelf behind him. "It's nice to see you again, Alex. If you'll excuse me, I've got to shelve this and—"

"Get back to work." He nodded. "I know."

He moved closer to her, so close that she could smell the cinnamon mints he'd always favored. The scent, once a balm to her nerves, now prompted a wave of sadness that hit her like a storm wall.

Tight-lipped, she waved the book in front of him and ducked her head to silently pass by.

"Here," he said, his voice soothing as he followed. "Let me help."

"I don't—"

"Please." Gina heard so much more than a simple word when he said it.

Avoiding his gaze, she held out the volume and Alex gripped it, his fingers grazing hers, their touch no less charged now than it had always been.

Pulling it gently out of her hand, Alex walked toward the bookshelves in the children's area, Gina unable to keep from following closely in his wake like a tugboat tailing a ship. He scanned the titles until he found the spot where it belonged, then used his thumb to mark the space.

"Ah," he said. "Here we go."

Reaching up, he almost had the book in place when suddenly, the little boy he'd brought with him appeared at his side and gave a tug on Alex's jeans. Startled, Alex dropped the book, which bounced right off Gina's head before landing on the carpet with a thud.

"Ow!" she cried out.

Gina had only just reached up to rub the newly sore spot when Alex's fingers grazed her hair, his hands gently cupping her face.

"Oh my God, I'm so sorry. Are you okay?" He bent down to stare into her eyes and all she could do was stare back, neither of them realizing for several seconds that any time had passed at all. He was comforting her, caring for her as he would have if they'd never parted ways, and she let him, completely unable to move herself to stop it.

When Alex caught himself and pulled his hands away abruptly, tucking them into his pockets as if they burned, his reaction smarted far more than the bump on her head.

Gathering her wits as she brushed stray curls from her brow, Gina nodded. "Yeah, I'm all right. It's just a little sore."

"I'm so sorry, Gina. I never meant to—"

The sound of giggling erupted behind them, and they looked down to see Alex's kids doing a very poor job controlling their laughter.

Alex frowned and chided softly, "Hey, guys, it's not nice to laugh when someone gets hurt."

But it was too late. The musical sound of the kids' giggling mixed with Alex's very serious expression, plus the need to release some of the morning's tension and the awkwardness of running into her childhood sweetheart, let something loose inside Gina. In a single moment she was laughing as well, and the kids were laughing even harder, and then Alex was laughing, too, and…

"It's really okay," she said when she'd calmed down enough to speak. "I know you didn't mean to hurt me."

"I truly didn't," Alex said. His smile faded and he looked at her for a long time, making her very self-aware. "And I am sorry."

"We're sorry too," said the little boy who looked like a miniature version of Alex. "We didn't mean to laugh. I hope you're okay." He glanced shyly down at his sneakers.

Gina's throat went dry, and there was a tickle behind her eyes. "Oh…that's okay," she said. "I know it's hard not to laugh when someone gets bonked on the head, and I'm not hurt."

"Aren't you going to kiss it?" the little girl asked suddenly, twirling a finger in her dark hair as her eyes darted between the grown-ups.

"Uh…what?" Alex asked, blinking as the tops of his ears turned pink.

Gina folded her lips together and put a hand over them, trying hard not to smile.

"Kiss the nice lady's head," the girl said, pointing toward Gina's noggin with an exasperated huff, as if she could hardly be bothered explaining the obvious. "When I get hurt, you kiss it and make it better. Aren't you going to kiss her head where you dropped the book? You have to make it better." She raised her palms as if to say, "Duh!"

Gina supposed she could have made things easier for Alex, but it was far more satisfying to watch him squirm. What happened next, though, she couldn't have prepared for.

"She's right, you know," Alex said, his eyes softening as he narrowed the distance between them, causing her breath to hitch. "I did in fact drop a book on you, and who knows, you might even have a knot there soon thanks to me, so the least I can do is…"

Reaching out to gently grasp the tops of her arms, he leaned over and pressed his lips to her crown, holding them there for longer than he should have, but perhaps not as long as she would have liked.

"All better now," Alex whispered, brushing his fingers against her cheek before pulling away slowly, his deep brown eyes meeting hers.

So much passed between them in that single look that Gina couldn't bring herself to speak, despite her mouth opening and closing several times. Alex, of course, noticed this and seemed to take joy in the fact that he still had the ability to undo her, a fact that would have annoyed her if she'd been able to feel anything other than pure shock.

The kids were staring wide-eyed when Gina finally regained control of her body and glanced their way. "I, uh, I guess I'll, uh…"

"It was good to run into you, Gina," Alex said, his eyes darkened with mischief. "We'll see you around."

Alex reached out his hands and the kids took one each, waving at her as the little family headed back through the store. When they reached the front door, he glanced back once before opening it to leave, his expression too complicated to read.

"Not if I can help it," she whispered to herself as the door closed behind them.

Seeing him this once had shaken the already wobbly ground she'd been teetering on since losing her job. Until a month ago, there had always been a next step, a new job in a new country, another destination to run off to. Gina didn't know if she had the courage to face the past, to unpack her troubled childhood and the people she blamed for looking the other way, to make amends for leaving Sophie—and Alex—for so long without ever stopping in to see if they were okay.

A question nagged at her from somewhere deep inside.

How will I cope if I have to stay still for a while?

Don't miss Starting Over at Trevino Ranch
by Amy Woods, wherever Harlequin®
Special Edition books and ebooks are sold.
www.Harlequin.com

#2983 FORTUNE'S RUNAWAY BRIDE
The Fortunes of Texas: Hitting the Jackpot • by Allison Leigh

Isabel Banninger's fiancé is a two-timing jerk! Running out of her own wedding leads her straight into CEO Reeve Fortune's strong, very capable arms. Reeve is *so* not her type. But is he the perfect man to get this runaway bride to say "I do"?

#2984 SKYSCRAPERS TO GREENER PASTURES
Gallant Lake Stories • by Jo McNally

Web designer Olivia Carson hides her physical and emotional scars behind her isolated country life. Until a simple farmhouse remodel brings city-boy contractor Tony Vello crashing into her quiet world. They share similar past pain...and undeniable attraction. But will he stay once the job is done?

#2985 LOVE'S SECRET INGREDIENT
Love in the Valley • by Michele Dunaway

Nick Reilly adores Zoe Smith's famous chocolate chip cookies—and Zoe herself. He hides his billionaire status to get closer to the single mom. Even pretends to be her fiancé. But trading one fake identity for another is a recipe for disaster. Unless it saves Zoe's bakery *and* her guarded heart...

#2986 THE SOLDIER'S REFUGE
The Tuttle Sisters of Coho Cove • by Sabrina York

Football star Jax Stringfellow was the bane of Natalie Tuttle's high school existence. A traumatic military tour transformed her former crush from an arrogant, mean-spirited jock into a father figure for her nephews. But can the jaded TV producer trust her newfound connection with this kinder, gentler, *sexier* Jax?

#2987 THEIR ALL-STAR SUMMER
Sisters of Christmas Bay • by Kaylie Newell

Marley Carmichael is back in Christmas Bay, ready to make her baseball-announcing dreams come true. When a one-night stand with sexy minor-league star Owen Taylor ends with a surprise pregnancy, life *and* love throw her the biggest curveball yet!

#2988 A TASTE OF HOME
Sisterhood of Chocolate & Wine • by Anna James

Layla Williams is a spoiled princess—or so Wall Streeter turned EMT Shane Kavanaugh thought. But the captivating chef is so much more than he remembers. When her celebrated French restaurant is threatened by a hostile investor, he'll use all his business—and romance—skills to be the hometown hero Layla needs!

YOU CAN FIND MORE INFORMATION ON UPCOMING HARLEQUIN TITLES, FREE EXCERPTS AND MORE AT HARLEQUIN.COM.

HSECNM0423

HARLEQUIN
PLUS

Try the best multimedia subscription service for romance readers like you!

Read, Watch and Play.

Experience the easiest way to get the romance content you crave.

Start your **FREE TRIAL** at
<u>www.harlequinplus.com/freetrial</u>.